NEVER *gonna* HAPPEN

DENVER ROYALTY

Sheridan Anne
Never Gonna Happen - Denver Royalty (Book 1)

Anne, Sheridan
Never Gonna Happen - Denver Royalty (Book 1)

Cover Design: Sheridan Anne
Editing: Heather Fox
Formatting: Sheridan Anne

DISCLAIMER

Never Gonna Happen was previously published as Logan - Denver Royalty (Book 1) 2018-2023

The content of Never Gonna Happen remains the same with new edits and tightening up of each chapter. The story within has not changed. Simply received a facelift plus new interior formatting, title, and cover.

Chapter One

LOGAN

My little sister gapes at me, her lips twisting in disgust. "You're not serious?" Cassie grunts from across the dining table of my Denver home.

A smirk stretches across my lips, all too prepared to exaggerate every little detail just to watch the way her bright, blue eyes fill with horror. "Hell yeah, I'm serious," I laugh, relaxing back in my seat. "We were dating a few weeks at most, and she was already talking about babies and marriage. What the fuck was I supposed to do?"

"Wait?" Jaxon laughs as he butts into the conversation, his hand resting against Cassie's thigh beneath the table. Both of them act as though the rest of us don't see it. "Is this the chick you brought to

Sean's wedding?"

"God, no. Got rid of that one ages ago. She was too needy. Though with how shamelessly you were drooling over Cassie during that wedding, I'm surprised you noticed anything apart from your own dick," I laugh, enjoying how he rolls his eyes before reaching over to grab my sister and haul her into his lap.

A beaming smile spreads across her face as she loops her arm around his neck and holds on as though she'll never let him go. And as awful as it is seeing your little sister with a guy, I'm glad it's Jaxon. These two have been together since they were kids, minus a few rough years in between. They sorted their shit out and have never been happier. Seeing the way Cass lights up every time he walks into a room makes it all worth it. It's a shame they lost those couple of precious years, but they both needed it to grow and discover who they really were before coming together as adults and truly committing themselves to one another.

"Yo, what's going on?" my brother, Sean, asks as he strides through my dining room with his wife tucked under his arm, making himself at home. Sean pulls out a chair for Sara and drops a kiss to her temple before sitting beside her and helping himself to my food.

"Logan just dumped another girl," Cassie says with a stupid grin, suddenly deciding she's more amused by my antics than disgusted. She drags her plate in front of her and jams her lunch down her throat like some kind of starved, wild animal. Some things never change. We Waters' are known for our competitive personalities, so I wouldn't be surprised if she were in competition with herself to see just how quickly she can annihilate her lunch.

"What's new?" Sean mutters, rolling his eyes and looking up with a teasing smirk like an asshole. "What's that? The third one this week?"

"Give me a break," I laugh, reaching for another bread roll and taking advantage of the spread. Once hockey season starts again, I'll be back on a strict diet plan to make sure I can perform to the best of my ability. "I was with her for at least four weeks."

Jaxon scoffs from across the table. "Bullshit. Two weeks tops."

"Nah, ten days would be pushing it," Carter, my other brother, calls from the kitchen, and by the tone in his voice, I know the fucker is enjoying the attention being on my love life rather than his for a change. Though, Carter started dating Cassie's best friend, Brianna, a few months ago, so unfortunately for me, when my dickhead brothers need someone to be the butt of their jokes, it's all been coming my way.

"Shut up," I announce to the table. "At least I'm not pussy whipped like the rest of you." At that, every male at the table rolls their eyes while the girls grin at their partners in delight. They know I'm right.

"So," Cassie says, getting up from Jaxon's lap and stacking the dishes on the table to clear away, not caring if we are finished or not, "what elaborate scheme did you use to break up with this one?"

I gape at her, my hand on my chest. "What makes you think there was an elaborate scheme?" I question as she reaches for my plate. Panic tears at me, and I desperately try to hold onto it, not nearly finished with my meal. I'm a growing boy-man. I have room for thirds and fourths. If I don't walk away from this table with a crippling stomachache, then I've failed in my mission to successfully stuff my face.

Cassie stops in her tracks and looks at me with a smug grin, her brow arching as though knowing me better than she knows herself. "You're not serious, right?"

A wicked smirk cracks across my face, and I give up on the plate, releasing it into the she-devil's grasp. We all fucking know she won't quit until she's won. "What's that supposed to mean?"

Cassie dumps the dishes on the kitchen counter before starting her scraping and rinsing routine, and I keep a sharp eye on exactly where she's putting those leftovers. "Hmm, let me see," she ponders with a stupid grin. "There was the time you told a girl you were caught up in a bank robbery and had to skip your date to give a statement to the police. And then there was that other time you faked a water-skiing accident and broke your leg. You made me go buy you crutches when the girl insisted that she wanted to come over and check on you."

I grin at the fond memory, but my response is cut off by Carter. "Oh, don't forget the time you told that chick your dog was going into surgery with appendicitis," he says with laughter in his voice.

"Oh yeah," I smirk, grabbing my drink and taking a sip.

"Huh?" Jaxon grunts, his gaze whipping toward mine. "I've lived next door for as long as I can remember, and I know for a fact that you've never had a dog."

"Exactly," Cassie laughs. "It was one of his schemes. He borrowed one of his friend's dogs, shaved half of it, and wrapped the poor thing up in bandages. I mean, if he bothered to google it first, he'd have known that dogs don't have an appendix."

"Hey," I say defensively as I get up from the table to help Cass with the dishes. "That dog loved all the attention I was giving him. Besides, how was I supposed to know the dog didn't have an appendix? A dog's anatomy isn't exactly common knowledge. I was desperate."

Booting Cass out of the way, I take over the dishes, hating when my guests try to clean up for me. I invited everyone over, so it's only fair that I am on dish duty. Besides, my parents would roll in their graves if I was a poor host.

The conversation drifts to Jax and how he'll be playing for the Colorado Thunder after having an amazing senior year with the Denver Dragons. Did I mention the Colorado Thunder just happens to be my team? I'm the captain and have been for the past two years. I worked my ass off climbing my way to the top, and because of that, I've just renewed my contract for another four years. I can't wait to get back into it. The new season is still months out, but I've never been so ready.

I grew up with a lake that ran behind our family home, and every year when the water froze, I would be out on the ice. When I was six, my father finally agreed to put me on a team, and I haven't looked back since. Joining that team was the best thing I've ever done, and I have my father to thank for that.

Luckily for Jaxon, he moved in next door when he was twelve, and I took him under my wing when I was sixteen. I turned him into the hockey star he is today . . . Well, he's not as good as me, of course. I couldn't let that little fucker move past me, even if it meant putting in extra hours on the ice just to keep myself ahead.

Talk of hockey has me looking up through the kitchen window to the man-made pond I had built on my property last summer. It's remained frozen since winter and since the off-season, I've been preparing it to create a whole new bunch of amazing memories, hopefully something I could share with a son of my own one day.

"Hey, Jax," I call out over the noise of their conversation.

His head whips up and meets my gaze across the kitchen. "What's up?" he questions as he grabs Cassie and pulls her back to his lap again, peering over her shoulder to hold my stare.

I nod my head toward the window. "Ice should be ready," I grin, excitement drumming through my veins. "Best out of ten?"

That same booming hunger for a win flashes in his eyes, and he practically throws Cass off him in his excitement. "Fuck, yeah," he roars before disappearing out the door, no doubt heading out to his truck to grab his skates.

Before I know it, Jax and I are out back tying up our skates while Cassie stands on the back deck, pulling on a coat. I roll my eyes, it's really not that cold. Hell, winter was over months ago, but the second someone mentions ice skating, Cassie's brain malfunctions and has her thinking she'll be freezing cold.

Looking up from my skates, I notice Sean slowly creeping out onto the pond, making sure the ice is still hard enough to skate on. "Dude, are you sure this is safe enough?" he questions, as usual, making sure to take over the role of safety officer. All he needs is a fluorescent vest, a hard hat, and a whistle, and he'll be right on track to claim the title of douchebag of the century.

"Yes, it's safe," I say, resisting the urge to roll my eyes at his back. I mean, I'm pretty sure it's safe. It was unceremoniously cold this winter, and the ice has somehow maintained its integrity. I've been out on it for the past two weeks trying my hardest to keep it smooth for the little time I have left before it melts, but with the rain last night, it's about as rough as day two or three of a recently shaven pussy.

During the hockey season, I didn't get a chance to skate out here, so considering today is my first real shot at it, I really couldn't give a shit if it's safe enough or not. I'm not about to miss this opportunity and will deal with the consequences afterward. Besides, I'm a fucking professional hockey player. I have pucks flying at my face day in and day out, I can handle a bit of uneven ice.

Jax and I grab our hockey sticks as Cassie pushes the box of pucks out onto the edge of the ice and slides it out further, being cautious not to get too close. She's always loved watching, but man, my sister can't skate for shit. She's blatantly refused to get on the ice, and I don't blame her. She's terrible.

Without a moment of hesitation, I step out onto my ice and the feeling is amazing. I've always wanted this, and the fact that it's here is incredible. Shooting myself forward, I fly around the man-made pond feeling like I'm on cloud nine. The cool Denver breeze whips past my face, and I notice a few divots in the ice that need a little work. I've considered buying my own Zamboni, but that might be taking the obsession a little too far.

"Fuck," I hear Jax holler from across the ice.

Whipping around, I seek out Jax to find him flat on his face, and I burst into uncontrollable laughter as I watch him pull himself to his feet and begin scraping off a large lump in the ice. "You could have done a better job," he calls out in frustration as Cass stands at the side, her hand plastered across her face, trying to muffle her laughter.

"My bad," I call back to him, glancing across at Sean and Sara and noticing that Sara just caught Jax's face plant on camera.

I can practically see Jax's eyes roll from clear across the pond, but I ignore it as I get back to enjoying my ice before it turns back into a beautiful, watery pond.

Carter convinces Cassie to pad out onto the ice with him, each of them slipping and sliding as they grab onto the homemade hockey goals that Jax and I so carefully built last summer. They push them into position at either end of the ice, and they somehow manage to do it without falling on their asses. Jax skates over and lifts Cassie into his arms, helping her to the side while leaving Carter to fend for himself.

"Come on, pretty boy," I call to Jax, more than ready to get this show on the road. "Let's get on with it."

Jax skates past with a cocky smirk that I know all too well. "Why are you so desperate for an ass kicking?" he questions. "Trying to get a feel for what this season is going to be like?"

"You've got no chance in hell, kid," I tell him, moving around the ice, unable to simply stand still. "I've got at least ten years of training on you."

"Ahhh, you see, that's your big mistake. Letting your ego get in the way. It's all about quality, not quantity, jackass." Jax drops a puck to the ice and tries to show off, no doubt because Cass is standing to the side, cheering him on like the devoted fiancé she is.

"That's Captain to you," I remind him before shooting past him and stealing the puck right out from beneath him. "Seems you still have a bit to learn," I laugh as I race down the other end of the ice and shoot the puck straight into the center of the goal.

"That doesn't count," Jax whines like the little brother I've always seen him as. "We haven't started yet."

"What's that? Do you need me to slow down so you can catch up?"

At that, Jax shuts up and presses his lips into a hard line, an intense concentration sailing over his face. He was the star of the Denver Dragons last year, but that was college hockey, and this is the big leagues. The NHL. He's only just getting started and still has a lot to learn, and when that happens, he'll be a force to be reckoned with. Hell, I hope that when he's ready, he'll be right there with me, challenging me for captainship, but until then, I'll be sure to remind him of his place.

Knowing neither Jax nor I will play fair, Carter stands firmly at the edge of the ice and plants a chair in the melting snow, declaring himself the official referee. With that, Jax and I meet in the middle and wait for Carter to get the game started.

Carter presses his fingers to his lips, and upon hearing an ear-shattering whistle, I drop the puck to the ice.

Jax scoops up the puck with lightning-fast reflexes and takes off, but he hasn't quite got the speed that I possess. I take off like a bat out of hell behind him, and it only takes a few short moments before I'm coming up beside him.

Jax darts to the left while showing off some fancy footwork that makes me think the idiot is better off in a pair of figure skates. As he gains on my goal, I drop back from trying to chase him so I can get in front before he shoots.

Seeing my plan in motion, Jax takes his shot while trying to beat me to the goal. As the puck flies through the air, I force myself forward, my lungs pumping hard in the cool air. The precious seconds are slipping away, and I dive for the goal, sliding across the rough ice just in time to capture the puck and prove to Jax that he's gonna have to try harder than that if he plans on besting me.

I quickly catch my breath as I look up at Jax with a grin. "Too slow, kid."

He rolls his eyes while he waits for me to get up off the ice, and I don't miss the way Cass makes a heart out of her fingers, silently encouraging him, despite knowing he couldn't possibly beat me. The game goes on, and even though I'd never admit it, I'm pleased that Jax is keeping up. That means good things are coming this season.

Half an hour later, we're both covered in sweat, panting heavily as we tie on nine points each. Cassie cheers and hollers from the side while Sean and Sara are playing tonsil hockey, and I'm pretty sure Carter has given up refereeing seeing as he's been playing on his phone for the last ten minutes.

The puck drops to the ice, and I make my move. There's no way I'm letting Jax beat me, especially after making such a point about kicking his ass. I would never live it down.

Flying down the ice with Jax thundering behind me like some kind of wild beast, he darts for the puck, but I'm too quick. I sidestep and fly around the slick ice, but Jax keeps right up behind me, as determined as ever. His next glide pushes him to my left, and I read him like a fucking book.

He darts for me once again while trying to cut me off. His stick flies out toward the puck, but I'm ready for it. I shoot the puck forward and watch as it sails smoothly under his stick before catapulting myself into the air and jumping right over it, narrowly missing a collision as he cuts across the ice.

"Fuck," Jax curses, though I'm not sure if it's from the shock of me jumping out in front of him or the realization that he's already lost the game.

A sick grin tears over my face as I race toward the goal, knowing he has no chance in hell of catching up now. Rearing back with my stick, I prepare to take my final shot, and as I push forward, my blade catches on the same fucking lump that Jax tripped over earlier.

Horror tears at my chest, and I try to catch myself, but I'm going too fast. I go down like a sack of shit, one leg slipping out to the left while the other shoots straight forward, sending me down into an awkward version of the splits. A sharp pain shoots up my thigh and into my groin, and I'm pretty damn sure I rip my ball sack in half.

The momentum from the fall has me sliding across the ice while

I try to curl into the fetal position, saving myself from any more pain. My whole body slams into Jax's goal as I let out a loud, roaring curse, the pain like nothing I've ever felt.

The force of my body slamming into the goal sends the whole thing flying back across the ice, and as I finally come to a stop, I try to move, only I can't. My upper thigh is aching, and I'm damn sure I've just torn my dick right down the fucking center, or at the very least, I'm certain I no longer possess a fucking ball sack.

"Fuck, dude. Are you okay?" Jax rushes out in a panic, barreling toward the goal, which is now a good ten yards down the ice. All fun and games have been replaced with nothing but fear for his captain. He knows what an injury could mean for our season.

He holds out his hand to help me up, but I'm not ready to move. "Nah, man. I'm good down here," I tell him with a pained grunt. "I think I tore a muscle."

Jax's eyes widen, realizing the seriousness of the situation. With the training starting in two months, and the season shortly after, a torn muscle could put me out, especially if it's not treated properly. Being the captain of the team, that could only mean bad news for me.

Fuck, I really need this to not be as bad as I think it is. The whole fucking season is riding on this.

"Where does it hurt?" Jax questions, hovering as I hear my sister trying to check on me from the sidelines.

"My fucking dick, man," I grumble, barely holding it together.

A wide grin stretches across his face, and it takes every last shred of control to not allow a booming laugh to tear from the back of his throat. "Shit," he says, quickly sobering before calling out for Carter to give us a hand. He looks back at me, cringing as he drags his hand over his face. "You really think the muscle is actually torn?"

"Yeah. No doubt about it," I say as Carter rushes out across the ice, trying to keep himself from sliding out. "Either groin or high upper thigh. I doubt the fucker is even attached to the bone at this point."

"Fuck."

My thoughts exactly.

Carter reaches us, and without hesitation, the two of them dive into the net to fish me out. I do what I can to not act like a little bitch as they haul me to my feet, but my dick aches, and it only gets worse as I put my weight down and try to hobble across the ice.

My whole fucking career flashes before my eyes, the heaviness of the situation weighing on me like never before. People always say to quit while you're ahead. I'm already in my prime. My last season was fucking sensational, but I'm not ready to hang up my skates just yet. This is nothing but a setback. I'll get myself looked at, put in the effort with the team physio to heal, and then I'll be right there, back on top where I was always meant to be.

Carter and Jax get me to the edge of the ice and Cass is right there with a chair for the boys to dump me in. "What's wrong?" she rushes out, wide-eyed and panicked.

"Logan broke his dick," Jax explains with far too much enthusiasm. "Do you think you'll ever be able to use it again?"

"Fuck off," I scold. "I've never had a problem using it before, and

I don't intend to start now."

Cass groans, thoroughly disgusted. "I don't want to hear about your fucked-up sexcapades."

I shrug my shoulders as I pathetically attempt to rid myself of my skates before Cass takes over and does it for me. She helps me put my shoes back on, the same way my mom used to when I was just a kid. "Are you really okay?" Cass asks, glancing up at me in concern.

I shake my head ever so slightly, refusing to let her know just how bad I think this really is. "I will be," I tell her, not wanting her to worry. "It's probably nothing."

"You'll have to call team management and let them know what's going on," she tells me.

"I know. I'll give them a call as soon as I get back up to the house," I say, looking back over my shoulder toward my home and dreading the walk up there. "They'll set me up with the team physio, and I'll be as good as new before the season starts."

Cassie scoffs as she helps me to my feet and allows me to throw my arm over her petite shoulder. I drop my body weight onto her, nearly making her crumble to the ground. "Isn't the team physio a sleazy asshole who's a little too . . . what's the word?"

"Arrogant?" I supply.

"Forward," she grunts. "The guy is practically a sexual predator. Way too inappropriate with his patients."

"Got that right," I mutter as my last stint in physio flashes back at me, and to say I was lucky it was an upper arm injury is an understatement. The last thing I want is to be dropping my pants for that asshole, but until someone has something concrete to be able to get his ass fired, there's nothing we can do.

Cassie cringes and I know without a doubt what's about to come flying out of her mouth. "Do you want me to look at it?" she suggests, sounding just as awkward as I feel.

"Fuck no!" The idea of having Cass in and around my junk just isn't right, but I should have seen it coming. She just graduated with her Bachelor of Applied Science and now has a further three years of study to complete her doctorate in physical therapy, but she's well on her way to becoming an incredible physio, and I don't doubt that she knows what she's talking about. But I can't bring myself to drop my pants for my sister. "Besides, you know as well as I do that my contract states it has to go through the team physio."

"I know," she says with relief clear in her voice. "I just hate the idea of you having to work with that asshat, especially with something so . . . sensitive. I just don't want him taking advantage of you."

"No one is gonna take advantage of me, Cass," I say, trying to ease her worries. He would be a fucking idiot if he ever tried anything on me, and he damn well knows it.

Seeing Cassie struggle under my weight, Sean and Carter rush in and take over, and before I know it, my brothers have got me on my couch while Cass fusses about, trying to make me as comfortable as possible.

"You know," Carter says as he flops down on the couch beside me, beer in hand and a stupid fucking grin stretching across his face. "You're never going to live down the whole broken dick thing."

Rolling my eyes, I tip my head back onto the couch and close my eyes, trying to breathe through the pain. "Trust me, I fucking know," I say with a heavy sigh, reaching for my phone to put in the dreaded call to management. "I can only imagine the shit you guys are coming up with."

"Just you wait," Carter says with delight. "Just you fucking wait."

Chapter Two

ELLE

My hand shoots out to the headrest in front, bracing for impact as my eyes widen with fear. "No, no, no," I scream, terror pounding through my veins. This can't be happening.

Torrential rain buckets down against the car, the sound pounding in my ears as we skid across the black ice. The tires screech as my father desperately slams on the brakes, my mother's piercing scream tearing through the car, but nothing can save us now. It's too late. We're going too fast.

My gaze flashes out the window, taking in the big oak tree, barely able to see it through the storm, before looking back at my sister Sammy. She's too close. She's going to take the brunt of it, and there's not a goddamn thing I can do to help her.

Time seems to slow, and the horrendous seconds seem to go on forever as my life flashes before my eyes. We're not going to make it.

The heavy thumping of my pulse is deafening in my ears, blocking out Sammy's terrified squeal, but I can't look away. Her face pales as she realizes what's coming—the fear in her eyes, the gut-wrenching terror in her tone.

The tree moves toward us like a demon in the night, ready to take everything I hold dear as my father grips the steering wheel, frantically trying to regain control, but it's too late. Far too late. We're already as good as dead.

My brother's arm shoots out, slamming against my chest and forcing me back in my seat as he tries to offer what little protection he can. My back rocks against the chair as I try to reach for Sammy, but Brendan's arm holds me down with a death grip. When the car finds purchase against the trunk of the huge oak tree, the impact feels like a blast straight to the chest.

Time slows as my head flies forward, crashing against the headrest of my mother's chair in front. Glass shatters and rain pours through the broken windshield as the sound of crushing metal assaults my ears.

I cry out, agony tearing through my body as my head spins with a pounding ache. Dizzy and disoriented, my eyes spring open. I have to blink a few times before they focus, and that's when I hear the distant noise of people rushing to get to us.

It's dark. So fucking dark that I can barely see. As black spots dance through my vision, I ease my neck to the right, ignoring the shooting pain and gazing over my brother. He's bleeding, and glass shards are protruding from his body, but he's breathing, and right now that's all that matters. "Brendan?" I breathe, zoning in and out of consciousness. Getting no response, my gaze focuses harder on his face, and I watch as his neck goes slack against his seatbelt, sending a wave of fear blasting through my chest. "Brendan," I croak again, my hand dropping to his thigh and shaking, but it's no use. I can't wake him.

Content with the fact he's still breathing, I ignore the ferocious ache in my neck and try to peer around Brendan. "Sammy?" I reach for her, but there's no one there. "Sammy?" I say louder, blinking back tears as my gaze flicks around the backseat.

The panic is like nothing I've ever felt, and I frantically search for the button to release my seatbelt in the dark as I search the front seats. My mom is gone as well. Where the hell are they? Why would she and Sammy leave us right now? If they are out of the car, they must be okay, right? Maybe I passed out a little longer than I thought.

Dad is slumped over the steering wheel with his head twisted my way. His eyes are open, but something's off. The eyes that are usually so full of life are . . . they're silent, lifeless.

Is he? No . . . No. he can't be.

"Daddy," I scream, now frantically searching for the button, only my jostling has the belt locked in place, holding me tighter against my seat as my hand clutches my throat, unable to draw a full breath.

I fight hard against the seatbelt until I finally manage to release it. Then wasting no time, I grab hold of the headrest in front and pull myself up, ignoring the screaming pain shooting through my head.

Reaching into the front, I shove my fingers against my father's throat, desperately searching for a pulse the way I was taught in my high school first aid class. I try to concentrate, but the sight of my mother lying twisted on the road catches my attention in the car's flickering headlights. My world shatters all over again, and a horrid darkness settles over my soul.

Tears fill my eyes as a wretched sound booms from deep in my chest, the agony and overwhelming grief like nothing I've ever felt. Strangers crowd around our car and rush to Mom's side on the road. I hear them calling out, asking if we're okay, but I can't find a single word.

My parents are dead.

Hands reach for me, tugging at my arms and locking around my waist. Before I know it, I'm out on the cold, drenched road, staring up at the mangled piece of metal that used to be my father's pride and joy.

Two strange men pull my unconscious brother from the wreckage and lay him down beside me. I scramble right to his side, gripping his hand with everything that I have left. I want nothing more than to pull the glass shards out of his body, but I don't dare. I've seen too many movies to know exactly how that would end.

As the men go back for my sister, I hear the sirens in the distance, and a shallow ray of hope spreads through my chest. Help will be here soon. We just need to hold on a little while longer. They'll take care of Brendan. They'll make sure he's alright and then Sammy and I will take care of him. It'll be hard, but we'll be okay. We have to be okay.

A man steps out from behind the twisted remains of the car with Sammy hanging limply in his arms. For just a moment, relief blasts through my chest— until I realize she isn't moving. My eyes widen, and my breath catches in my throat as the stranger gently lays her on the ground, only he doesn't step away.

Why is he hovering over her?

Move away from her. You're scaring her. She doesn't like strangers.

Releasing Brendan's hand, I scramble across the asphalt, the rough road scraping up my knees, but it doesn't matter to me. How could it? Rushing to Sammy's side, my hand flies to her precious face, realizing she's hardly breathing. Blood stains her clothes, pooling on the road beneath her. Broken bones, deep gashes, *half her body all but crushed from the impact.*

"Sammy," I cry as I grab hold of her shoulders and give her a shake. "Wake up. You need to wake up. You're going to be okay. I promise, just . . . please."

The strangers try to pull me away, but I don't dare let go. I'll never let go.

Tears stream down my face, and I try to hold myself together, frantically glancing between Brendan and Sammy, terrified they'll leave me here alone. "Hold on just a little while longer," I beg of Sammy, listening intently as the sirens grow closer. "The ambulance will be here soon."

Sammy's eyes begin to flutter, and a moment of relief takes over before it quickly starts to fade. Those big blue eyes look up at me in pain and devastation before the life begins to drain away. "No, Sammy. Don't go. I need you," I tell her with a broken sob. "Hold on."

The ambulance comes screeching into view, the red flashing lights casting an eerie glow across the wet road, but I keep my eye on Sammy, watching as the life fades from those sweet eyes. "No, no, no, no," I cry, suppressing the overwhelming need to shake her when her eyes grow heavy and her head lolls to the side. "Don't give up."

I scream out for my sister as the paramedics come to a stop, dropping to their knees beside me, but it's too late.

She's gone.

Sammy's gone.

S weat drenches me as I wake with a gasp and sit up in bed, my heart pounding in my chest.

Holy shit. Today is not the day to dream about my dead family.

Dragging myself out of bed, I suck in a heavy breath and let it out before trudging into the bathroom, trying to shake away the images that continue to haunt me. Leaning over the sink, I splash cold water over my face and glance into the mirror, more than rattled by the chilling reminder of my past.

Just great. My first day on the job, and I look like a complete train wreck. Perfect.

My eyes are bloodshot, and my hair looks like a hot mess, but that's got nothing on the heavy bags below my eyes. It's going to take something more than just a little TLC to fix this walking disaster.

Padding back to my room, I grab my phone off my bedside table and quickly check the time. 6:03 a.m. Not bad. I don't need to be at work until nine, so I could try sleeping for another hour and get the extra sleep I've been neglecting, or I could try and make myself somewhat presentable for my first day. It's a no-brainer. Besides, the thought of closing my eyes so quickly after that dream is terrifying. It's one thing having to relive the agony of seeing my parents' lifeless bodies, but having to watch the life fade out of Sammy's eyes like that is the single hardest thing I've ever had to experience. Having it on constant replay sure as hell doesn't help either.

Wanting to make a good first impression at my new job, I jump in the shower and put in the extra effort to wash and condition my hair. I brush out all the knots and even go the distance to shave my legs—not that anyone is going to see them, but it's the thought that counts, right?

After stepping out of the shower, I wrap my towel around my body, and knowing I still have all the time in the world, I add a little extra pampering to my routine before getting started on my hair and makeup.

Within a few short minutes, I'm more than ready to get my day started. Making my way into the living room, I head over to my birdcage and take off the blanket, letting my little Louie know it's time to wake up and start living his best asshole life. "Morning, Louie," I sing.

"Morning, Fucker," he replies in his little parrot, bird voice.

Frustration burns through me, and I glare at the little shit. "Stop swearing at me, you little bastard."

"Little bastard. Little bastard," he mimics before repeating it another million times, his new favorite saying.

Great. Just fucking great. Out of all the words Louie can say, curse words seem to be his favorite. Though, the hardcore rap my neighbor plays all day long comes in a close second.

Deciding to give him a little freedom until I need to leave, I unlock his cage and reach in, letting him hitch a ride out on the back of my hand. "You know, if you weren't such a jerk, I'd get you a girlfriend," I tell him.

With another hour to waste, I make myself a decent breakfast and start on my chores, but keeping busy doesn't calm the nerves creeping in.

Today is going to be massive. I keep having to pinch myself to believe it's actually happening. Things like this simply don't happen for me. Not anymore.

After years of working and struggling my way through college, studying to become a sports physiotherapist, I finally made it. A month ago, one of the best hockey teams in the NHL posted about an opening for a junior physiotherapist position. So naturally, I gathered up every ounce of my courage and shot for the stars. There must have been hundreds of applicants, yet for some reason, the Colorado Thunder saw something in me, and after weeks of intimidating interviews and background checks, I was offered the job.

It's a dream come true, but it's also terrifying. This is the chance of a lifetime, and I won't be able to live with myself if I screw it up. Not to mention, this position comes with a hefty paycheck. It's not as nice as what the senior therapist would be earning, but it's sure going to go a long way in helping pay off the mountain of debt I've accrued over the past seven years of college and life.

With my hours quickly dwindling to mere minutes, I get Louie back in his cage before grabbing my bag off the kitchen counter and heading for the door. "Bye, Jerk," I call behind me.

Louie's little head turns in my direction before letting out an ear-shattering squawk, confirming that yes indeed, that little asshole really is a jerk, but I can't help but love him.

After sinking into my beat-up car, I jam the key into the ignition and hope like fuck the old girl kicks over. The car rumbles to life as I twist the key, but she chokes and falls silent the next moment. I let out a shaky breath before trying again, and this time, she fires up as though she were brand new. Breathing a sigh of relief, I pull out into the busy Denver traffic and get my ass across town.

The Thunder's training center isn't far, but the closer I get, the worse my nerves become. Life hasn't exactly been easy for me. I've been delivered blow after blow, and now that I actually have something to be proud of, something exciting and new that could help pave the way to a great career, I'm terrified of it being taken away from me.

This is what I've been training for. I know the human anatomy like the back of my hand, and I know exactly what to do with it when it's under stress. I've got this. There's no reason to be nervous. Every day during those long college hours, I gave it everything I had. I didn't want to just earn my degree and be some mediocre physio; I wanted to be at the top. When positions started opening up, I wanted my name at the top of every list, and now, here I am, exactly where I was always meant to be. My hard work is finally paying off. Though, I'd be kidding myself if I thought the hard work was over. This is only the beginning.

Glancing down at the small screen on my dash, I press my brother's contact and listen as the call connects over Bluetooth. It rings twice before Brendan's voice fills my car. "There better be a good reason why you're waking me at eight in the morning," he scolds on a yawn.

"It's my first day with the Colorado Thunder," I remind him, my voice shaky and filled with nerves.

"And?" Brendan questions. "You'll be fine. There's nothing to worry about. You were practically born for this job."

"I know," I say with a groan. His confidence in me knows no bounds. I just wish that confidence was able to rub off on me. He's my brother, the only family I've got. It's his job to believe in me, the same way a father is supposed to tell his little girl that she's the prettiest darn thing he ever did see.

"I wish you knew just how ridiculous you sound when you doubt yourself," he tells me. "But now that's settled, can I go back to sleep?"

Rolling my eyes, I go to relieve him from his brotherly duties when I hesitate, my face scrunching up, knowing just how much he hates it when I ask how he's doing, but what other choice do I have? It's my right as his big sister to bug him however much I please. "How are you?" I question. "And don't even think about giving me a bullshit response."

Brendan lets out a heavy sigh, and I can practically hear his eyes rolling in his head, but instead of hitting me with his usual groaning *I'm fine,* he pauses, the silence so loud through the phone. "You had the dream again, didn't you?" he questions a moment later, the soberness in his tone dropping a weight over my shoulders.

My back stiffens. "How'd you know?"

"Elle," he starts, the sadness in his voice making me wish for the millionth time that I could go back to that night and change it all. "You only ever ask how I'm doing when you've had that dream. It's like your reminder to check in with me. Otherwise, you avoid asking because you know I hate talking about it."

"Hey," I argue. "I check in with you all the time."

"I know," he says with a soft chuckle. "But you only hit me with the hard shit when the grief comes up and sucker-punches you right in the gut."

Letting out a heavy breath, I find myself grappling with what to say, but I force the words out of my mouth anyway, knowing the little turd will hang up if I don't. "Shit, Bren. I didn't realize I was that easy to read."

"Like a fucking book, Elle."

"Oh, shut up," I scold, resisting the urge to reach through the phone and smack him on the back of his head. "Would you answer the damn question? You know I'm only going to keep bugging you until you do, and you better be honest with me. Otherwise, I'm skipping out on my first day just to come over there and kick your ass."

"Fine," he groans, knowing just how serious I am. After all, he learned the hard way just how far I would go to protect him and make sure he's happy and pain-free. "I'm doing alright. A little stiff and sore, but nothing I can't handle."

"Are you sure?" I question as I feel the worry creeping over me. "Did you want me to put in a call with your doctor? Maybe you need to be moving around a little more often. Last time you were stiff, you weren't getting enough blood circulation."

"Believe me, there's nothing wrong with my blood circulation if you know what I mean," he jokes, never skipping an opportunity to gross me out. "I'll book in for one of those extra special massages. That should make me feel better in no time."

"Ugh," I groan, knowing he's joking just to mess with me, but goddamn, it works every time. "You're so gross, Bren. But seriously, don't you dare pay for a massage. Those girls barely know what they're doing. I could come around after work and do it."

"Don't be stupid. You're going to be exhausted after work, and besides, I wouldn't want to miss my weekly rubdown with Stacey. She has magical fingers, you know."

"I'm hanging up now," I tell him.

"About time. I'll see you on the weekend."

I can't help but smile at the idiot. "Yeah, I'll see you then."

The call goes dead, and I find a smile spreading across my face. My brother was my rock after the accident, and that has never changed. Not when we buried our parents and Sammy, not when we were sent to live with our aunt and uncle, and not when I moved away for college.

No matter what, he's always been there and always will be, no matter what bullshit curveballs life wants to throw at us.

Pulling up at the Thunder's training arena, I bring my car to a stop, and just like the few times I've come for interviews, I'm caught off guard by the sheer magnitude of the training facility. It's huge like *craning your neck just to see the top of the building* kind of huge.

After shaking off the nerves and pulling my shit together, I let out a heavy breath, grab my bag, and push out into the cool morning breeze.

I've got this.

Standing tall with my chin held high, I make my way inside the impressive training facility, and I'm met at the door by the senior physiotherapist, Dave. He's big, sweaty, bald, and gives me the creeps. He's the kind of guy who holds onto your hand a little too long and whose eyes always seem to be looking at your ass. But then, he really seems to know what he's doing when it comes to physio. So with that in mind, I can ignore his flaws for the chance to learn. I just hope he makes a good teacher. Hell, I hope I'm just overthinking things.

Dave sets me up with a uniform and introduces me to a few people in management who I promptly forget the names of, but they seem too flustered to spend time focusing on me. Apparently one of the players was injured yesterday, and it's a big deal, though I'm sure I'll know all the ins and outs of that one before the day is out.

I've never been good with names, but after a week or two, I'm sure things will start to stick. Dave goes on to explain that the season is still a few months out, with training starting up again in August, so I won't be too busy. Until then, there are a few small injuries and stressed muscles to relieve along with the usual daily post-workout massages, so I should use the downtime to learn the ropes. It's the perfect way to ease into this crazy, new position and get to know each of the players.

With that, I get straight into it, determined to prove just how much I belong here.

It's just after lunch, and the day has flown by. Dave has been very professional, and I'm pleased to report that he's making an excellent teacher. I stood in while he worked on two of the players this morning, and after explaining their issues, he allowed me the chance to show him exactly what I was made of.

I'm just coming out of the lunchroom when I find Dave hanging outside our office, his phone in his hand as he paces back and forth. My brows furrow in hesitation. I don't want to pry, but it's not in my nature to ignore when someone looks stressed. "Everything okay?" I ask, keeping my voice cheery.

"Yeah, just peachy," he scoffs with a deep sarcasm that puts me on edge. He notices his tone and immediately checks himself, letting out a heavy breath and dragging his hand over his face. "Sorry. You didn't deserve that. It's my son. He just got suspended from school for starting another fight."

"Shit," I say, inwardly wondering what kind of kid he's got. Though who am I to judge? Brendan was the same when he was younger—before his trauma forced him to grow up so quickly—and he turned out alright . . . mostly. He's only an asshole some of the time.

"Yeah," Dave agrees. "Listen, I've got to go pick him up. You'll need to cover the afternoon appointments, but don't worry, you were great this morning. It's clear you know what you're doing."

"Sure," I say, not wanting to let on how my nerves just spiked and are swirling around my stomach. "Anything I need to know?"

Dave goes on to explain the appointments I'll be covering and reminds me what exercises I should be recommending. He makes a point that the captain is coming in with a fresh injury and that I'll need to do an initial assessment to determine the severity of it, and not to lay a finger on him unless I am positive of my treatment plan. I agree with everything he says, but I listen intently anyway, not wanting to screw up anything on day one. With that, he double checks he has his keys, scrawls his number on a slip of paper in case I need to reach him, and then hauls ass toward the door, leaving me to fend for myself.

After sending my two o'clock appointment on his way, I drop into my desk and get familiar with my next player. I scan the paperwork and realize the next guy through my door is the captain of the team, Logan Waters, the very appointment that has the whole management team scrambling.

My gaze scans down the paperwork until I get to the information detailing his injury. My eyes widen, horrified by just how serious this one is and understanding just how painful it must have been. Hell, he's no doubt still in a lot of pain. It only happened yesterday, so I'm going to have to be careful with this one.

From what I can tell, it's an inner thigh and groin injury, but I'm going to have to get extremely close and personal to work out the severity of his injuries. I mean, one slip and BAM—I'll have a handful of NHL penis.

I did not come prepared for this. Arms, legs, backs, and asses. Easy. Captain's junk . . . not so much. Sure, I can handle it. I know what I'm doing, and after properly assessing him, I'll be able to work out my game plan, but I can't deny that I'm intrigued.

Shit. Be professional, Elle.

This should be interesting.

Chapter Three

LOGAN

I would rather shove my dick in a meat grinder than be here.

Okay, that was a slight exaggeration, but my point is valid. There's nothing quite like having a middle-aged asshole accidentally brushing past your dick for an hour on a Monday afternoon.

If it wasn't stipulated in my contract that I see the team physio for assessment and treatment, I'd even consider letting my sister take the reins on this one. Yeah . . . okay, maybe I wouldn't, but anything is better than Dave.

I let out a heavy sigh as I pull up at the Thunder's training arena in Denver and reach into the back to grab the crutches that Cassie was able to find on short notice. I insisted I didn't need them, but apparently, she doesn't take no for an answer, and honestly, I can barely fucking walk. I need them more than I could ever admit. She also made a point to remind me that if I stay off it and let the muscle rest, I will heal faster, which in turn means that I'll be back on the ice sooner. She then proceeded to give me a list of exercises I should be doing, which is when I promptly tuned her out.

I love my sister, but sometimes, I just need to smile and nod while reminding myself that she loves me and only wants what's best.

Feeling like a fucking dork on my crutches, I make my way into the arena and head straight for the physio. Glancing down at my watch, I double check the time. It's three o'clock on the dot. I wonder if Dave will cut the appointment short if I just happen to be late. Probably not. I'm the star player, the captain of the team. All eyes will be on me this season, and it's imperative that I'm at the top of my game. Dave is bound to spend extra time on me. A player getting around with a limp is going to reflect poorly on him, and he'd never allow it.

The next few months are going to be hell on earth having to deal with him. I can only imagine how many times the fucker is going to slip, but I'll suck it up if it means getting back on the ice.

I have no idea why management hasn't sacked him yet. At least half the team has made complaints, but I guess there isn't anything they can do until they have concrete evidence of misconduct. I'd like to say this world is dominated by the game alone, but it's just a bunch of bullshit politics just like everything else.

I hobble up to Dave's office, doing what I can to shake the bullshit from my head and attempt to go into this with an open mind. There's no denying it though, Dave is the best physio the NHL has ever seen, so I try to give him the benefit of the doubt. "Yo, Dave," I call as I attempt to open the door while balancing the crutches in one hand and trying not to put any weight on my leg. I learned that one the hard way and fell flat on my face after getting up this morning, and trust me, falling flat on my face with morning wood wasn't fun.

"Oh, sorry. Not Dave," a feminine voice replies from within the room.

My head snaps up, and I follow the voice to a petite brunette across the room. She's fucking gorgeous, and I find myself staring. Soft strands of her hair fall down in her face, perfectly framing it, but it's those big blue eyes that send my heart racing.

My gaze sails over her, starting at the top and working my way down, taking in her stunning perfection. A soft flush spreads over her cheeks, and realizing I'm gawking at this woman, I reel it in before I make a fool of myself. "Sorry," I smile, fixing the crutches back under my arms and making sure to turn on the charm, giving her the panty-dropping smile that's never failed me. "I was expecting Dave."

"That's okay," she says trying to avoid eye contact, but she can't, not without appearing rude. "I'm Elle. Dave had to rush out, so I'll be taking your appointment today. Is that okay?"

Music to my fucking ears. "Baby, that's more than okay," I murmur as my smile turns into a devilish grin. "I'm Logan."

Elle nods and gives me a tight smile. "I know," she says, waving my file. I hold her stare, and the flush on her cheeks darkens, driving something within me. I need to see more, need to know what makes this girl tick. But it's clear Elle is shy, and if I were anyone else, the next hour would be very awkward for her, but luckily for me, I plan on having a little fun.

"So, before we start," she says as she fumbles around in her papers and pulls out a form. "Two things. One, I need you to sign a consent form for me to work on you. And two, I'm not your *baby*. Let's get that clear."

Ooh, maybe not as shy as I assumed.

Leaning my crutches up against the wall, I meet her gaze and wink. "Noted. Not my baby," I say before hobbling across and taking the consent form from Elle. I look it over, my brows slightly furrowed before glancing up, only to find her studying me.

Her bright blue eyes flick away before that flush reappears on her cheeks. If she weren't my new physio and working for the Colorado Thunder, I'd already be in her space, finding out exactly what it is she likes, but I need to take it slow with this one. Something tells me she's going to be a hard one to crack, but when I do, I have a feeling it'll be worth every fucking second of the ride.

"Haven't I already signed all this shit?" I ask as I reach for a pen.

"Yes," she murmurs. "However, that covered Dave and the last junior he had working with him. This one covers me."

"Right," I say before signing the form. "So, you're here for good then?"

"Looks like it," Elle says as she takes the form from me and slips it into a manila folder, giving me a great view of her perfect ass and making me want to sink my teeth into it.

She hesitantly turns back, worrying her bottom lip, unknowingly making it clear she's nervous. "So, umm . . . this injury of yours?"

"Yeah?"

She glances down at her papers once again, probably wondering how to be professional about asking a guy she just met about his dick. "Your paperwork says you tore your right upper thigh and groin?" she questions.

"Sure did," I confirm, leaning back against the massage table for balance.

"And how did you do that?" she asks with a smile that completely throws me off guard, clearly both amused and intrigued by this fucked-up little situation I've gotten myself into. There's no way in hell I'm leaving this room in an hour without a date for dinner tonight.

I grin at the fond memory while also very aware that I've already given these details to management. There's no doubt she already knows what happened. Any good physio would have read the full report before the patient had even walked through the door. No, this beauty just wants to hear it directly from me. "I challenged my sister's fiancé to a hockey match, best out of ten," I explain, confused as to why I'm so hungry to see her come alive. "And for the record, I kicked his ass."

Elle's smile widens as the smallest chuckle escapes her lips. "That's a little unfair, don't you think?"

"How so?"

She looks at me as though I've grown another head, leaning back against her desk. "Aren't you the captain of the best NHL team in the country? Surely the poor guy didn't stand a chance."

I laugh, wishing that were true. "Jax can hold his own, hence the injury."

"Ahh, and it all makes sense. He nearly had you, didn't he?" she laughs.

"I suppose we'll never know," I tell her, not about to admit just how right she is.

Elle grins as she steps over to the massage table and rests her hand on a towel, trying to bring things back to the reason we're here. "Okay, you'll need to undress from the waist down and lay on your back. You can cover yourself with the towel," she says before giving me a professional nod and stepping away. "I'll give you some privacy to get ready."

"No need," I say as I flick the button on my jeans and allow them to clatter to the ground, my belt heavy against the ground.

Elle's eyes bulge out of her head, that bright blue stare locked on my dick. "Where the fuck is your underwear?" she shrieks, momentarily forgetting she's supposed to be professional about this, but the moment I walked in here and saw that gorgeous face, I knew there was going to be absolutely nothing professional about this appointment.

With a soft chuckle and a smirk, I get up onto the table and lay back into position as she gapes after me, her mouth open in shock. "Figured I wouldn't need them," I tell her, not bothering to hold back on it. But truth be told, they were too hard to put on.

Elle shakes her head as if trying to force herself not to look again. "Right, um . . . okay," she murmurs to herself as I brace my hand behind my head, making myself at home. "We'll get started then."

She turns and starts making her way toward me, and the hunger within me is like nothing I've ever known.

Don't get hard. Don't get hard.

Keeping my gaze locked on her bright blue stare, I reach for the towel and studiously position it over my junk, more than ready to get this shit started.

Her face flames and she hastily turns away to grab the massage oils, giving herself a moment to find her composure. When she turns back around, she's back to the professional physio that she's trying so hard to maintain.

"Where exactly are you experiencing pain?" she asks, striding toward the table.

Realizing a lot more than just a date with the hot physio is at stake, I decide it's best to get serious now. I explain exactly how the injury happened, where the pain stems from, and exactly what I've done to start the healing process. She hits me with question after question, being incredibly specific, and considering how young and fresh out of college she is, she really knows what she's talking about.

Elle makes a move to get started on her initial assessment, stepping right up beside the table and glancing over my thigh. "I'm not going to sugarcoat it. This is going to be uncomfortable," she warns me, referring to how painful this massage is going to be, though I don't miss the double meaning.

"Yeah, I know the drill," I tell her, hoping my carefree attitude can somehow help put her at ease. After years of being a professional athlete, this is far from my first stint in physio. I know exactly how painful it can get.

Elle places her small, cool hands on my skin, and a brilliant warmth spreads from her touch, sending electric pulses throughout my body. I can't tear my eyes off her. Who is this girl? It's clear she's frazzled by me, but there's no telling if it's because she's attracted to me, or if maybe she's just nervous about this new job. Either way, I have to find out.

She starts to move her hand over my thigh, getting a feel for my injury, and it's like pure magic. Her hands roam higher, and I'm almost begging for her to keep going, which is when I realize, this isn't right. She's hesitating. This should be hurting like a motherfucker.

"It's okay," I tell her quietly. "I can handle it."

Her bottom lip is pulled between her teeth as her eyes focus heavily on my thigh while mine remain on hers. Elle lets out a nervous breath, and it's as if I can see her making the decision to get over her nerves.

With skilled fingers, she presses down into my muscle, getting a proper feel for the extent of my injury, and I want to scream like a fucking baby. I turn my face away from her as I try not to cringe. I was worried about losing control of my junk earlier, but I can honestly say that it's not even close to being something I'm concerned about now.

Fuck me. This is worse than I could have imagined. I take back my earlier comments, I really would prefer to shove my dick into a meat grinder. This is pure agony.

"Sorry," she mutters as she continues to torture my thigh.

Letting out a shaky breath, I try to school my features. "No pain, no gain, right?" I say, trying to sound at ease, but the pain comes through my voice loud and clear.

"Right," she agrees.

"Tell me about yourself," I practically demand, desperately needing to focus on anything other than the way her hands seem to have a death grip on my thigh.

"There's not much to say," she comments as her hands slip a little higher into a tighter part of the muscle, both exploring the depth of the injury while also starting to work it out.

"Make it up if you have to," I beg through a clenched jaw. "Otherwise, you're going to see a grown man cry, and I'm going to be really fucking pissed at myself if that happens."

"Okay," she says with a smile in her voice that somehow manages to calm me. "What do you want to know?"

"Why physiotherapy?" I question.

"Oh, shit," she cringes. "Start with something easier."

"Touchy topic?"

"Kind of," she admits, only meeting my gaze for a moment. "I love how physio has the ability to help someone with simple techniques. To me, it's an art form, a sort of magic. I've seen it transform lives, and I guess I want to be able to give that gift to others." The pressure on my leg starts to lessen as she talks about her work, and I realize that while it feels much better, it's not very productive. The way she speaks about her job, it's clear that she has an incredible passion for it, but while I'm trying to distract myself, I can't be distracting her. I'll have to change the topic.

"Yeah, I understand that," I say. "What do you do for fun?"

"Fun?" she scoffs. "I don't have time for fun."

At that, the pressure on my thigh returns, and I cringe at the pain. Holy shit. I'm going to die on this table. "What do you have time for?" I ask, gripping the side of the table tighter and forcing myself not to weep like a child.

"Um . . ." she says before pausing, really thinking it through. "To be honest, I'm not really sure. Until I got this position, I was working two jobs to get myself through college and pay the bills, but now I guess that can change."

"Good," I say, meeting her stare and letting a wide, seductive smile spread across my face, using every opportunity to my advantage. "Then you have time to come to dinner with me."

She instantly flushes and looks away, and there's no doubt she's intrigued by a date with me, but I see the rejection in her eyes before a single word has come out of her mouth. "Never gonna happen," she says as she presses just a little harder.

"Is that a challenge?"

"No," she laughs.

"Why not? I think you could use a night out."

Elle's hands pause on my leg as those blue eyes flash to me. "I don't think you have a clue what I need. And besides, I know guys like you, Logan Waters, and I'm not interested in being someone's play toy, especially at the risk of my job."

Curiosity gnaws at me, and I push up onto my elbows to watch her more clearly as she works. "What makes you think I'm like that?"

A wide grin settles over her face, and it's the most dazzling thing I've ever seen. "Are you telling me you're not?" she counters, her brow arching as if daring me to lie to her.

"Not at all."

"Hey Siri," she calls out. "Is Logan Waters a manwhore?"

My eyes widen, panic booming through my chest as I hear Siri come alive. "No, no, no, no," I say, horrified at the bullshit Siri could possibly dig up about me. "No need to come in hard with the Google searches. That's just cold."

Elle gives me a triumphant grin before grabbing a warm towel and wiping off the excess oil. "We're done here, Romeo. You can put your pants back on."

I swivel around on the table and sit up to face her. "I'm going to change your mind, you know," I tell her in all seriousness.

Elle looks back at me, and once again, her beauty blows me away. "Honestly, you can try all you like, but in the end, this is my dream job, and I'm not about to do anything to risk that. So, unfortunately for you, that means I won't be going out with the star player any time soon," she explains, letting me know exactly how it's going to be. Though, the interest in her eyes tells me that this is far from over. She's intrigued, and the attraction burning between us is as clear as the blue Denver sky.

After hopping off the table, I pull on my jeans as Elle slinks over to her desk and starts making notes on today's session. I hobble over to her and step in beside her, reaching toward her and pressing my fingers to the bottom of her chin. Elle sucks in a shallow breath as I lift her chin, bringing those bright blue eyes to mine. "Challenge accepted," I tell her, letting her see just how serious I am.

My fingers fall away, not wanting to crowd her, and I watch as her full lips press into a hard line, carefully considering everything that's happened during our appointment. Resignation flashes in her eyes, realizing that I'm not backing down, not until she explicitly tells me to at least.

Letting out a heavy sigh, she gets back to her feet and hands me a slip of paper with a list of exercises scrawled across the front. "You want the good news or the bad news?"

"Hit me with the bad news."

"It's bad. Your injuries are extremely severe and you're going to be up for months of rehabilitation to regain the type of function you require for the intensity of your sport. It's going to be a lot of work, and I don't doubt management will be freaking out. I'll leave it up to Dave to decide on the game plan. However, I would assume you'd be up for three or four physical therapy appointments per week, daily sessions with a specialized personal trainer, a weekly standing with a sports masseur, and an intense stretching routine."

"Shit. It's really that bad?"

"Yeah," she says regretfully. "But the good news is, we have until August before training starts, and assuming Dave is in agreement with my assessment and you're strict with your rehabilitation, I don't see why you can't be back on the ice by then."

Blowing my cheeks out, I scan over the list she's given me. It's all straightforward. "Three to four times a week, huh?"

"That's right."

My gaze lifts back to hers, and I can't help the wicked grin that stretches across my lips. "It's a date."

She smirks right back at me, her eyes dancing with silent laughter. "Call it what you want, but it will be with Dave."

Her comment is like a bucket of iced water tipped right over my head. "What?" I question, the thought of not seeing her at my next appointment sending a wave of disappointment firing through me. I don't want to come back to see Dave, not when I know Elle is here.

"Dave is the senior therapist. You're the captain. I can guarantee that you'll be seeing him next time. I was only filling in because he had to run out," she reminds me. "Besides, I doubt management is going to pin all their hopes and dreams for their upcoming season on the new chick straight out of college."

Damn it. She's right. As good as she is, management would want me working with the senior therapist, someone who's already proven themselves time and time again. Though, if I put in a good word and insist, they might let me continue working with her, even if it's just for the basics.

"Don't you worry about that," I tell her as I grab my stupid crutches and hobble toward the door. I glance back and send her my signature wink, and her cheeks flush with a brilliant red. "I'll see you around, Elle."

She stutters out a shaky goodbye, visibly swallowing before forcing herself to look away, and with that, I give the girl a break and limp out of her office, knowing damn well I'll be seeing her again.

Chapter Four

ELLE

Holy shit! What a day. I knew I'd be diving headfirst into this insane world, but I didn't realize I'd be launched right into the deep end. I wouldn't have it any other way, though. I loved every part of it. Well, I certainly loved one particular part of my day, but shit, that was intense.

Logan Waters is a force to be reckoned with. When he sets his mind to something, he won't stop until he gets it. And as intriguing as he is, knocking back that ego of his is going to be the best fun I've ever had. Every chance he got, he hit on me, and I continued to cut him down, yet somehow, it only made him try harder. There's no doubt about it, the man is persistent.

But damn. He's so much more than a heartbreaker. He's sexy as sin and one hell of a smooth talker. He's dangerous. The second I saw him, something inside of me fell into place. It's a feeling I've never had before, and to be honest, it scares the shit out of me. I need to keep my distance.

As much as I enjoyed working on him today, feeling his warm skin under my fingers and massaging his strong thigh, I'm glad Dave will be back to take the rest of his sessions. I don't know what to do with these feelings, but it's nothing I can't sort out with a large glass of wine . . . actually, this calls for the whole bottle.

His good looks and wicked charm are enough to steal a girl's heart and rip it right out of her chest, which I'm sure is exactly what he's done countless times before. Hell, Siri was all but ready to confirm it for me. But I meant what I said—I absolutely love my new job, and more than that, I need it. I won't be risking this for anything, not even Logan Waters. Though something tells me he's going to be a reoccurring performance for a while.

I have to be strong and hold my ground. The captain of the Colorado Thunder is not going to break me. He will not tear down my walls, and I will not risk my position just to have a fling with what must be the most attractive man I've ever met—no matter what the heavy pulsing in my core is begging me to do.

Being a physio for one of the world's biggest sporting teams is a dream. People work their whole lives just to be presented with an opportunity like this one. Any new graduate would kill for it, and here

I am, as lucky as ever to have the position drop into my lap. I will not mess this up. Besides, this job will go a long way in paying off the massive debt hovering over my head. Like I said, I need this so much more than I need one night with Logan, no matter how good that night could have been. Though, I have it on good authority that his dick is going to be out of order for a little while.

I'm halfway home when I realize that I really do need that bottle of wine, and I pull over to run into the liquor store. Making it quick, I scurry around, scanning over the labels for the cheapest, yummiest shit I can find. Moments later, I come out holding two bottles by the neck because one simply wouldn't do.

Once I'm home and walking down the hallway toward my apartment, I stop a few doors up and knock. My best friend, who I met in this very hallway four years ago, opens her door in her pajamas, looking disheveled and exhausted.

I don't say a word, I simply hold up the bottles for Jaz to see.

Relief flickers in her stare. "I'll be there in two minutes," she grins before closing the door. Satisfied, I make my way down to my apartment.

After unlocking the door and barging my way in, I dump my bag on the floor and make my way across my cramped apartment. "Sup, Louie?" I say as I pass the little asshole.

"Sup, Louie," he mimics in his little bird voice before promptly starting to whistle.

I place the two wine bottles on the kitchen counter before heading down the short hallway to my room. Sending my uniform flying over my bed, I hastily pull on a pair of well-worn sweatpants and a tank before striding into my bathroom and washing off what's left of my makeup.

I'm halfway through pouring two glasses of wine when Jaz waltzes through my door, her gaze locked on her phone, hopefully busy ordering pizza.

Jaz collects her glass off the table, grabs a blanket out of my cupboard, and makes herself comfy on the couch as I stash the bottles in the fridge and go to join her. "Did you have a shit day, too?" she questions, hitting play on her favorite Spotify playlist.

"Just the opposite," I tell her, lifting my glass to my lips and taking a small sip, loving the fruity goodness.

"Oh?" she asks, tossing her phone down between us, her brow arching in curiosity.

Grabbing my half of the blanket, I pull it over myself and get comfy, preparing to tell her all about my day. "I had my first day with the Colorado Thunder," I remind her.

"Oh, shit. That's right," she says, her whole face lighting up before her eyes go wide. She gasps loudly, her glass freezing halfway to her mouth. "I didn't wish you luck this morning. Crap, I'm such a bad friend. I'm so sorry."

"Don't be ridiculous," I tell her. "You're absolutely fine. It's not a big deal."

Jaz rolls her eyes, and I see her need to fight me on this, but her curiosity for the team gets the best of her. "It is a big deal, but please, God. Tell me you met the players?"

A beaming smile stretches wide across my face, and without even saying a word, she knows I've got a story buried here somewhere. It's only a matter of getting it out of me. "I might have met a few of them."

"And?" she prompts, knowing me too damn well. "Don't hold out on me, Elle. Give momma what she's looking for. I bet they were all sexy pieces of muscled man meat, ripe for the choosing. They were all horn dogs, weren't they?"

"That, they were," I laugh before I go on to explain every last detail about my experience with the elusive Logan Waters. "There was this one guy. He tore a muscle and was in for his first appointment, and good God, Jaz, he was so hot. Straight up image right out of the Men's Health magazine. If I could, I would have licked him from head to toe, and the vibes I was getting from this guy—he would have let me. He was so persistent, even asked me out. Though there's no doubt this guy is a manwhore."

Jaz sips her wine, peering at me over the top of the rim. "So? What's the problem?" she questions. "When he's in next, bend yourself over that table like a pretzel and let him rail you. Your hoochy is in desperate need of attention. You're probably growing cobwebs up in there. I mean, is it possible to grow your virginity back? Because babe, if it is, I'd be concerned for you."

"My hoochy does not have cobwebs in it," I defend.

"Bullshit. I hear it crying at night, screaming for a good pounding."

"Jaz," I shriek as I throw a cushion at her. "Shut up!"

Jaz awkwardly tries to dodge the cushion while attempting not to spill her wine all over my couch, but the roaring laugh tearing from her throat is the most contagious sound I've ever heard. "It's true," she throws back at me.

I've got nothing. She's right. It is true. My vibrator and ten-inch silicone dildo have never seen so much action in their life. They're amazing, some of my best friends in the world, but let's be honest, they're not what I'm really craving.

Now, Logan's tongue . . . I could only imagine what that could do.

Little does Jaz know, I'm a 25-year-old who still has her V-Card. At least in the traditional sense. Does getting railed by a ten-inch silicone dildo count as losing one's virginity? It's purple and veiny, if that helps. Circumcised, too.

Don't get me wrong, I'm no prude. I've fooled around with plenty of guys, but no one has ever given me that overwhelming need to give myself up for them. Not in the way Logan did the second he walked into the room. If he weren't such a manwhore and one of the Thunder players, today sure as hell could have ended differently.

Men have come and gone, and the second they realize my life is far from easy, they're straight out the door. I suppose I realized a long time ago that I'm going to be one of those girls who has to be okay with it being just me and my battery-operated boyfriend.

Well, that's not entirely true. I have Jaz and Brendan, and of course, Louie. Though the way that rat-bastard keeps cursing me out, I wouldn't be surprised if he were looking for his opportunity to up and leave me too.

"If you think he's such a player, then give me one good reason why you couldn't just play with him back?" Jaz continues, not prepared to let this one go. After all, he's the first guy I've shown even a slight interest in for years. "Clearly, that's what he wants. So what's the harm? You use each other for a good time and move on. No one would have to know and then your job is safe."

"You know that's not how I do things," I tell her with a heavy sigh. "Besides, Logan Waters is not the kind of guy you could simply walk away from. He's a heartbreaker through and through. He has one of those cocky, sexy smirks that just draws you in, and if I let myself go there, I'm going to end up devastated. So, I'll pass."

"Girl, you need a thorough dicking. With those moth balls growing in your hooch, you don't get the luxury of passing. Take what you can get and enjoy it while it lasts," Jaz tells me, taking another sip. "What's this guy look like anyway?"

Finding it physically impossible to describe him well enough to do him justice, I grab my phone and do the dreaded Google search. A grin rips across my face as I recall our conversation from earlier today. He didn't want me to look him up, yet, here I am, and there's no denying just how right I was. There must be hundreds of pictures of Logan with different women on his arm.

I hold my phone out to Jaz and turn it around, letting her take in the perfection that is Logan Waters. "Holy shit," she shrieks, her eyes going wide as she takes the phone from my hand and zooms in.

"Holy shit," Louie mimics.

"If you're not going to screw him, then I will," Jaz declares. "Fuck, I would do anything to be in your position right now. That man would have me spread-eagled over the desk within two minutes of the appointment. You must have some serious willpower, girl."

I roll my eyes, but my comment is cut off by Louie's foul mouth. "Holy shit," he repeats again. "Holy shit."

"Shut up, you little bastard," I call out.

Damn it. I cringe knowing the error of my ways. I've just added fuel to the fire. "Little bastard. Little bastard," he starts.

Jaz looks over the back of the couch to admire my foul-mouthed best friend. "That bird is fucking amazing," she sighs, giving him a fond smile. "If you ever get sick of his twisted ways, I'd be happy to take him off your hands."

I roll my eyes before snatching my phone back and looking at the photos once again, zooming in just as Jaz had. He truly is breathtaking. "The fucker is a jerk, but he's my jerk," I say, referring to Louie. Putting my phone down, I glance up at Jaz and lift my glass to my lips. "Why was your day so shit?" I ask as a knock sounds at the door.

Getting up and checking the door, I find our pizza delivery and a thrill shoots through me as I grab the boxes and send the driver on his way. With the pizzas in hand, I head back to the couch, passing Louie's cage to let him out. He instantly flies over to the couch and makes a home out of the backrest before promptly trying to tear it to shreds with his beak.

"I had the tiny tots dance class this afternoon, and the assistant dance teacher called in sick. We were doing choreography with a full class of twenty kids who were all exhausted and whiny, and I had to handle it on my own. It was literally hell on earth. I usually enjoy the tots class, but today I couldn't wait to send them home." Her bottom lip pouts out, and she reaches for a slice of pizza as she looks back at me with sad eyes. "I swear, I had the biggest headache. I mean, I love the kids, but days like today make me want to never have them."

I cringe, hating that she's had such a shitty time. "I'll take rubbing up the sexy hockey players over twenty exhausted kids any day."

"Right," she sulks. "I had my adult's class after, so at least that gave me a chance to relax. But I have to admit, wine, pizza, and Louie are going a long way in making me feel better."

I hold up my glass to her. "Cheers to that," I say as she brings up her own to clink against mine.

An hour later, we've annihilated a bottle and made the sensible decision to leave the second one for Saturday night. Jaz leaves with a promise to chat tomorrow, and I go about my night, locking Louie into his cage and fixing his blanket over the top before cleaning up from dinner.

After double checking the door is locked and bolted, I head to bed and slip between the sheets when my phone buzzes with an incoming text from Brendan.

Brendan – How was your first day?

With a smile, I quickly hit reply, knowing if I were to wait, he'd likely throw his phone down and then I'll be waiting for another response between three to five business days.

Elle – Amazing. A few awkward moments with the captain's junk, but otherwise, I absolutely loved it.

Brendan – What the hell are you doing getting close to the captain's junk?

Elle – Long story.

Brendan – Is this Logan Waters? Stay away from him. He has a reputation.

Damn it. I forgot how closely Brendan follows the NHL. I shouldn't have said anything. Now he isn't going to stop bugging me about it.

Elle – Hey! I'm the older sibling here. I'm supposed to be warning you off girls, not the other way around.

Brendan – Tough shit. You're all I got. Deal with it.

I roll my eyes as I picture him saying that.

Elle – Fine, but don't stress. There's nothing to worry about with Logan. I'm not stupid enough to fall for his charms.

Brendan – Yes, you are.

Elle – You're a loser! Night Bren.

Brendan – Night.

With that, I plug my phone into the charger and place it on the bedside table as thoughts of Logan creep into my head.

I need to stop thinking about him.

I. Am. Not. Interested.

Ahh, shit. Who am I kidding? I'm so interested.

I'm screwed, and not in the good way. I have never been so affected by a man before, and why does it have to be a man like Logan anyway? One I can't possibly avoid. Come the start of the training season, he's going to be at the arena every single day, in and out of physio all the time, making me clench my thighs together while pretending there isn't an itch I really, desperately want him to scratch.

My job is too important.

But seriously, that body! I only saw the bottom half, which was mind-blowing. Not to mention the size of his . . . shit. No. I must not think about that huge, mouth-watering co—fuck. I swear, a body like his only comes from a lifetime of dedicated training. His muscles were like rocks, so defined and hard. The second I touched him, I melted. I can't wait to see the rest of him.

No. No. No. I have absolutely no reason to be seeing more of him. Though, it's bound to happen at some point, right? I don't think there's any stopping Logan Waters when he's made up his mind.

Before I even know what's happening, I'm reaching under my bed and feeling around for my trusty vibrator. My eyes close, images of Logan swirling around my mind as the soft buzz sounds through my quiet room. My hand travels down, and I hook my thumb into the waistband of my pants before sliding them down my legs, sending a thrill shooting through me.

I've never done this while thinking about someone before, but I have to admit, it makes it that much better. I can almost imagine it's real. The vibration rocks through my body, and I tip my head back, my eyes already rolling to the back of my head.

I didn't realize just how on edge Logan Waters has me.

Thinking about him in this way, imagining his hands on my body, his lips, his tongue, his lengthy cock pushing inside of me—every last bit of it—is only going to make resisting him that much harder. But I'm too far gone and can't find it in me to stop.

My orgasm builds until finally it's too much, and I come hard, my pussy turning into a spasming mess, convulsing as my back arches off the bed. But I don't dare ease up, determined to see this through right to the end.

I press the little button on the vibrator, increasing its power, and the intensity skyrockets, making me cry out his name before finally bringing me back down. And it's then I realize just how right Jaz is. I definitely need a good pounding from something so much more than the friends under my bed, but at least that should hold me off for a little while.

I hope.

Chapter Five

LOGAN

"Hey," I call out as I struggle to walk into the home I grew up in with these damn crutches. "Anyone home?" Jax and Cassie have been living here for a few months, and I must admit, seeing this home filled with life again is something I didn't realize I needed.

When my parents were alive, this place was always filled with joy, but over the past few years, it's been a ghost town. Now that we've got Cass back from New York and they're starting this new phase of their life—it's all theirs.

Well, for now, at least. Jax wants to build Cass a home to have something to call their own, but I don't see the point, especially when this place is available. I guess I understand their reasoning. After all, Jax's parents live next door, and while it's a trek to get there, it's still a sore point. I don't blame them for needing a space to call their own, somewhere they can build a life together.

"We're in the kitchen," Cass calls from inside, and I'm glad she's finally learned to say what part of the house she's in. After all, the place is a fucking mansion, and while I don't mind the exercise, I would have been walking around for ages trying to find her. And as I can't seem to get the hang of these damn crutches, that really isn't something I want to be doing.

Finally making it to the kitchen, I find Cassie and Brianna with flour spread from one end of the kitchen to the other. "What the fuck are you doing?"

"We're making apple pie," Cassie says with a beaming smile, so damn proud of herself. "Do you want some?"

I look around at the state of the kitchen. Apple peels are scattered everywhere, mostly on the floor, while flour and sugar cover the counter, and it looks sticky as shit. I head over to the oven and peer inside, but the smell that comes out resembles something that smells like roadkill. "Ahh . . . I might pass," I say with a disgusted cringe.

"What's that look for?" Bri questions.

"Because it looks and smells like an apple pie massacre happened in here," I tell them.

"What?" Cass says, completely baffled by my comments. "It does not."

"Yeah, it does," I confirm, more than happy to hit her with tough love. If she was looking for someone to cater to her feelings, then she should be asking Jax or Sean. They're both little bitches when it comes to Cassie.

At that, a familiar sulk sets across my little sister's face. "Whatever," she mutters under her breath, getting back to her baking. "It's not for you anyway."

"Thank fuck for that," I grin.

Cass rolls her eyes, as I head for the fridge, searching out something decent to eat, but apparently, the inquisition isn't over. "Did you go to physio?" my sister asks as she takes a pile of dishes to the sink and drops them in the water, making half the water overflow and spill out onto the floor. She shrieks, her eyes bulging out of her head as Bri races around, searching for a towel to help.

"Yeah," I respond, watching the two of them try to get on top of their mess.

"And?" Cass prompts.

"And what? It was fine."

"Fuck's sake, Logan. You've gotta give me more than that," Cassie whines as she drops to her hands and knees to soak up the water with the towel.

With that, a smile cuts across my face, and I let out an amused breath. "Well, what do you want to know? The senior therapist wasn't there, so I got the new chick and thought about how quickly I could get between her legs the whole time."

Cass gives me a hard stare, the disapproval in her eyes eating at me, but I don't dare let her know that. "Did she know what she was doing?" Cass questions, ignoring my comments. "Cause if she didn't, she could have caused more damage."

"Relax," I say as memories of Elle come rushing back, and I try my hardest to mask it. "She was really good. Knew exactly what she was doing. It hurt like a fucking bitch, though."

"Yeah, that will get better as it heals," Cass says, bringing out her I know what I'm talking about because I'm a professional too voice.

"It's not my first rodeo, kid," I remind her. "I have three sessions a week, five specialized personal training sessions, a masseur, and an intense stretching schedule. Trust me, I've got this shit handled."

"That's expected," she replies as a thought occurs to me.

"Hey, she looked young, maybe a little older than you. Perhaps you know her. She's fresh out of college. Probably just finished her doctorate in physical therapy."

At that, Cass gets up off the floor and dumps the soaking towel on the floured table and faces me, her brow arched in curiosity. "I don't know. There wasn't an overwhelming number of girls in my classes, but she's three years ahead in her studies. I doubt we would have crossed paths. What's her name?"

"Elle. I'm not sure of her last name."

Cassie's brows furrow as she thinks back. "Elle? Hmmm. There was a TA in all of Professor McGillins lectures. I think her name might have been Elle. Like, super pretty. Petite brunette, has big blue eyes?"

"Yeah," I say, standing up a little straighter. "That's her."

"Hold on," Bri cuts in, looking at me funny. "What gives? You're way too interested in this. Have you got the hots for your physio?"

I roll my eyes as I look away from her and back to Cass, unable to stop the grin stretching across my lips. "What do you know about her?"

Cass shrugs before checking on her failed apple pie. "Not much. I didn't really know her. She generally kept to herself. People said she was shy, but I think she just didn't want to deal with other people's bullshit."

Hmm, that sounds about right. She sure didn't put up with any of my bullshit.

"But Bri's right," Cass continues. "You never ask questions about girls. You usually don't give two shits about them. Why's this one special?"

"I don't know," I mutter, leaning back against the counter. "There's just something about her. I can't put my finger on it, but I need to figure her out."

Cass gives me a knowing smile as if I've fallen madly in love with the girl, but she couldn't be more wrong. I just want to know her, take her out, and head back to my place. Once I've done that, I'll move on. Though, maybe I won't. I don't know.

All that matters is the second I walked out of that appointment yesterday, I was dying to turn right back around and demand she go out with me, not taking no for an answer.

"Well, if it helps," Cass says. "A friend of mine said she knew her from high school, and apparently, she hasn't had it easy."

My brows furrow as I watch Cass a little more closely, something sinking heavily in my gut. "What's that supposed to mean?"

"I don't know, they weren't close. She was a few grades above her. But I got the feeling it was bad. Though considering she scored that position with your team, I can only assume things are good for her now. Working for the Colorado Thunder is going to set up her career for the rest of her life."

Cassie's words have me more curious than I have the right to be. Why should it matter to me what Elle has been through? I only met her yesterday, yet here I am practically drooling over every word that my sister has to say about her. But more than that, I need to know exactly what Cass meant when she said Elle hasn't had it easy. What does that even mean? Countless possibilities swarm through my mind. Does she come from a bad family? Has someone treated her wrong? Put her down? Maybe she's been in a bad relationship? That would make sense why she was so ready to push me away without a second thought. You know, apart from the whole refusal to risk her job thing. That makes sense, and I have high respect for that.

Elle said she was working a lot until now, so she probably has student loans and rent to pay, which I'm sure is a lot. Cassie is in the middle of the same course. Four years of college to gain her bachelor's degree—which she's completed—followed by another three years to gain her doctorate—which she's just starting now. It's not cheap, but now that Elle has finished her schooling and has a great job, things must be getting better for her.

I'm comforted by my inner thoughts, though who knows if I'm even on the right train of thought. But again, it shouldn't matter to me.

I just wish I understood why it does and why Cassie's conclusion of her has me so wound up.

Whatever it is, I need to figure it out for the sole purpose of squashing it.

"You got her number?" I ask on impulse.

Cass raises her brows at me with yet another smug look. "Why the hell would I have her number?" she throws back at me. "Besides, even if I did, I wouldn't be giving it to you."

"What? Why the hell not?"

"Because if you want to win this girl over, I'm not going to let you do it by being some creepy stalker. You need more class than that. Besides, I don't need to remind you how stupid it would be to get involved with your physio. Not to mention how risky that is for her. If she gets caught messing around with one of the players, she'll be done for."

Damn it. She's right. But that doesn't do anything to ease the raging curiosity burning within me. "You know I wasn't made for class," I remind her.

"I know," Cass laughs, rolling her eyes. "You were made for one-night stands, just like Carter."

"Hey," Brianna scolds. "I resent that. Carter's been a good boy since meeting me."

"True," Cass relents, shaking her head in wonder. "I still don't know how you did it."

"It's simple math," I explain with a shrug of my shoulders as they each look at me with impatient stares. "Brianna must be kinky as shit."

"It's true," Bri muses. "But I like to think I have a few more appealing qualities than that."

A grin stretches across my face, more than prepared to mess with her. "Yeah . . . I don't know about that."

Bri grabs a handful of flour and sloppy, left-over apples and launches them clear across the kitchen as my eyes widen in horror. A disgruntled roar tears from the back of my throat as I try my hardest to avoid the onslaught of mess, but my injury keeps me from going far, and within seconds, I'm covered from head to toe in flour as Cass and Brianna cheer.

"What the fuck happened to the kitchen?" Jax asks, looking horrified as he comes in through the side door.

Cassie throws her arms around his neck and gives him a quick peck on the lips. "We're cooking," she boasts proudly. "Do you want some?"

Knowing her cooking skills are as shit as they come, Jax looks over her shoulder to meet my stare, and I hastily shake my head, horrified by the apple pie roadkill taking up residence in the oven. Jax glances back down at Cass, giving her a regretful smile. "Sorry, babe. I just ate. Maybe later," he tells her.

"Sure thing," she says, pushing up onto her toes to kiss him again, and with that, she unwinds herself from him and continues cleaning up the kitchen with Brianna. Jax crosses through the mess, joining me at the dining table as I attempt to get the flour out of my hair. "How's your dick, man?"

"Better than ever," I grin, knowing this was coming. "I'm flattered you care so much. Are you jealous you've never had a turn?"

"Oh, yeah," he laughs as he scoots closer to me and slips his hand under the table, placing it high on my thigh before meeting my hard stare. "Is that an invitation, big boy?"

"Ugh," Cass groans, gagging from the kitchen sink. "I'm sure you're not missing much. I accidentally walked in on him with Marcie Lovegold when he was fifteen, and let me tell you, he had no idea what he was doing."

"Well . . ." Brianna says, glancing at Jax as she bounces her brows. "If he fucks the same way Carter does, then yeah, you're definitely missing out. Get in there while you still can. Though be warned—use lube. Lots of fucking lube, because he's gonna tear that ass up."

"Gross," Cass whines with a disgusted cringe. "This conversation is over."

I can't help but laugh at her disgust, but she's right, this conversation has definitely taken a turn for the worse. "I still have a few hours to log in the gym for the week. You in?" I ask Jax.

Jax looks to Cass with longing before realizing that she's going to be stuck in the kitchen for ages. "Yeah, alright." He gets up from the table and hands me my crutches before heading for the door, and as I follow, I can't help but laugh as Bri calls out after us with a recommendation for the strawberry-scented lube she picked up online.

Following Jax down to the home gym in the basement, I take a good look around. Each time I'm down here, there seem to be extra additions. This week he's installed more cardio equipment, though I'm not sure why. Jax generally prefers to do cardio outdoors like the rest of us, but I'm not about to question his dedication to his work.

I get straight to business, working through the list of exercises Elle gave me yesterday, despite my workout with the specialized trainer this morning. After all, I want nothing more than to get this injury healed, but then if I play it smart, I could stretch out the appointments. Though, I'm most likely going to be having those appointments with Dave, so maybe it's best to recover as quickly as possible.

I get through the exercises slowly, making sure to do each one exactly the way Elle wants before starting over again and being as thorough as possible. After finishing off with the stretches, I head over to the free weights to get some real training done, and after an hour, I reach my max. My chest, arms, and back are more than ready to call it a day.

Glancing over at Jax, I find him lying on the cool concrete trying to catch his breath, and a laugh rips from the back of my throat. "You're going to have to work on your cardio if you want to keep up this year," I tease.

"Shut up," he huffs. "My cardio kicks your cardio's ass."

"Whatever helps you sleep at night," I murmur as I offer him my hand and hoist him to his feet, nearly falling over in the process.

"Do you really want to know what helps me sleep at night?" he questions.

"Fuck off," I say, releasing him just a moment too early and letting his bitch ass fall back to the ground. Leaving him behind, I make my way back up to the main floor of the house in desperate need of a shower. It's one thing working up a sweat in the gym but doing it while covered in flour isn't ideal.

With my slow pace on the crutches, Jax catches up to me in no time, and we follow the noise out to the den to find the girls putting a movie on. I hand Cass my credit card and she instantly knows to reach for her phone. "Dinner's on me," I tell them. "How do you feel about Chinese?"

"Hell, yeah," Bri says. "I'll call Carter."

I nod and as I turn to head for the bathroom, determined to shower more now than ever, I look back at the girls and Jax as they get comfortable on the couch. "I'll call Sean."

Chapter Six

ELLE

It's Thursday morning, and I've been dreading this next appointment all week. My only saving grace is that Dave is here and will be taking the lead during the appointment, but I still have to sit in and pay attention to every last bit of wisdom Dave has for me.

As gross and weird as the guy is, professionally he has a lot to offer someone like me. I'd be a fool not to soak it all up. He didn't make his way to being Senior Physiotherapist for the Colorado Thunder for nothing.

My gaze flicks to the clock for the millionth time over the past few minutes. "Is there somewhere else you need to be?" Dave questions without looking up from his paperwork, making it damn clear he's annoyed by my distraction.

"No, not at all," I tell him.

"Then you should be reviewing the notes from Logan's trainers and going over his progress reports," he says. "Might I remind you that he's the captain of this team, our star player, and it will not fare well for us if we cannot get him into prime condition before the start of the season."

If only he knew that I have his whole file memorized. Well, only the relevant stuff. I wouldn't dream of snooping through his personal information, that just seems so wrong. Interesting, intriguing, and so damn enticing, but wrong. Definitely wrong.

"Of course," I say, before diving back into Logan's already memorized notes.

A few moments later, there's a knock at the door before the man of my nightly fantasies waltzes in, looking like sex on legs. His gaze immediately comes to mine, sending heat through my cheeks. In an instant, that signature cocky grin takes over, and I can't control the need that pulses deep inside me.

Shit. With one look, he's got me right where he wants me.

Those dark eyes flash with a wicked, seductive secret, holding my gaze hostage for only a moment before he turns his attention on Dave, reminding me that the asshole is in the room. "Dave," he says with a nod, simply to be polite before glancing back at me. "Elle." Logan purrs my name as though it was made to roll off his tongue, and as his eyes become hooded, my world all but falls out from below me.

Fuck, I love the way my name sounds on his lips.

"Ahh, if it isn't our star player," Dave says, getting up from his chair and clapping his hands together in delight. "Sorry I missed you on Monday. How are you feeling? Been keeping up on your exercises?"

"Yeah, I'm doing good," Logan says with a cocky attitude that I'm sure is usual for him, even though I know with one hundred percent certainty that his response is complete and utter bullshit. I've felt how bad his injury is, and there's no doubt in my mind that he's still in a shitload of pain.

A scoff escapes my lips, and my eyes bulge out of my head as I quickly try to cover it up, but it's far too late. Both Dave and Logan whip around to face me, one watching me with irritation, the other so damn amused. "Do you have something to say?" Dave questions, annoyance thick in his tone.

Oh, shit. I may as well go for it.

"Yeah, sorry," I start as I turn to Logan. "It's just that you're clearly not doing good. You have a really serious injury that could impact your future, and I'm sure it's causing you a lot of pain and discomfort. Despite doing your exercises, you're not doing yourself or your career any favors by pretending it's not as bad as it is."

Logan looks at me with curiosity, and it's obvious he's deep in thought, but he doesn't respond. "She's right," Dave says. "Are you keeping off it?"

"Yes," he groans as if he's had this exact conversation with Dave a million times before.

"And you're doing the exercises Elle gave you on top of your specialized training?" he queries.

Logan gives him a look that suggests he's a moron for even asking. "Come on, Dave. You know me better than that," Logan says. "I take my career seriously. There's a lot riding on me getting this healed. I'm not here to fuck around. If I tell you that I'm doing my exercises, then I'm doing my exercises."

"You're right. Let's get on with it," Dave replies before patting the table. "Drop your pants and climb on board."

My eyes widen in shock as both Logan and I take pause. Did Dave really just say that to the captain of the Colorado Thunder? Drop your pants and climb on board? What the actual fuck. No wonder he has such a horrendous reputation among the players.

A few of the guys have mentioned in passing to watch out for Dave, but I figured they were exaggerating. After all, he's never said anything to me that would make me think differently. He gives me the creepy pervert vibe, though I had nothing to back it up with. But the way he looks excited about getting his hands on Logan is just weird, and to do it so openly with witnesses in the room tells me he has gotten away with this shit for far too long.

Disgust crosses Logan's face, and I can practically see him wanting to walk right back out of the room. But we both know he has no other choice but to complete his physiotherapy in order to be cleared to skate come the start of the season.

A strange feeling flutters through me, wanting to save him from Dave's creepy hands, but I have no idea how I'm going to swing that. Dave is already oiling up his hands, preparing for the appointment while

Logan reluctantly unbuckles his belt—no offer of privacy extended to Logan beforehand, despite his openness to flaunt his body.

I go to look away when Logan catches my eye, and unlike every other time he's looked at me, there's nothing but a strained heaviness now. A silent message passes between us, his warning for me to be cautious around Dave clear as fucking day.

I nod, letting him know I understand exactly what he's trying to tell me, and before I get the chance to turn away to offer him that sliver of privacy, his pants are already gone. Logan makes his way to the table, and I can't help but notice how he still has his underwear on, unlike our appointment on Monday, only confirming just how uncomfortable he is about following through on this appointment. It breaks my heart. None of the players should be made to feel this way.

If only I knew what the fuck I could do to help him.

Logan gets comfortable on the table, propping his strong arm behind his head, and I just can't help myself. My gaze roams over him, and that feeling hits me once again, that overwhelming desire to climb up on that table and give him everything I've got.

My stare trails over those thick, strong thighs, then further up over his torso, and across the stubble decorating his sharp jaw. He's perfection, absolutely gorgeous. My gaze lifts just a little more, roaming over his face and shifting to find his dark, knowing stare already resting on mine, that familiar cocky grin quickly stretching across his ruggedly handsome face. Shit.

Sprung.

Logan raises a questioning brow as if to say, see something you like? And I want nothing more than to go out onto that ice and lay down in front of the Zamboni, hoping like fuck it crushes me whole.

Caught checking out the guy I insisted I wasn't interested in. Just great. It's like throwing fuel on the already blazing fire, and now there's no way in hell he's going to back off. But to be honest, I don't want him to. Maybe I should take Jaz's advice and let him have his wicked way with me until we get bored of each other. But there's no way a woman could get bored of that. It's physically impossible, and after realizing just how inexperienced I am, he'll walk away without a backward glance.

Dave finally turns around and steps up beside Logan on the table before glancing across at me. "Elle," he says. "Come join me. I want to show you some different techniques."

Thank God. It seems Dave has regained some type of professionalism. I do as I'm told and feel the heat of Logan's eyes as he watches me cross the room. I get in position on the opposite side of the table so I can watch exactly what Dave is doing.

He gets straight into it, and true to his word, he shows me a few techniques that I've never seen before. I can't wait to try them out on my next client. "How's the pain, Logan?" Dave asks.

"Fine," he grunts, but it's clear that it's not fine. Nothing is fine about any of this.

"Excellent," Dave replies before continuing with his work.

I watch on with a stark interest as Logan's hand subtly falls down beside the table and comes to a stop at the back of my thigh. Goosebumps spread across my skin, a dangerous need pounding through me, even more so as his big hand squeezes my leg. My knees weaken, and I grip the edge of the table to keep me standing, refusing to look down and meet Logan's heavy stare, knowing exactly what I'll find there.

Logan doesn't remove his hand, and good God, I don't want him to. I work double time, trying to maintain control as the fire and electricity from his touch burns through me, my body already craving so much more.

Finding the courage, my gaze shifts up from Dave's hands to meet Logan's dark stare, and I find a soft smile playing on his lips. "Save me," he mouths with desperation.

I think about it for a moment, but the look in his eyes makes it impossible to turn him down, and I realize that right now, I would do anything for this man. "Dave, do you mind if I give your techniques a go?" I ask. "If that's okay with Logan, of course. I'm intrigued by the artistry of your work."

"Indeed," Dave says, reaching for a towel and wiping the oil from his hands as he steps back from the table. He glances down at Logan. "You're okay with Elle taking over?"

Logan nods without hesitation, and I make my way around the other side of the table before squirting oil into the palm of my hand. My hands circle one another, warming the oil, and I watch as Logan's eyes catch the movement as they rub together. Desire pools in his stare, and I have to look away, unable to handle his intensity.

"Alright," Dave says as he comes to stand by my side. My fingers drop to Logan's strong thigh, and it's all I can do not to let out a low, hungry groan. Trying to maintain professionalism, I focus on what I'm doing as Dave talks me through his techniques and allows me to take the reins. "You're a natural, Elle. You're going to go far in this industry."

"Thank you," I say, more than happy to accept the compliment on my skills.

Deciding I know what I'm doing, Dave takes a seat at his desk and gets busy filling out Logan's progress reports while I try my best to think of anything other than the way my fingers are pushing right up into his groin.

I work on Logan for twenty minutes before Dave stands, the progress reports completed. "If you're good here, Elle, I might head out for lunch," Dave says, pulling my attention back to him.

"Oh, sure," I say as anxious nervousness begins pulsing through my veins, the tension suddenly so thick in the air between us.

"Make sure to go over his exercises and book in his next appointment," he reminds me, but there's simply no need, it's standard procedure. I might have only been here a week, but I know the routine by now.

"Got it," I murmur.

With that, Dave takes off out the door, and I watch in amusement as Logan's body instantly relaxes. "Thanks for that," Logan says, referring to my complete takeover of the appointment.

"No problem," I smile. "You looked a little uncomfortable."

"That's the understatement of the year," he scoffs, that arm propping back behind his head. "He's a great physio, but there's just something . . . I don't know . . . off about him."

"Yeah, I've picked up on that."

"How do you mean?" Logan asks, his body going rigid as a sharpness enters his deep tone. He sits straight up, his gaze locking right onto mine with a fierce protectiveness. "Did he do something? Touch you?"

"No," I gasp in horror, my eyes widening. "Nothing like that. I just get a weird vibe from him. Not to mention, the way he asked you to lose your pants and climb on board like you were about to catch the train to pound town was . . . uncomfortable."

"Good," he says, relaxing once again before laying back on the table and allowing me to continue my work, needing to force him to relax his body as I recall his reaction. I can't understand why he seems protective over me, but for some reason, I like it.

As I move across his thigh, working my way deeper into the core issues, Logan groans, gripping the side of the table, but I have to admit, he's doing well. I've had four of his teammates in tears this week. "Shit, this sucks," he mutters.

"I know, but it won't take long to heal, especially if you keep up with your rehabilitation plan," I remind him, certain he's already heard this a million times by now. Hell, I can only imagine the type of check-ins he's had with team management.

Logan sighs. "I just want to get back on the ice already. It's barely been a week, and I don't know what to do with myself."

His comments are asking for a smartass response, and I don't have it in me to hold back. "I'm sure you can think of something to do that will drain all your pent-up energy."

Logan looks at me with that knowing smirk, and I have to resist biting my lip. "You offering?" he questions, his tone so low and deep my knees almost fall out from beneath me.

"You wish," I tell him, but let's be honest, he knows damn well just how interested I am. "I know we're just coming off the back of Dave's perverted ways, but call me curious. I've been thinking about your explanation on Monday, when you told me exactly how you fell, and I couldn't help but wonder—"

"I swear to all that's holy, Elle, if you're about to ask me if my dick still works, I'm going to bend you over this table and show you just how fucking good it gets."

My fingers dig deeper into his thigh and he groans, knowing exactly what's at risk if he wants to keep talking to me like that. "Try all you'd like, Captain," I murmur, feeling bolder than ever before. "But you'll have to catch me first, and something tells me you couldn't even make it to the door without succumbing to the pain. At least, not without those crutches."

Logan stares up at me, the challenge in his eyes only becoming more intense.

"On that note," I continue. "When you hypothetically bend me over this table, is that going to be done with or without the crutches? I mean, how's that going to work? You're either holding the crutches and free-handing everything else—hoping you don't accidentally poke someone's eye out with that thing—or you ditch the crutches and flail around on one leg, trying to fuck while hoping you don't fall. Neither option seems very appealing to me."

"Are you sure?" he asks as his eyes become hooded, more than ready to throw my sarcasm right back at me. "I have days' worth of energy to burn. I'll make sure you enjoy yourself, crutches be damned. Just say the word and we'll get you some protective eyewear."

Fuck me. Breathe, Elle. Breathe.

I purposefully press harder into his thigh, and he lets out an amused groan. "Okay, okay," he laughs, and the way his eyes light up makes me wish I could stand and watch him forever. "I'll behave. But only if you tell me something else about yourself."

"No way," I grin, enjoying this banter between us far too much, despite knowing I'm pushing the limits of my professionalism. Hell, I more than crossed it, but Logan's different. He knows I'm serious about my work, but he also understands that we're just having a little fun to get him through the pain. "It's your turn to do the talking."

"Fine, I guess that's fair," he groans. "What do you want to know?"

"Um, I don't know. Surprise me."

"Okay," he smiles as if he truly has something that could surprise me. "I'm an identical triplet."

"What?" I grunt as my hands pause on his thigh. I couldn't have heard that right, and I'm sure with all my googling over the past week, that would have surely come up. "You're telling me there are three of you?"

"Yeah," he says. "Me, Sean, and Carter. Sean's the sensible one, but Carter's worse than me."

"Bullshit. Worse than you? Impossible," I laugh, so hung up on this. Three Logan's. Shit. His poor mother. I can only imagine the number of women who would have been showing up on her doorstep, desperate for her sons' attention. "Is it just you three?"

"Nah, we have a younger sister, Cassie. She just completed her bachelor's degree in applied science at Denver and is just about to start her doctorate in physical therapy."

"No way," I say. "I was a TA for a few years. I probably would have run into her at some point."

"Yeah, she mentioned that."

My brow arches, something sparking deep inside of me at the thought of this man chatting about me to his little sister. "You've been talking about me, huh?"

His eyes widen, realizing he let that slip. "Uhhh . . . you might have come up," he tells me. "You know, because she was asking about my physio."

"Riiiight," I laugh, deciding to let him off the hook. "I didn't really know many of the girls in college. I mainly kept to myself."

"Why's that?" he questions.

"Just had a lot on my plate is all," I find myself saying before my hands pause on his warm skin. "Wait, did you say her name was Cassie? I remember one girl. Everyone was raving about her practically being a famous YouTube singer."

"Yeah, that's her," he smiles fondly before meeting my gaze, his brow arching in question. "Care to elaborate on the whole, have a lot on your plate thing?" he asks so casually, but I see his need to dig deeper into my world, and it puts me on edge. I don't open up about my life to anyone. It's too hard, and all it does is cause me pain. Apart from my brother, Jaz is the only one I've managed to open up to, and that was hard enough.

I shake my head ever so slightly, and I'm relieved when he doesn't push.

We finish off the appointment with mindless chatter, and I exit the room to give Logan a chance to pull his pants back on, the way he should have been offered in the first place. I come back in to find Logan leaning up against the desk, and I take him through a few more exercises before booking his next appointment.

He walks out the door and gives me a cheeky-as-fuck grin before it closes behind him with a soft thud, leaving me a mess of emotions, unsure what the hell to think. This man is something else. Just the physical attraction is enough to draw me in, but now that I've spent two hours over the past week talking with him; I've learned that he's one of the funniest and most intriguing guys I've ever had the pleasure of meeting, and that scares the shit out of me.

I'm treading in dangerous waters, and soon enough, the rapids are going to drag me under.

I'm just thankful Logan didn't try to ask me out again because I don't have the willpower to turn him down twice. Every chance he got, he had something cheeky to say, and no matter what I did, I couldn't wipe the smile off my face. The way he so effortlessly throws that quick wit right back at me, not afraid to hold back no matter how risky it might be. It's so carefree and honest. Hell, just being in his presence makes me feel so much lighter.

There's something refreshing about him, something that helps me forget about the pain and hurt of the world I live in, and I find myself excited for his next appointment.

Sitting down at the desk, I fill in the few things Dave left for me when I notice my phone beeping on the desk beside me. I unlock the screen and find a new message from Jaz.

Jaz – Fuck the girls' night in on Saturday. I want to go out and party. New club on Main?

A grin spreads over my face. I could really use a night out to let loose and get my mind off Logan. It's exactly what I need.

Elle – Hell yes. Count me in.

Chapter Seven

LOGAN

After seeing that text come through on Elle's phone on Thursday morning, I've been struggling big time. To be a creepy-as-fuck stalker or to not be a creepy-as-fuck stalker? The struggle is real.

It's not as though I meant to look at her phone. I wasn't intentionally snooping through her messages. Her phone chimed and I just happened to glance that way when the message appeared on the screen.

In the end, I've allowed my stalker tendencies to fly free. I've thrown my how to not be a creepy fucker textbook into the fire, despite knowing that I need to let this go. But I can't. Every fucking waking minute I spend thinking about what this girl is doing.

Unlocking my phone, I bring up my best friend's number and press call. It rings twice before Jace's tone sails through the phone. "Yo, fucker. What's up?"

"Any plans tonight?" I question as I head out my back door to sit by the frozen pond that I can no longer skate on. At least for the next few months, that is. But I have all faith that Elle's magic hands can turn those long, painful months into mere weeks. Though, whether it's weeks or months, the integrity of the pond isn't going to last that long. Just over the past few days, I've watched it begin to succumb to the warming weather.

"Yeah, I'm taking Lacey out," he says. "Why?"

"Ugh," I grunt, not exactly thrilled with Jace's new girlfriend. "Scratch that. We're going out."

"Nah, man. I can't bail on Lacey again. She'll kill me and then have my balls for dinner," he says. "Man, she still hasn't forgiven me for ditching her last month, but it wasn't my fault. It's not like I intentionally forgot I'd organized to meet her at that bar. I don't know about you, but having your balls pulverized ain't all that fun."

"Don't talk to me about sore balls, man. You've got no fucking leg to stand on until you've felt the pain of your sack almost tearing right through the center," I tell him. "So find wherever the fuck Lacey put yours and bring your girl with us."

Jace lets out a reluctant groan, knowing this will probably end in some kind of argument between them, but he simply can't resist, especially considering he can bring her along. "Fine," he finally relents. "What's the plan?"

"We're hitting that new club on Main."

"Yeah, alrig—wait. You can't be going out to a fucking club in your condition," he says. "Aren't you on crutches or some shit like that? Carter mentioned you lost all functionality of your dick. Tough break, man."

Fucking Carter.

"There ain't nothing wrong with my dick. It works perfectly fine," I say with a grin, recalling last night in the shower after I couldn't get Elle out of my head. Especially after hearing her talk about the way I would fuck her on the table, with or without my crutches. And while I know she was insinuating that it would be awkward, messy, and embarrassing, all she managed to do is make me want it more.

"You sure, man?" Jace continues. "You can't fuck yourself up. There's too much riding on this."

"I won't. I'm good."

"Alright," he says. "We'll meet you at your place in a few hours."

"Sure," I say before ending the call.

A light drizzle starts, so I head back up to the house and kick back on the couch to watch ESPN. I feel like a dick going out to this club. It's not like I saw her reply. I'm just assuming she's going to be there, but if she is, I hope it doesn't mess with her head. I just need to see her outside of that room, and having a few drinks at a club to let loose is the perfect way to do that.

I fall asleep to the sound of last year's championship game and am woken later by the sound of my phone screeching by my ear. I hastily sit up with a groan and answer the phone without looking at the caller ID.

"Hey, fucker," Carter's annoying voice says through the line.

"What's up?" I say on a yawn, reminded that at some point, I need to kick his ass for telling Jace that my dick doesn't work.

"Not much. Bri and I were going to head around to your place for dinner," he tells me.

"No can do, brother," I say. "Jace and I are going out."

"Oh, yeah," he says with interest. "Where are you going?"

Dragging my hand over my face, I try to wake myself a bit, wondering if this is somehow going to turn into a fucking party. "That new club on Main," I tell him, more than ready to get him on board, especially considering Carter likes to get wild and fucked up when he lets loose. Though I'm not going to lie, his wild antics have landed me in trouble a time or two with clueless paparazzi who couldn't tell the difference between us.

"Fuck yeah, count us in," Carter says before calling out to Bri. "Babe, call Cass. We're going out tonight."

"What?" I grunt, realization dawning that not only is this going to be a fun night, but it was supposed to be my opportunity to run into Elle, and I don't need to be doing that with my whole fucking family watching over my shoulder. "That wasn't an invitation."

Fuck me. There's no stopping them now. The second Cass finds out about this, she'll have Sean and Sara on the phone too. I can just imagine it now, the second Cassie recognizes Elle in the club, she's going to know exactly why we're there, and when she does, I can guarantee that Jax will know too.

"Tough shit, bro," Carter says, probably grinning like a fucking idiot. "Bri has been begging for a night out to get messy, and I'm sure Cass has been too."

Well . . . this is going to be interesting. I can just see it now. Tonight is going to turn into the Waters family train wreck.

"Fine," I grumble, pulling my phone away to double check the time and realize that Jace and Lacey should be coming around soon. "Jace is bringing Lacey. We're meeting at my place before heading in."

"Oh, he's still with that chick?" Carter asks in distaste.

"Yeah," I laugh, a little caught off guard. "Do you even know her? What's your problem?"

"Dude, remember that chick in high school I screwed in the science labs before getting sprung by her boyfriend?"

"Yeah?"

"That's her," he says proudly.

Ahh, fuck.

"Shit," I sigh, tonight really is going to be interesting. "I'd forgotten about that. Are you sure it's the same chick?"

Carter scoffs. "Come on, brother. You know me better than that. I don't forget my conquests."

"Don't let Bri hear you saying that," I warn him, needing to cut this call short. It's getting late, and if I don't have a shower now, I won't have a chance before everyone starts piling in. "I got to go, man."

"Yeah, alright. We'll be there in an hour," he says before ending the call.

With that, I hobble up the stairs and get myself showered and presentable before heading back down to the living room and ordering a few pizzas. The girls are going to be drinking before we leave, and I'd rather they had a little food in their stomachs before they get absolutely wasted at the club. I can already tell it's going to be an unforgettable night. I just hope it's unforgettable for the right reasons.

Within the next half hour, everyone shows up. Cassie comes waltzing in with Jax first, followed by Carter and Bri, Sean and Sara, then Jace and Lacey. The second Lacey walks in, her eyes widen in shock quickly followed by pure panic as she notices Carter smirking at her from across the room, and it's clear Jace doesn't know shit.

Carter looks at me with a wicked grin, and I realize he's going to be the designated shit-stirrer tonight. Just fucking great.

Cassie makes herself helpful and starts pouring drinks as everyone devours the pizzas. That's when the inevitable fight over who's going to be the designated driver rears its ugly head.

A funny look passes between Sean and Sara before she lets out a heavy breath and puts her hand up, offering to drive. Only it doesn't solve our problem since there are nine of us to squeeze in an eight-seater car. But Carter does what he does best and crawls into the trunk and hides.

"Nope. No way," Sara says, shaking her head at my brothers. "I am not driving with that idiot in the back."

"Come on," Carter calls as his head pokes up and appears in the back window. "Live a little. What happened to the badass I knew from high school? You haven't turned into a little bitch, have you?"

Sara clenches her jaw, glaring at Carter, but fuck, he plays her so well. He knows exactly what strings to pull.

"Babe?" Sean questions. He would never make her do something she isn't comfortable with, so if she says no, then the plan is about to change.

She lets out a loud huff. "Fine, but if I get arrested, I'm telling them you're all hiding little baggies of cocaine up your asses so you get cavity searched."

Carter whoops and laughs as the rest of us pile into the car, and before we know it, we're pulling up outside the newest club in town, more than ready for a good night.

As we file out of the car, a strange nervousness spreads through my gut, and I have no idea why, but it fucks with my head.

Why the hell am I nervous? I've been with a million girls and never once felt this way. There's just something about Elle. I need to know her. I need to be next to her and find out what makes her tick. What does she like? Who are her friends? Where does she live, and why the fuck hasn't she agreed to go out with me yet? You know, apart from the obvious.

I shake it off as we make our way toward the door. "What's up with you?" Jace asks as he reaches for the door, holding it open for the girls. "You look . . . sick."

"Nah, I'm fine," I tell him, stepping in front of him and cutting in front of Sean, not prepared for Jace to look any closer. The second I step into the club, my gaze lifts around the room, taking it all in.

Disappointment begins gnawing at me as I scan over the dance floor, hastily taking in the many faces. But as my attention shifts toward the bar, I find Elle reaching for her drink, and a pounding force blasts through my chest.

Bingo.

She's fucking radiant in those tall, thigh-high boots. Just the sight of her has my cock painfully twitching in my pants. She's wearing a skintight black mini dress, showing off the sweet curves of her body, and I can't help the low groan that tears from the back of my throat. I'm used to seeing her in her uniform, which she looks fucking amazing in, but this. This. Goddamn. That tiny dress is going to send me to the deepest pits of hell, and I'll go willingly.

Elle stands with a friend, laughing as they sip on fancy cocktails, and I find myself mesmerized, unable to look away. The club's flashing lights illuminate the subtle chestnut hues in her hair, making her look like the only person in the room. My nerves disappeared the second I laid eyes on her, and now all I feel is an overwhelming need to stand right at her fucking side.

At this moment, I'm exactly where I need to be.

"Hey," Cass says, stepping in beside me, nudging me with her shoulder as she looks up at me. "What's up with you? You look strange."

"Nothing," I say defensively, but my argument is cut short the second she turns her head toward the bar and notices the fucking bombshell who's having the time of her life.

Cassie's eyes bug out of her head and she gapes up at me, a wicked, smug grin stretching right across her face. "HOLY FUCKING SHIT," she squeals, bursting into roaring laughter, knowing damn well she just caught me out. "You're here to see Elle, aren't you?"

"No," I say. "It's a coincidence. I didn't know she was gonna be here."

"Bullshit," Cass laughs before turning back to our group and hollering loud enough for the whole fucking club to hear. "Logan's girlfriend is here."

"Girlfriend?" Sean grunts in question, disbelief thick in his tone.

I shake my head. "She's not my girlfriend," I say, but it's already too late. Cass blatantly points her out, making damn sure that each and every one of the fuckers around me knows exactly why I concocted this plan.

"Fuck, bro. She's hot," Carter says. "Why don't you go for it?"

"It's not for lack of trying," I tell him, unable to keep my eyes off Elle. "She's the new junior physio on the team and doesn't want to get caught messing around with the players." Understanding dawns on his face, but he knows damn well that I'm going to give it a go anyway.

"Alright," Sean says as he takes Sara's hand. "Let's get this night started."

"Fuck, yeah," Carter calls as he grabs Brianna and yanks her toward the bar.

I stay back with Jace and Lacey and find a table while the others stock up on drinks and snacks to keep us going for hours on end. I watch as Carter and Bri walk by Elle, and I grin in amusement as her eyes instantly latch onto Carter like she's seeing a ghost. Her gaze follows him, which is when she sees Bri's hand in Carter's and disappointment flashes in her eyes before she covers it up and points him out to her friend.

I've never been so fucking amused in my life.

It's damn clear Elle thinks I'm Carter, and for a moment, I feel as though I should let her sweat it, but the need to put her out of her misery takes over, and I make my way across the club. The two girls are still busy ogling Carter when I step in between them and throw my arms over their petite shoulders. "See something you like, ladies?"

Elle's gaze snaps up toward me before recognition hits and a curse comes flying out of her mouth. "Holy shit, Logan. What the hell are you doing here?"

All I can do is grin, caught off guard by her beauty, when her friend cuts in. "Huh?" she grunts, looking at me before hooking her thumb in Carter's direction. "I thought that was Logan?"

"No, no. He's not as devilishly handsome as me," I say with a cheeky wink in her direction.

Her face flushes, and she makes a show of fanning herself. "My, oh my," she grins, quickly glancing at Elle before fixing her hungry stare back on me, slowly trailing up and down my body. "You're right about that. I'm Jaz."

"Hey," Elle grunts, cutting off whatever smartass response I was about to give before fixing me with a hard, suspicious stare. "What are you doing here?"

I can't help but smirk as it becomes devastatingly obvious that I knew exactly what she was doing tonight. "I'm here with the family. We're checking out the new club," I tell her.

Elle's suspicion only grows. "Right . . . and what do you think of it so far?" she asks, amusement beginning to shine in those bright blue eyes.

"Fucking stunning," I murmur, holding her stare captive, letting her feel the weight of my comment and watching as her cheeks flush with the most stunning shade of pink. "Why don't you come join us?"

Elle's head is shaking before she can even get the words out. "No. No way, Logan Waters. I know what you're up to, and it's never gonna work."

"You know what?" Jaz grins before giving Elle a look that says, I dare you to stop me. "We'd love to join you."

"Ugh," Elle groans as she looks up at me. "Fine, but you need to behave. Hands to yourself at all times."

With her shoulder still tucked firmly under my arm, I lead her and Jaz toward our table. "I can't make any promises," I murmur for only her to hear as my thumb gently skims across her shoulder. A shiver sails over her skin, and I know she feels it too, that same pull that's driving me right now. I just wish she wasn't so stubborn and would give in to my wicked charm.

We make it to our table, and I introduce the girls to everyone and make sure I let Elle know exactly who Jax is on the team since they are bound to meet in a professional capacity eventually. Carter and Sean make their way back to the table and Jaz practically loses her mind.

"Far out, these men are like . . . wow," she says as she practically starts drooling. "Why is everyone here taken?"

"It must be your lucky day," Elle says. "Logan here is as free as a bird. Have at him. Though be warned, the jury is still out on whether his dick actually works or not."

I give Elle a hard stare before letting my hand fall to my belt buckle, the challenge heavy in my eyes. "You wanna settle this right now, babe?" I ask as Cassie and Sara blanch in horror, but Elle's not having a bar of it, more than ready to call my bluff. She just stares, a smirk pulling at the corner of her lips as if daring me to continue, assuming I won't. Her mistake.

I slowly begin releasing my belt before gripping onto the button and making a show of popping it open, not once taking my eyes from hers. Elle's expression sobers, her face falling every passing second, realizing I'm not the type to bluff.

Gripping the small zipper, I start dragging it down until she's had enough. "Holy shit, Logan," Elle rushes out, scolding me as she steps into me, trying to mask my almost exposed dick from the crowd around. "Are you trying to get your dick splashed all over every news outlet in the country?"

"I'd prefer to put it somewhere else to be honest, but if it's gotta break the internet for you to accept that it's a fucking beast, then that's what I'll do."

Her cheeks flush, and she shakes her head, desperately trying to hold back a grin. "I can't with you," she says, lifting her cocktail to her lips and taking a long sip. She bites down on her lip, her gaze locking onto mine as she leans in, so very clearly feeling the effects of her cocktail. "For the record, I know damn well it's a beast. The question is, what the hell are you gonna do with it?"

My hand captures her waist, and I pull her in a step, her body flush against mine. Elle raises her chin, her lips barely a breath from mine, and the need to kiss her eats at me. But she's made her stance on this well known, and I'm not about to take advantage of that just because she's had a few drinks and her guard is down. "Just you fucking wait, Elle," I murmur, my fingers skimming her waist, over her hip, and down to the soft exposed skin of her thigh. "When I fuck you, when I open these pretty thighs and take that sweet little cunt, I'm going to have you screaming until your lungs give out, until you're coming so fucking hard on my cock that your walls are shaking. When I touch you, Elle, I'm not just going to fuck you. I'm going to claim you."

Elle falters, sucking in a breathy gasp, her fingers hooking into my belt loop and holding on for dear life. "Careful now," she whispers, somehow impossibly closer, the feel of her body against mine like fucking magic. "Don't make promises you can't keep."

My fingers trail back up her body until my arm is locked firmly around her waist, caging her against me, right where she's meant to be. "Wouldn't dream of it."

Elle slowly shakes her head, forcing herself to look away as she creates just a fraction of space between us. She lets out a deep breath, her cheeks blowing out. "You're gonna get me in trouble, Logan Waters."

I smile down at her, desperately wishing she'd move back into me. "You're damn right I am, and you're going to love every fucking second of it."

Chapter Eight

LOGAN

Tonight has been a fucking adventure. The whole table is a mess of sloppy, drunk girls while the guys are talking over one another, desperately trying to be heard over the noise. Elle's more than relaxed after having a few drinks. Hell, she's fucking tanked, and I can't get enough. She's fallen right in with my family. My brothers seem to like her, and Cass is already head over heels in love with the girl.

Another round of cocktails ends up on the table, and Elle reaches across to hand them out to the girls. She reaches over Sean, offering one to Sara, who waves it off. "Designated driver," she rumbles, looking longingly at the cocktail, probably wishing she could let loose and join in on the girls' ridiculous shenanigans. Though, I'm sure she could. We would just get an Uber for the way home.

Elle gives her a knowing smile, and as she goes to put the cocktail back on the table, Bri swoops in, clutching the drink. "I'll take that," she declares, a glass in each hand—one pink and one blue.

"That's right, babe. Drink up," Carter encourages with a stupid grin.

Elle laughs, watching as Bri takes the straw from each glass and sips on them at the same time before glancing at Carter. "Aren't you supposed to discourage your girlfriend from drinking so much?" Elle questions, laughter dancing in her eyes

Carter smirks right back at her. "Nah, not this one," he says, all too proudly. "Brianna gets real kinky when she's drunk."

"Oh, God. I want that," Jaz says as she gets up from the table. "I need to find a man to take home tonight. Who's with me?"

At that, the six girls get up as though they're tied at the hips. They grab their cocktails and shimmy out onto the dance floor. I watch them go, only to find one sticking around, her hand already falling into mine.

Elle hauls me up off my chair, and I'm so fucking grateful that I've been able to walk properly tonight, otherwise, I'd already be flat on the ground. She beams up at me, the feel of her hand in mine so fucking right.

She drags me out onto the dance floor, and I let out a heavy breath, not sure how the fuck this is going to go. Sober Elle would be scolding my ass for even considering looking at a dance floor, let alone stepping out onto one of them, but drunk Elle can't seem to fucking wait.

Bumping into Cass and Bri, Elle stops and spins around, falling into my arms as her body begins to move to the music. I don't let go of her hand, and as I spin her around, I notice the rest of the guys must have followed us out.

Elle dances like no one's watching, grinding up against me, and goddamn, she has me right on the fucking edge. She turns in my arms and grins up at me just as the music changes to something a little slower. "You knew I was here, Logan Waters," she accuses, more than happy to call me out on my shit.

"Yeah," I laugh, no point denying it now. "I saw the message come through on your phone. Is that going to be a problem?"

"Not right now," she smiles, "But I'm sure it will be tomorrow."

I can't help but laugh, not doubting that for even a moment. "For the record, it's not like I was actively looking. I just needed to brace myself against the desk chair to be able to get my fucking pants on, and there it was, Jaz's message just staring right up at me."

Elle chuckles and throws her arms around my neck, rubbing her perfect body up against mine. "Why'd you come?" she questions, a fierce curiosity in her blazing blue eyes.

My fingers brush along her waist, unable to resist touching her. "I can't answer that."

"You can't or you won't?"

"Can't," I confirm. "Because I have no fucking idea why I came. I just knew I needed to see you again, and the fact that you were going to be here, outside of work. Well, fuck, Elle. How the hell could I pass that up?"

She grins up at me, her cheeks slightly flushed, but the alcohol keeps her rooted right to the spot, refusing to look away. "You're a smooth talker, Captain."

"You like it," I challenge her. "In fact, you fucking love it."

She watches me back, refusing to say a word because she knows just how fucking right I am. "Don't deny it, baby. I know you're not ready, and that's okay. You will be soon, and when you are, I'm gonna have you begging on your knees for more."

Her eyes meet mine, and I see a real fear behind them. "You're a heartbreaker," she says, telling it how she sees it, and it all becomes abundantly clear to me. She's scared I'm going to hurt her, scared to give up a piece of herself only for it to be destroyed within my grasp. She thinks I'm just like all the other players out there, and that's on me. I haven't given her anything to believe otherwise, so I'm going to have to prove to her that I'm not. I mean, I've definitely had my moments in the past, but this girl is different. The idea of having her only for a moment doesn't feel right. When I take her as my own, it'll be forever. I don't want to give her up.

Elle's going to be mine. There's no doubt about it, but she just has to realize it first, and when she does . . . Well, that's when the real fun is going to begin.

A few hours later, Carter and Bri are practically screwing on the dance floor. Jax has taken Cass home, and Sara is yawning at the table. I have no idea what happened to Jace and Lacey, but I know Lacey is upset after Carter dropped the bomb on Jace and let him know about their past.

Elle and Jaz collapse into their seats while Elle pulls out her phone. "I'm going to order an Uber," she tells Jaz, who nods along while downing a glass of champagne.

My back stiffens, and I look at Elle, the thought of her disappearing in an Uber not sitting right with me. "Let me drive you home," I say to Elle, reaching out and pressing her phone down until she places it in her lap.

She glances up at me with a raised brow before scoffing. "Oh, because showing Logan Waters my home is such a great idea," she says. "Besides, I thought she was driving," Elle adds, nodding toward Sara, who's now asleep on her husband's shoulder.

"Yeah, that's not happening," I tell her, gaining Sean's attention. "Come on. I'll drop you guys home, too."

Trusting that I would only offer to drive if I were sober, Sean nudges Sara and lets her know we're leaving. Her face crumples, annoyed to be moving around as she fishes through her purse and hands me the keys before letting Sean help her up.

As we get up, I glance down at Elle with an expectant stare, knowing there are only two ways this is going to go. She's either going to get up and walk out to the car like a good girl, or I'm going to carry her ass there myself. "Are you coming?"

Elle presses her lips into a hard line before shaking her head. "Nope," she finally says.

I stop in my tracks and look down at her, realizing she's just being stubborn. "Why the hell not?"

"Because I'm not a damsel in distress. I don't need you to come in and save me. I've been taking care of myself long enough," she tells me.

"Babe, you're being stupid. Get your ass out of that chair. I'm taking you and Jaz home." She presses her lips together in consideration, and I can see she's still leaning toward no, but unfortunately for her, I'm not taking no for an answer. "I'm not trying to work an angle to get in your pants. I just want to make sure you get home safe."

She rolls her eyes as she gets to her feet. "Fine. You win this round, Captain, but only because I don't want to sit in the back of a dirty Uber." She strides past me, going to follow Sean and Sara out, when she stops and turns back. "And for the record, if I find you showing up at my door unannounced because you insisted on taking me home just so you could work out where I live, I'm going to . . . Ummm, I haven't worked that part out, but just know, it's bad. Very bad."

A grin tears across my face, more than ready to do exactly what she's warning me against. I'll take my chances. "Noted."

Logan: 1

Elle: 0

Chapter Nine

ELLE

The blinding sun streaming through my bedroom window is bright enough to wake the dead, and I realize that maybe I drank a few too many cocktails last night. My head aches, and I'm pretty sure if I don't make it to the bathroom within the next few seconds, I'll be seeing last night's dinner all over my bed . . . wait, did I even eat dinner?

A loud groan rumbles through my chest as I get myself up out of bed. My legs are wobbly, my feet ache from hours of dancing, and I have to use the wall to keep myself balanced as I find my way to the bathroom.

After quickly finishing my business, I splash water over my face and glance up into the mirror, horrified by the person staring back at me. I'm a train wreck. My hair looks like Louie has been living in it for the past few months, mascara is smudged all over my face, and for some reason, I'm wearing a shirt that certainly is not mine.

What the hell happened last night?

The last thing I remember is being in the club after that big buffoon crashed my girls' night with Jaz. He ordered round after round, we danced, he said something that is way too blurry for my mind to recall, and then I somehow got myself home. I should probably check in with Jaz to make sure she made it home safely, though I never would have left without her.

The shirt falls down to my knees, and I try to remember why it's so familiar to me. I know for a fact that it's not one of Brendan's. It's way too expensive for our kind of budget. And besides, I buy all his clothes for him, and I certainly didn't get him this.

I wrack my brain as I brush my teeth and scrub the mascara from under my eyes. I'm halfway through brushing the nest out of my hair when it hits me—this is the shirt Logan was wearing last night.

I suck in a loud gasp, gaping at myself through the mirror. How the hell did I end up wearing Logan's shirt?

Please, God, tell me nothing happened last night.

Why the hell am I in his shirt anyway? And why the hell do I like it so much?

My eyes widen, and I grip the shirt before yanking it up and double checking my underwear is still firmly intact. Finding them exactly where they're supposed to be, I let out a relieved sigh, gripping the edge of the sink and dropping my head. Thank fuck for that.

I couldn't have lost my virginity without knowing, right? I'm sure if we slept together, he would still be in my bed . . . or maybe he's the kind to screw me and leave, but then he would have left with his shirt on, right? You know, assuming his dick actually worked.

I doubt anything happened though. Logan doesn't seem like the type to take advantage of a woman who's been drinking, and he sure as hell doesn't seem like the type to just slip out during the night. No, Logan Waters is the type of man to fuck a woman all night long and then again in the morning.

The desperate need for coffee pounds through my veins, and I trudge out to the kitchen as bits and pieces of my night filter through my head. The dancing, the joy, the way his arms would lock around my waist.

Fuck, I'm already in too deep.

Bypassing the kitchen, I make my way across the back of the couch before stopping in front of Louie's cage and lifting the blanket off to say good morning. "Hey, little guy. Did you miss me last night?" I ask, opening the cage and reaching in to get him out.

Louie instantly hops on my hand, hitching a ride out of his cage before making his way up to my shoulder. He squawks like a motherfucker, and the sound is like nails on a chalkboard. "Jesus Christ," I mutter, making my way into the kitchen. Reaching up to grab a mug, I try to remember if I picked up painkillers from the store this week.

I get busy making my coffee as Louie flies off my shoulder and perches on the back of the couch, his favorite spot. "You wouldn't believe my night, Louie," I say as the smell of coffee begins to fill my kitchen. Taking my mug, I lift the rim to my lips, and just as I go to take a sip, a loud creak comes from the couch.

My body stiffens as I freeze on the spot, my eyes widening with fear. My heart begins to pound as I slowly turn around, my gaze shooting to the couch. All I see is the back with Louie perched on top, and I hold my breath as I slowly move across my kitchen to get a better angle.

A big body comes into view, and the fear quickly fades as my brow arches. "Holy fucking shit," I murmur as I stare at the gorgeous man taking over my couch.

What the fuck is Logan Waters doing here? And why the hell is he sleeping on my couch?

I take a moment to take him in and study his impressive body before reality hits me. Maybe we did have sex. That would explain why he's here and why I'm wearing his shirt, but I thought I'd be sore after the first time—or at least remember it.

Disappointment rumbles through me, taking grip of my heart and squeezing for all it's worth. I really wanted the first time to be special, something meaningful with a man I was desperately in love with, not a drunken one-night stand.

Letting out a sigh, I lift my coffee mug to my lips again and take a sip, trying to figure out how the hell I'm going to get Logan out of here. As if reading my mind, Louie hops off the back of the couch, landing right in the middle of Logan's bare chest.

Louie lets out an almighty squawk as Logan's eyes spring open, his whole body jolting. Logan's arms fly out, clutching onto the sides of the couch as he stares up at the most stunning bird I've ever seen. "What the—"

"Bastard. Little bastard," Louie says in that adorable bird voice, cutting Logan off.

Astonishment comes over Logan's face as he takes in the foul-mouthed bird perched on his chest. That strong arm moves behind his head as the corner of his mouth lifts in a cocky smirk. "Well, shit. At least give me your name before you start climbing on top of me."

Pressing my lips into a hard line to keep from laughing, I clear my throat to gain his attention, and those dark eyes instantly snap to mine. There's an intensity in his stare, something powerful I'm not prepared for, and remembering I'm in nothing but his shirt, a deep flush spreads over my cheeks.

"What the hell are you doing on my couch?" I question as I cross my arms over my chest, doing everything in my power to try and mask the effect he has on me.

Logan rubs a hand over his face before running it through his dark hair, his bicep rolling with the movement. He slowly sits up as Louie walks up his wide chest and perches on his shoulder. "Good morning to you too," he rumbles in a deep, husky tone that makes my insides quiver.

His gaze roams up and down my body, slowly trailing over my bare legs and to his shirt that covers my body. A deep hunger flashes in his eyes as a fierce desire pulses through my veins. The way he's looking at me . . . damn, I could get used to this. "Logan," I say, forcing his gaze back to mine. "My couch. Why?"

He smirks before getting up off the couch and walking over to me, a slight limp from the night of being on his feet. I freeze as he steps into me, invading my personal space. Logan leans in, and I catch my breath as he presses a kiss to my forehead. My hands grow shaky as he closes his big ones around mine and takes the coffee mug right out of my grasp. "Thanks for this," he says, his right hand falling to my waist as he lifts my coffee to his lips—the very lips I haven't been able to stop thinking about. "Your couch is not very comfortable. I'll get you a new one."

I lift my chin, barely a breath away as I meet those dark eyes. "You're not getting me a new couch, Logan," I tell him. "Why are you here?"

His gaze sails over me again, starved for my touch. "You look ravishing," he murmurs in my ear before finally stepping back and allowing me my personal space, but the distance between us is almost painful.

"Ravishing," Louie repeats in his little bird voice, making Logan grin in approval.

I give him a hard stare, raising my brow before crossing my arms over my chest, impatiently waiting for an answer, and the longer he makes me wait, the wider his smirk becomes. "You don't remember, do you?" he questions, amusement thick in his velvety tone.

"If I remembered, I would have gone to much greater lengths to make sure I didn't come out here in nothing but your shirt."

"Mmmm," he groans as he looks me over with hooded eyes. "That would have been a tragedy."

"Logan," I demand, reaching out and taking my coffee back. "Concentrate."

He lets out a sigh before backing up and leaning against my kitchen counter, crossing his leg over the other. "I drove you and Jaz home after I detached her from some random asshole. Then I walked you to your door like the perfect gentleman, and you nailed me in the balls when I tried to kiss you—as if they haven't already been through enough trauma."

My hand comes up, covering my mouth as my eyes widen in horror. "Oh shit," I breathe. "You're lying. Tell me I didn't."

"Sure as fuck did, babe," he says, reaching forward and plucking the coffee right out of my hand again. "Then you started crying because you felt bad about it and were worried you caused more damage. So, you insisted on trying to fix it before attempting to strip me."

"Oh, Jesus," I groan.

"It was very endearing," he teases.

"I'm never drinking again," I say, covering my face, completely horrified by myself. "So, we didn't . . . umm?"

"Have sex?" he laughs. "No. Not for lack of trying on your part. I'm not really into taking advantage of a woman who was so drunk that she walked straight into her own front door."

"Oh, thank God," I breathe in relief, though I shouldn't be surprised. I knew Logan wasn't the kind of man to take advantage of me in that way, and I should be ashamed that I even asked him, but I had to be sure.

"Well fuck," he scoffs. "Thanks for the vote of confidence. It wouldn't have been that bad. Hell, you would have even enjoyed yourself."

"With your broken dick and all?"

"Fucking hell," he mutters under his breath, dragging his hand over his face.

I can't help but laugh. "It's not that. I'm sure I would have enjoyed myself and probably came back for seconds. It's just—" I let out a breath and glance again. "It's nothing. Forget I said anything."

Logan narrows his gaze on me, and I sense his need to question me, but I move across my kitchen, not allowing him the chance. I go about making myself a new coffee before I start blabbing about my virginity, and as my mug fills, I glance back at him over my shoulder. "You still haven't explained why you slept on my couch."

"Well," he says leaning back against the counter with a smirk that just doesn't seem to be disappearing. "After you mauled and attacked me, I could hardly walk, so you insisted I come in, and then you wouldn't let me out of your apartment. You all but kidnapped me."

I fix my stare on him, certain he's exaggerating. "How so?"

"You sat on me, Elle," he states bluntly.

Embarrassment floods me, and I find my jaw dropping as the mortification hits. "Ahh, shit. I'm so sorry," I tell him with a cringe.

"Oh, believe me. I enjoyed it," he says with a wink. "You fell asleep. I took you to bed, but apparently you're not a fan of doing laundry.

You had no pajamas, so you got my shirt instead."

My mouth drops open. "You dressed me?" I shriek. "And went through my laundry?"

"You're welcome," he says proudly.

"You didn't look, did you?"

"Are you serious?" he questions. "Of course, I fucking looked."

I can't help but laugh. I should have known better. "Well . . . thanks for mostly being a gentleman. You didn't have to do all that. You could have just dumped me at the door like most men would have."

Logan steps toward me, taking my waist and pulling me right into his wide chest. My heart races, and I catch my breath, completely frozen against him, hating just how right this feels. "I wouldn't do that. Not to you."

I shake my head, trying to make sense of this incredible man. "I don't understand you, Logan."

"You will, baby," he says. "Just give it time."

Flashbacks of the very first time I met him come rushing back, and a smile spreads across my face. "I'm not your baby," I remind him.

"Oh, but you are," he says, lifting his hand to push my hair back off my face, and as he does, I catch sight of his watch.

My eyes widen, and I grab hold of his wrist, double checking what I'm actually seeing. "Shit. I'm late," I shriek, knowing this is going to bite me on the ass. "You've got to go."

"What?" he grunts, slight disappointment in his tone. "Where are you going?"

"I'm meeting my brother," I tell him as I turn him and push him toward the door. "Or at least, I'm supposed to be."

"Cool, I'll come along," he says, putting on the brakes as I realize I'm trying to kick him out with my bird still perched on his big shoulder.

"Ha," I scoff, imagining how that would go down with Brendan as I reach up for Louie and let him step onto my hand. He climbs up to my shoulder and I get busy pushing Logan toward the door again. "No chance in hell. Besides, if I recall correctly, I'm pretty damn sure I told you that this was never gonna happen. I've got a job to protect, and unfortunately for you, that means getting your ass out of my apartment."

He lets out a laugh as I finally get him to the door. "Yeah, I thought that was a long shot," he says as he stops and turns in the doorway to look at me. "So, are you going to give me my shirt back?"

I glance down at myself, all too aware that I'm not wearing a bra. "You expect me to just take it off right here?"

"That would be nice," he says with that signature grin, making butterflies swarm through the pit of my stomach.

"You know what?" I say, grinning right back at him, "I'd rather keep it."

He watches me for a short moment, fondness shining so damn bright in his eyes. "I'll see you around, Elle," he says with a wink before finally turning and heading down the hallway, leaving me an absolute mess of emotions.

Closing the door behind him, I fall against it and let out a shaky breath, my head squished against the wood. What the hell am I doing? Innocent flirting at work is one thing, but this . . . We crossed a line.

I've allowed him to get too close.

Not having time to dwell on it, I shove Louie back in his cage before racing through a shower and getting dressed. Before I know it, I'm in my old, beat-up car, rushing down the highway.

I pull up at my brother's rehab facility and give myself a moment to breathe. Coming here is always hard, even years down the track. It reminds me of everything we've lost, but it's also a place of hope, somewhere we get to reclaim our strength. At least it is for Brendan.

His spinal cord was damaged during the crash that killed the rest of our family, and he's been in a wheelchair ever since. But six months ago, while we were having breakfast, his big toe moved. He didn't feel it, so we're damn lucky Louie had shit on the floor and I was on my hands and knees trying to scrub it clean while it happened.

So here he is, in a rehab facility, draining any and all spare funds that I have while he works on regaining some movement in his legs. It's hard financially, and it was the reason I was working two jobs up until now, but it's worth it.

I rush inside and hurry down the hallway until I come to Brendan's room, not hesitating to barge right in. "Hey, little brother. How are you?"

"You're late," he says through a narrowed gaze, sitting in his wheelchair by the window. "You're never late. What's going on?"

"Nothing," I say defensively. "I overslept."

"Bullshit. You were with a guy, weren't you? Logan Fucking Waters," he accuses. "I told you not to go there with him. He has a reputation."

"Chill out, Bren," I say, dropping into the chair beside his bed. "Nothing's going on between me and Logan. I went out to a club with Jaz last night."

"Liar."

"I'm not lying."

"So, how come you blushed the second I mentioned his name?" he questions.

I avert my stare, knowing just how well he sees through me. "Shut up. There's nothing going on."

Brendan just scoffs and grins, knowing he's right.

Rolling my eyes, I lean back in my chair and look over my brother, checking his face for any signs of discomfort or pain. "How are you feeling? Has the doctor been around today?"

He shakes his head. "He usually comes around eleven on a Sunday. You haven't missed him yet."

"Perfect," I smile. I mean, Brendan is more than capable of telling me how his progress is going, but there's something soothing about hearing it directly from the doctor himself. "How'd your therapy go yesterday?"

"Good," he grins before rolling out past the bed on his wheelchair. "Watch this."

Sitting forward in the chair, I watch with anticipation as a fierce concentration spreads over his face. He breaks out in a sweat, and I'm about to tell him to cool it when his whole right foot moves. "Holy shit," I squeal, jumping out of my seat. "That's fucking amazing."

"I know," he grins. "I'm actually getting somewhere this time."

"You sure are," I grin, never having been so damn proud of the kid in my life. He was hesitant to try after his last stint in rehab. He was able to get his toes moving then, but nothing further. When I took him home, he was so down on himself that he stopped his exercises and all progress was shattered, but this time is different. He's in a better place now, and I know if he continues to assert himself, he'll be able to achieve greatness. "I'm so proud of you."

"I know," he laughs. "I'm pretty fucking amazing."

We spend the next hour discussing my new job and how it's all going, though I strategically manage to leave all talk of Logan out of it. I tell him about Dave and what kind of guy he is, and I laugh as Brendan vows that he's going to kick his ass when he can walk again.

At eleven, the doctor comes in, and I sit up a little straighter and listen intently while enjoying just how good the man looks in his white coat. "Ahh, Elle. It's always a pleasure to see you," he says, laying on the charm, only today I don't seem to be eating it up like I usually would.

"You too, Doctor Ellis. How's our special little guy going?"

"Ugh," Brendan groans. "You gotta stop calling me that. I'm twice the size of you now."

"Sorry, Kid," I laugh. "Can't help it."

Doctor Ellis steps up to Brendan and does his usual prodding and poking while giving us the latest verdict. "Brendan's been doing incredibly well. We have high hopes for him. His tests and labs have all come back with positive results, so it's all up to him now. He needs to stay focused, continue his therapy and exercises, and at the rate of his progress, he should have no issues getting up on his feet within the next few months. That's with assistance, of course."

"Are you serious?" I rush out, my eyes wide.

Doctor Ellis nods. "Just keep him in high spirits and don't let him do too much. It's common for patients to push harder when they see progress. Brendan mustn't do that. This is going to be a long road, and he needs to take his time. Otherwise, he could do more harm than good." He turns to Brendan. "Have you been sticking to the therapist's program?"

"Sticking like a fly on shit," Brendan confirms.

"Bren," I scold, completely horrified before turning to the doctor in embarrassment. "Sorry."

"It's fine," he says. "If using sayings like that is going to keep him in high spirits, then by all means, have at it."

"This is why I put up with you, Doctor Ellis," Brendan says.

"Oh, geez," I mutter under my breath.

The doctor heads out, and I'm left with a grinning Brendan as my eyes fill with unshed tears. "You could walk again."

"Yeah," he smirks, the grin across his face wider than I've ever seen it. "Then I can kick Logan's ass as well."

I can't help but laugh. "You are such an asshole."

"You're damn right," Brendan laughs. "But you love it."

"I sure do."

Chapter Ten

ELLE

I walk into work on Monday morning with the world in the palm of my hands. With this new job and Brendan's progress, I've never been so happy. Life couldn't be better for me.

After parking my car outside the Thunder's training facility, I make it through the front door and am greeted by Tony, one of the many suits from management. I give him a small smile and go to walk on by, but he falls in step with me. "How are things going, Elle? Are you enjoying your work?"

Nervousness rockets through my body. I've never been one to enjoy talking with the higher-ups, but I haven't done anything wrong.

I've been the perfect junior, apart from grinding on the captain and waking up in his shirt. "Oh, yes. I am very much. It's like a dream come true."

"That's great news. I'm glad you're settling in well," he tells me. "How do you feel about the workload? Too much? Too little? Do you feel as though you could handle more?"

Oh, shit. I hope this conversation is going somewhere good.

"The workload has been great," I tell him. "I'm handling everything so far and nothing has been out of my depth, but I could definitely handle more."

He nods as he takes it all in, and he seems to be deep in thought. "I'll cut to the chase here," he says as we stop outside the physiotherapy rooms. "Dave is going to be taking a little time off, and I need to know if you're capable of taking on the workload without him. If not, I'll hire a temp to fill in, but it would mean extended hours, which you'll be compensated for, of course."

Woah. That's a surprise, but at the same time, a little nerve-racking. It means I'm not going to have Dave there to act as a buffer between me and Logan, but then I won't have to deal with Dave's creepy vibes.

"Oh, I didn't realize he was taking time off," I muse, my brows furrowed. "But yes, I can handle it. I'll just have to shuffle a few appointments around so there are no double-ups. Considering it's still the off-season, I don't see why it should be an issue. However, once training starts up again, there's physically not enough hours in the day for me to handle it by myself."

"Yes, don't worry. We wouldn't leave you hanging like that," he says, chuckling at the absurdity of it. "However, you're certain you can handle the workload? I've heard only glowing reviews from the players. They've shown a lot of confidence in your abilities."

"Yes," I tell him, needing just a moment to wrap my head around that, my chest swelling with pride. "Apart from Logan, there are no major injuries. Mainly just the usual after-training aches and pains. Nothing I can't handle."

"Exactly what I wanted to hear," he says. "Tell me, how's Logan's progress coming along? I've noticed he ditched the crutches."

"Yes, he did indeed," I say, feeling strange about discussing a patient's progress, but in a team like this, when it comes to an injured player, especially one who happens to be the captain, there is no privacy. Management requires to know every detail of his progress, every setback, every time he so much as sneezes. "It's only been a week, but he's already regained some movement and the muscle is in the early stages of its healing process. He's on a strict rehabilitation program, which he has been sticking to religiously. As long as he continues as such, I see no reason why he shouldn't be back on the ice in as little as six weeks for light training, back to normal in eight to ten."

"Excellent, that's what I like to hear. You won't have any problems with Logan. He's serious about his career and will do anything to ensure he gets back on his feet. As for the other guys . . . don't be intimidated by their personalities. Most of them are single and tend to enjoy female attention. They're harmless."

"I can handle them," I laugh.

"Good to know," he says, reaching out and giving my shoulder a small squeeze. "I've got to run, but let me know if you're in over your head and we can find someone to help you out until Dave's return."

"Sure thing," I say with a nod before he turns and walks away, leaving me gaping after him. Not wanting to look like an idiot standing out here in the hall, I hastily duck into my office and promptly start freaking out. Not only are the players expressing their confidence in me to management, but that same management is willing to let me take the reins while the senior therapist is off. Sure, it's the off-season and not a huge deal, but these are professional athletes I'm dealing with, and their confidence in me to handle this is huge, especially after being here for only a week.

I have free rein of the place. Any other junior might be intimidated by the task, but I know what I'm doing, and I know exactly what I'm capable of. I trust my instincts and my training, and I know I'll kick ass.

I just wish I knew that Dave was planning on taking leave so I wasn't so blindsided by it. I could have used my Sunday afternoon to go through the notes of the players I'll be tending to this morning, but there's no time like the present. My first appointment is at ten, and until then, I've got some reading to do.

This is the perfect opportunity to see what I'm made of, and I have no doubt that I'm going to make this job my bitch.

Chapter Eleven

LOGAN

Pulling up at the training facility, I meet with a few of the boys before we head into the conference room. It's been four weeks since my injury, and the whole team has been called into a mandatory meeting. Training will be starting up again next week with the start of the season just around the corner. We do this every year—a formal welcome to our new players and making sure everyone is on the same page. We'll go over the expected training schedule and any dates we need to be aware of.

Walking into the conference room, I find all of our management team here, even the bigwigs. All of our players are here, but what I don't expect is to see Elle sitting in the corner, looking way out of her comfort zone.

Those gorgeous blue eyes lift to mine the second I walk through the door, and a secretive grin crosses her lips. Not wanting to be caught, she quickly glances away, doing what she can to try and smother the intense need within her eyes. Hunger blasts through my veins. God, I want to be with her. With Dave out on leave, I've been seeing Elle more over the past few weeks, and that tension between us has only gotten stronger. My ability to keep away from her is quickly dwindling, but I'm trying so fucking hard to respect her need to protect her job. She set boundaries, and I'm gonna respect them.

The need to go to her comes over me, but I know she wouldn't want that, especially right now with management here to see. Instead, I find Jax in the back of the room, helping himself to the spread of food on offer, and I go to join him, knowing management likes to go all out on their buffets.

With a full plate on my lap, I get comfortable as the rest of the team, complete with the trainers, coaches, players, and even the PR team, make their way through the door.

It's been twenty minutes of meeting Elle's eyes across the room when Tony, one of the higher members of management, finally gets off his ass and gets the party started. "Thank you all for being here on such short notice. I know it's a Saturday, and for most of you, that means it's your day off, so we'll make this as quick as we can."

A few of the guys call out and give Tony a hard time, but we all know they're joking and Tony takes it in stride, but what do you expect from a group like this? The room is full of testosterone, and above all, our team believes in an enjoyable environment.

"Alright, settle down," Tony says, shaking his head at his players. "First item on the agenda. Our new recruits are here, sitting within our ranks. We have six new additions to our team, and I encourage each and every one of you to go out of your way to make them feel welcome and show them the ropes. These players are the future of our team, your future replacements."

With that, Tony goes around one by one and introduces each of the new players, which of course, includes Jax, who naturally plays it cool. Tony makes sure to let everyone know Jax is engaged to my little sister, which only sends a wave of ribbing toward me. Elle's face brightens at Jax's introduction, and something about it warms my heart.

"Alright, other changes this year," Tony continues. "A few of you may have already had the pleasure of meeting with our new junior physiotherapist, Elle." With that, Tony indicates to Elle at the back of the room, and a chorus of wolf whistles follow. Elle's face flames, but she manages to give a quick wave before her eyes settle on me once again.

"Shut it," Tony demands. "Elle is one of the best therapists we've had, so you guys better keep it in your pants and treat her with respect. The last thing we want is to scare her away. Though, something tells me she can handle herself, and let me tell you, you don't want to be the one who ends up on her table after disrespecting her. It's not going to be pleasant."

The message is well received as the guys pull their shit together. Which I'm grateful for, to be honest. I know Elle is freaking dynamite, but I don't want all these bastards appreciating her. She's mine.

"Now, speaking of physio," Tony says. "You may have noticed that Dave is not here and has also not been here for the past few weeks. I know many of you had issues working with Dave—and for good reason. I wanted you all to hear it from me first and not the media. However, Dave is currently being investigated for possession of child pornography. With that being said, his contract with the Colorado Thunder has been terminated."

What. The. Fuck?

Gasps and shock echo around the room while others voice their opinions. I knew he was a fucking dirtbag, but I never realized it went that deep. I mean, fuck. He has a family. A son and a wife.

I look over at Elle and raise my eyebrow, silently asking if she knew about this. She shakes her head, shrugging her shoulders, but it's the horror in her eyes that brings her message home. She had no fucking idea.

Disgust crashes through me, feeling as though I should have spoken up, pushed for action earlier, and the fact that I didn't weighs heavily on my shoulders. I had a duty to protect my team, and I failed them. The only relief I have is knowing that management was smart enough to terminate his contract, but that was inevitable. He'll be spending his time in prison from now on.

After giving us a moment to come to terms with the news, Tony continues with the meeting. "Now, if this situation affects any of you or you feel that you need to talk, the team counselor is on hand and you know my office is always open. With that being said, Elle will be holding down the fort until the start of the season, and in the meantime, we'll be interviewing for the senior therapist position."

The words spill out of my mouth before I can stop them. "Why don't you hire Elle as the senior therapist?"

My gaze cuts to her to find her jaw practically on the floor. "Umm . . . what?" she mutters.

"Why not?" I ask looking back at Tony. "Like you said, she's one of the best physios we've had. I know for a fact that I wouldn't have come this far without her. I'm a week ahead of where I'm supposed to be. Hell, I'll be back on the ice with the rest of the team next week. Fuck knows I couldn't have done that without her."

Tony rubs his hand over his face, deep in thought as he slowly turns his gaze toward Elle. "I don't mean to put you on the spot, but is that something you'd be interested in?"

"Well . . . Yeah, but a position like that is usually reserved for someone who possesses a lot more experience than I have. I mean, I just graduated."

"That you did," he says, watching her closely, clearly considering this. "Hypothetically, if you were offered the senior therapist position, would you feel prepared to take on the responsibilities that come along with it?"

"Yes," she says, sitting straighter in her seat.

"I'll make you a deal," he says slowly, a grin lifting the corner of his lips as the whole team watches the show like it's prime-time television. "You've been here three weeks, so I can't promote you to senior therapist without you doing your time first. So, I'll give you one year. During that time, I will hire a senior therapist on a twelve-month contract, and it will be your responsibility to learn from them. And if you can prove to me and this team that you are deserving of becoming our new senior physiotherapist over the next twelve months, then come next season, the position is yours."

Her jaw drops open, and she gapes at Tony. "Are you shitting me?" she breathes.

"No, Elle," Tony laughs. "I'm not shitting you."

"Holy crap. Yes. Of course, yes," she grins as the whole room bursts out into whoops and hollers, more than happy to have her on board. "I won't let you down."

"See to it you don't," he says, his vote of confidence stirring something within me and making me so damn proud of her.

Elle looks at me with absolute joy in those blazing blue eyes. "Thank you," she mouths before the guys crowd her. Her chair is suddenly thrust up into the air, and she lets out a squeal as she holds on for dear life. Laughter rips from her throat, and the look on her face has me ready to drop to my knees, but if even one of those bastards hurt her, they will have to deal with me.

I couldn't be happier. If anyone deserves this position, it's Elle. She's already proven to me that she has what it takes, and now she has a shot to show the rest of the world, and I know without a doubt, she'll do just that.

"Hey," Tony calls out. "I want to get out of here just as badly as you guys do. Put Elle down and get your asses back in your chairs."

With that, the team slowly calms down and takes their seats as Tony gets on with his meeting. "Now, Logan," he says, focusing his attention on me. "What's going on with this groin injury?"

Snickers break out across the room, but I ignore them the best I can. "Upper thigh," I correct him. "And it's doing well. Like I said, I'm ahead in my progress and I'll be back on the ice next week."

Tony glances at Elle for confirmation. "Is that right?"

"Yeah," she agrees. "Logan's recovery is miraculous. I have approved him to start training along with the rest of the team next week, but only for basic training, nothing too strenuous just yet. I don't want to risk him pulling the muscle again. I'll be assessing him during that time, and I assume he'll be back to normal training within a few weeks."

"Perfect. That's exactly what I wanted to hear," he says before addressing the rest of the room. "With all of that out of the way. There's just one more thing to cover before I let you go." He glances around the room, and the look in his eyes tells me he's nervous to break whatever news it is he is about to break.

"Let's hear it," one of the guys calls from the back.

Tony swallows before letting us have it. "Okay, with all the new changes this year, management has come together and decided a bonding experience will benefit you all as a team. So . . . We're going camping."

What?

Every eye in the room looks at Tony in disbelief. "You're kidding, right?" one of the boys asks.

"No. I am not kidding," Tony says. "This trip is mandatory. Every last person in this room will be in attendance. That includes managers, coaches, trainers, and therapists. Every single one of you."

I can't help but look at Elle and have to cover a laugh at how her jaw is hanging wide open for the second time during this meeting. This trip isn't looking so bad.

"Alright. This is happening next weekend, so call your wives, your girlfriends, your moms. I don't care, just clear your schedules, and I'll see you then." Tony smirks, and with that, gives us all a smug grin before heading right out the door with the rest of management on his heels, his booming laugh echoing up the long hallway.

Getting up, I start heading out with Jax at my side when that sweet, velvety voice calls out to me. "Logan," Elle says, pushing through the crowd of players, ducking and weaving as she makes her way over to us.

My gaze sails over her and her cheeks flush in that gorgeous shade of pink I've come to crave. "What's up?" I say, forcing myself to keep distance between us.

"I, uhh . . . I just wanted to say thanks," she says. "You didn't need to do that for me, but I appreciate it nonetheless."

Warmth spreads through my chest, and I don't miss the way Jax discreetly steps away, giving us what little privacy this room can offer. "You've got nothing to thank me for. They would have seen that you're the right person for the job," I tell her.

"Yeah, but you spoke up for me," she says, looking up at me with wide eyes, thick with emotion. "No one has ever done that for me."

A smile pulls at my lips, and I point out the door. "Come on," I tell her, pressing my hand to her lower back and gently guiding her closer to me, desperately wishing I could reach out and kiss her. "I'll walk you out."

For once in her life, Elle actually lets me have my way and walks with me while Jax trails along behind us. We get halfway up the corridor when I hear someone jogging behind us. "Hey," Max, one of the younger players, calls out. We stop and glance back, watching as he quickly catches up. Max stops before us, his gaze sailing over Elle with appreciation before he gives her his signature cocky smirk. "I'm Max," he says, thrusting his hand out in front of her.

Elle reluctantly takes his hand to be polite, but when he grips it tightly and attempts to bring it to his lips, she yanks it right back, clearly uncomfortable. I find myself inching forward, discreetly putting myself between Max and Elle. "She's not interested, man."

His eyes flick between us with curiosity. "Ahh, now your little ploy to get her promoted makes sense. You're together, right?"

"No," Elle cuts in, clearly irritated with Max. "Logan is my patient, that's it. Just as you'll be my patient if and when the time comes."

Max's hands fly up in surrender, amused with the whole encounter. "Sorry, my bad. Wasn't meaning to make assumptions," he says before turning to Jax as we start walking again, Elle now more than ready to get out of here. "So, what's up, man? What's your story?"

"Not much to say," Jax says a bit standoffish, and after knowing him since he was twelve years old, I can tell he doesn't care for Max, nor should he, the guy's an asshole.

"Are you excited about the camping trip?" Max continues, not getting the hint.

"Yeah, I guess," Jax says, but I know he's lying. Camping's not his thing. "Should be good."

"You got some bitch to clear it with?" Max asks with a grin, proving he wasn't listening during Tony's introductions of the new players, because if he had, there's no way in hell he would have been stupid enough to refer to my little sister as a bitch.

Anger spreads through my veins, and while I know Max is just trying to get on board with Jax, this shit ain't gonna fly. Not to mention, if I don't intervene, Jax will annihilate him for calling Cass a bitch, and that's not how any of us want to start the new season.

"Watch it, Max," I say, the threat in my tone immediately gaining his attention. "That bitch you're referring to is my little sister."

Max's face drops, his eyes widening in horror. "Shit, I'm sorry, man," he breathes, glancing between me and Jax before backing up. "I, uhh . . . yeah. I'll see ya 'round."

With that, Max takes off at a jog, leaving Jax shaking his head. "What a fucking douche."

"I couldn't agree more," Elle says under her breath as we reach the main doors and step out into the midday sunshine. Jax takes off, probably wanting to soak up as much time with Cass before the season starts, and I'm left with Elle looking up at me, not impressed in the least. "What do you think you're doing giving Max the impression that something's going on here?"

My lip kicks up in a crooked grin. "Because something is going on here."

She rolls her eyes and lets out a frustrated groan. "You're impossible."

"I've been called worse."

"I don't doubt that," she murmurs as we reach her car.

She stops at her door and turns to face me, those big blue eyes staring up at me, even brighter in the sunlight. I step closer, moving into her personal space before slowly leaning in. Elle's breath catches, and I have to stop from grinning in victory as her gaze drops to my lips, longing flashing in her eyes. "I'll pick you up on Saturday. We'll go together."

"Yeah . . . no," she says. "There's no way in hell I'm going camping."

"Sorry to break the bad news, babe, but it's mandatory. You don't get a choice in the matter."

Coach Robinson hollers from across the lot. "Logan. Leave the poor girl alone and get your ass home. You've got a groin injury that needs healing."

A wicked grin stretches across Elle's face, and her eyes sparkle with silent laughter. "You heard the man, Captain," she smirks. "You need to get home so your dick can heal."

I resist the urge to fold her over my knee and spank that firm ass. "I'll pick you up at nine," I say with a smirk of my own before backing away, not leaving her the chance to object. Cutting across the lot, I listen to the fiery groans that tear from her throat before climbing into my truck and taking off.

I'm going to see her at least three times during the week for my regular physio appointment, but I can't fucking wait for next Saturday.

Chapter Twelve

ELLE

A knock sounds at my door on Saturday morning, and I groan as I throw myself out of bed. Reaching up, I slide my eye mask up my forehead and trudge down the hall, my legs wobbly from sleep. If this is Jaz coming to raid my coffee jar again, I'm going to kill her.

Walking out past Louie's cage, I step in front of the door and unlock the deadbolts before finally pulling the door open with more force than necessary. "What do you . . . fuck," I grunt, realizing it's not Jaz at my door, but a very tall, very sexy, very intense hockey player. I come up short, frozen to the spot. "What are you doing here?"

"Camping trip," Logan reminds me, his gaze dropping down my body. A devilish grin spreads over his face, and it stirs something deep within me, making me want him that much more. I hate when he looks at me like this. It's as though he's starved for my touch, and the fact I can't give that to him kills me.

Glancing down to see what's got his attention, I see nothing but my body, wrapped in his shirt with my nipples protruding in the cold, like targets begging for his attention. I knew I should have given it back straight away, but I couldn't part with it. It smells like him for God's sake. How the hell could I give that up?

A smile pulls at my lips as I clear my throat. "My eyes are up here, Captain," I murmur, ignoring the elephant in the room—the elephant otherwise known as his shirt. "I could have sworn I told you I wasn't going camping."

"Well, fortunately for me," he says, moving past me and into my apartment. "You have no choice. So really, I'm saving your ass here, and I'm sure you will find an appropriate way to thank me."

After closing my door, I turn around to find Logan pulling the blanket off Louie's cage and opening the door to get him out. I lean against my front door before crossing my arms over my chest, hating how much I love having him in my space. "Make yourself at home."

"I will," he says with a very happy Louie on his shoulder. "Coffee?"

Logan makes his way into my kitchen and searches through the cupboards before I put him out of his misery and grab the mugs for him. "I'm assuming you haven't packed yet?" he asks, fidgeting with my coffee machine, clearly having no idea what he's doing.

"Why would I pack for a trip I'm not going on?" I question.

"Because you are going."

"The only place I'm going is back to bed," I say with a yawn.

Logan hands me my coffee before giving Louie a little scratch and looking back at me. "Cool, I'll come with you."

Frustration burns through me, and I lift the mug to my lips, needing the caffeine hit more than ever before. "Do you have any idea how frustrating you are?" Logan simply grins before striding down my hallway, and all I can do is gape after him. "Umm . . . what do you think you're doing?"

"You said to make myself at home," he says over his shoulder. "We're going back to bed . . . or, we could pack for the mandatory camping trip for the job you wouldn't dream of risking. Take your pick."

Logan disappears into my room, and I blow my cheeks out with a frustrated breath, but hearing him rifling through my things gets my ass moving. Busting through my room, I find him searching through my drawers, a black lace thing hanging from his fingers. "Get lost," I groan, shoving him out of the way. "I can pack my own bag."

Logan smirks as he gives in and leans against my bedroom wall, knowing damn well I played right into the palm of his hand.

With a sigh, I give in. I guess I truly don't have a choice but to go on the stupid camping trip, after all, he's right. It's mandatory, and I don't want to fuck things up by not showing up. Especially so soon after Tony promised me a twelve-month deal.

Opening my closet, I reach up to grab a bag, only it's just out of reach. I push up onto my tiptoes and have to jump a few times before my fingers finally latch onto the fabric, but I get there in the end.

"I could have helped with that," Logan says in that smug-as-fuck tone that I equally love and loathe. "All you had to do was ask."

"Never going to happen," I tell him as I start throwing the contents of my drawers into the bag only to have Logan come and empty it all out. "Are you serious?" I whine.

"You've clearly never been camping," he laughs, heading back to my closet and launching hoodies and sweatpants at me. Once he's satisfied with the contents of my bag, he asks the most ridiculous question yet. "Where's your tent?"

I give him a blank stare and don't even bother with a response. A tent? Is he for real?

His brows furrow. "Swag?" he asks, a little more hopeful.

Again, I don't respond.

"You've got to at least have a sleeping bag, right?"

At that, the grin rips across my face. "Come on, Logan. You seem like a smart man. At least, mostly. There's no telling just how many pucks you've taken to the head, but honestly, do I look like the kind of girl who owns a sleeping bag?"

He presses his lips together. "You're right. Stupid question. You can share with me."

Oh, God. I can't catch a break with this guy.

Against my will, Logan slings my bag over his shoulder and drags me out of my apartment, barely waiting even a second for me to put Louie away and lock the door behind me. Hell, I barely got a chance to pull on some clothes before he dragged me out of there.

We pass Jaz's door just in time to see her kicking out her one-night stand, and she leans against the doorframe, watching us with a smirk. "What's going on here?" she questions with a smile that threatens to tear her face in two.

Logan grins at my best friend, slinging his arm over my shoulder. "I'm taking my girl camping," he says, making it sound more like a date than a work thing.

Jaz bursts out in laughter. "Good luck with that," she says before meeting my gaze. "I'll kidnap Louie." I give her a grateful smile before tossing her the keys to my apartment, and within seconds, she's at the other end of the hall, jamming the key into my lock.

Logan helps me up into his beast of a truck, and the second he's settled in beside me with nothing but cramped spaces and an open road ahead of us, the tension begins to fill the truck.

It's a short drive, barely an hour outside the city limits, when we pull up at some kind of reservation. Logan brings his truck to a stop among the other players' vehicles. Eyes swivel our way when the guys notice the team physio jumping out of the star player's truck, which is exactly what I wanted to avoid, but Logan couldn't look happier. To these guys, I must look like a desperate whore, trying to win over the captain like the majority of the women who are interested in these men.

I more than took pleasure out of the drive with him, and I absolutely love the way he seems to keep showing up in my life. There's something about him that's wearing me down, and it's scaring the shit out of me. I want him. I want to know what it'd feel like to be his whole world, but if something is going to happen between us, I need to know that it's the real deal. I won't risk it all for nothing.

Logan and I join the rest of the team and wait for the stragglers to show up. "Everyone here?" Tony asks ten minutes later.

"Looks like it," one of the players says from the back of the group.

"Alright," Tony says with way too much enthusiasm for a Saturday morning. "We have a mile hike to our campsite, so let's get a move on."

My mouth drops as I turn to Logan. "You failed to mention a hike," I scold.

"Don't look at me," he says in surrender, but the grin on his face tells a different story. "I had no idea."

Liar.

Oh well, I may as well make the best of this. Though I can't exactly agree that a mile hike is what's best for Logan's injury, but something tells me there's no telling him that. He's determined to see this camping trip through.

Looking up at Logan, a wide grin stretches across my face, and as his brows furrow, wondering what could possibly have me grinning like this, I turn back toward the group of management behind us. "Tony," I say, watching as his head snaps up, his eyes coming directly to mine. "Listen, as much as I want to encourage Logan to keep active during his recovery, I cannot condone a mile hike through uneven ground. One slip and your captain could be out for the start of the season."

Tony's face sobers as Logan shakes his head. "I'm fine," he says, holding up a hand to start his objection, but Tony's not having it.

"You're right. It completely slipped my mind," Tony says, pausing as he glances back toward the cars behind us. He drags his hand over his face, regret in his eyes before glancing back at Logan. "I'm sorry, Logan. You'll have to sit this one out."

"Oh no," I rush out. "He shouldn't have to miss this. I'm sure we can figure something out."

"Any suggestions?" Tony asks, clearly on the same wavelength, wanting the team's star player to be here for their pre-season bonding ritual.

I make a show of looking around at the other players, particularly Jax who hovers close by. "I mean, you have a lot of players here," I say, subtly eyeing Logan before turning back to Tony. "I'm sure between the lot of them, there's enough muscle here to carry Logan in."

"Hmm," Coach Robinson says, cutting in as Logan shakes his head. "I like it. Jaxon, you're up."

I have to spin around so that Tony or Coach Robinson don't catch the wide grin tearing across my face, but Logan sure as fuck sees it, and he is not impressed. But before he can say a word, Jax is right there, turning and offering Logan his back. "I always knew you wanted to mount me," Jax says, a smirk playing on his lips.

Logan meets my eye as he steps up behind Jax and takes his shoulder. "You and I," he says, in warning, "we're gonna talk about this."

I bat my lashes, as innocent as ever. "I'm just looking out for you, Captain."

He grumbles something I can't quite make out and next thing I know, the great Logan Waters is being piggybacked through the woods by his future brother-in-law. Then just to make sure I remember this moment for the rest of my life, I pull my phone out of my back pocket and hold it up. "Say cheese."

Jax gives me a wide, beaming smile as Logan just stares, and I take the picture—one I know I'm going to treasure for the rest of my life.

The whole group gets a move on, and I have to admit, it's really not that bad. The only annoying part is having the eyes of Max constantly on my back. I made it clear I'm not interested, and Logan kind of won that pissing contest, not that there was anything to win.

Half an hour later, we make it to the campsite, and Jax is drenched in sweat. He all but drops Logan to the ground as I look around at our massive patch of grass surrounded by trees. It takes me all but two seconds to realize there's no bathroom, nowhere to shower, and nowhere to give me any sort of privacy.

It also doesn't go unnoticed that there's a dirt road leading right in here, meaning management fooled us all, and the one-mile trek was all a part of the bonding experience.

Once the whole group makes it into the clearing, they all scatter to find the best spot to set up their tents. With nothing to set up, I consider heading into the trees and searching out the best hiding spot to use as a bathroom, but instead, I head over and help Logan and Jax with their setup. And as I have absolutely no idea what I'm doing, I get put on pole duty, right there in my comfort zone.

As I stand and hand the guys their poles, I find myself in awe. They find these tasks so impossibly easy, while something like this is an absolute nightmare to me. There's a reason I don't go camping, apart from the fact I have no one to go with. Jaz would laugh in my face, and it would be way too hard with Brendan.

"What are you staring at?" Jax asks, breaking me out of my inner thoughts.

"I just don't get how something so big fits into that little thing," I say as I point out the tent bag discarded on the ground.

Logan lets out a stupid laugh from the opposite side of his tent before calling out. "Babe, big things were meant to fit into tight spaces."

Oh, God.

"Stop calling me that," I call back, but I struggle to keep the laughter out of my voice.

"I would if you didn't like it so much," he quips.

I let out a huff because let's face it, I do like it.

From here on out, I ignore Logan as best I can. "How'd you learn to do all of this?" I ask Jax as he finishes up his tent, making it look so damn easy.

"That guy," he says, nodding his head in Logan's direction. "The triplets were like my big brothers growing up, but I was closest with Logan. He taught me how to skate."

"Really?" I ask in interest. "So, you know him pretty well?"

"Yep," he says, lowering his tone and taking a step in my direction, "That's how I know he likes you." My eyes widen as I meet his cautious stare, an unspoken demand that he explains himself. "Look, I can't begin to understand what goes through Logan's mind. I don't think anyone can, but it's perfectly clear to me that you mean something to him. You're not some random chick he wants to just fuck and toss away. He's already in deep, hoping like fuck that one day you'll be ready."

"What makes you so sure?" I question, quietly.

He looks at me intently, begging me to figure it out. "He has never chased a girl before, yet he's showing up at clubs for just a slight chance he might see you there, turning up at your place to offer you a ride, and from what I hear, you even dropped him with a shot to the balls, but he's still looking at you with fucking puppy dog eyes. He's used to women falling at his feet, but you keep cutting him down, and the fact he keeps looking for more tells me that you're it for him. He doesn't want anyone else, just you."

I think it over, but Jax isn't finished just yet. "Logan is an amazing guy, and I think you'd be an idiot if you turned him down before you got to know him. He's not the dumb jock people expect him to be."

"I know," I say with a nod. Anyone who has spent any time with the guy would be able to see he isn't a dumb jock, and I'm not blind. I can tell he likes me, but I have no idea why. What worries me is that he'll take me out a few times before he realizes that I'm nothing special, just a messed-up girl with an even more messed-up past. I come jam-packed with the type of baggage that scares men away.

"What's going on over here?" Logan asks as he struts over, looking like sex on legs.

"Jax and I have fallen madly in love. We were planning on running away together and would have made it if you didn't interrupt us," I tease. "Please, extend my apologies to your sister."

"I would have believed that a year ago," Logan grunts. I turn to

Jax with a raised brow, sensing a story that needs to be told, but from the tone of Logan's voice, it could be a touchy subject. "Come on," Logan says as he nods in the direction of one of the trucks that came in through the dirt road.

Taking off with Logan, I look up ahead at the dirt road. "I can't believe they made us walk when there was a road that leads right in."

"Yeah, they're dickheads like that," he chuckles as we reach the truck. "But I have it on good authority that you're a dickhead like that too. Honestly, a mile piggyback ride? I had my dick grinding up against Jax's back for half an hour."

I press my lips into a hard line, smothering the grin that's trying to tear across my face, watching as Logan reaches into the back of the truck and pulls out two folding chairs and an axe.

My eyes widen just a fraction. Why in the hell do we need that?

"I knew it. You're too good to be true. You're gonna drag me out into the woods and kill me in my sleep, aren't you?" I ask as he passes me one of the chairs and throws the axe over his shoulder like some kind of lumberjack.

"Too good to be true, huh?" he smirks, those dark eyes sparkling with silent laughter. "But no. If I was planning on killing you, I would have done it the night I crashed on your couch."

"Ha. Ha. Very funny. Besides, you can't kill me, Louie needs me too much."

"What Louie needs is a good speaking to," he laughs.

"Leave Louie alone," I grin as I roll my eyes, but it's true, Louie is one hell of a bad birdy. "What's the axe for?"

"You and I are on firewood duty," he says proudly.

I gape at him, certain he's joking. "Bullshit," I grunt.

"It's true," he says. "Tony made up a roster if you'd like to check."

I let out a groan. "This isn't going to be one of those things where they make you do those stupid games like the three-legged race and that one where you have to catch eggs?"

"No," he laughs, "but I'm sure if you suggested it to Tony, he'll find a way to add it to the schedule."

"Noted. I'll keep my mouth shut."

We take our chairs and place them down in front of the tent before heading out into the trees to find some wood . . . and not the good kind.

I get started on our task and pick up as many sticks as possible. "Babe," comes that deep voice from behind me. "What are you planning on doing with those twigs?"

"Huh?" I ask. "What do you mean? I'm getting firewood which is a hell of a lot more than what you're doing right now. You haven't got any wood."

He gives me that annoying I-know-best grin that drives me insane, but with the axe over his shoulder and the tight-fitting shirt and denim jeans, all I can think about is throwing myself into his arms and begging him to take me.

Logan steps up to me and forces me back against a tree. The twigs fall to the ground as Logan presses his strong body up against mine. I catch my breath, my heart starting to race as I meet those dark eyes, the world fading away around us. "Trust me, babe," he murmurs, his fingers brushing down the side of my waist. "I've got all the wood you need."

Oh, dear God.

Logan places the axe down beside us and cages me against the tree with his arms, those dark eyes focused so heavily on mine. The tension grows between us, and my hand slides up to find purchase against his warm chest. "What are you doing?" I whisper, knowing I won't be able to stop if those full lips were to come down on mine.

God, he smells so damn good.

"I can't wait any longer," Logan rumbles, torturous need flashing in his eyes. I suck in a breath, and just like that, Logan closes the gap between us. His warm lips come down on mine, and it's pure heaven, but as his hand tightens on my waist, claiming me as his own, every last bit of my resolve crumbles.

Intense need blasts through me, and I kiss him back, giving him everything I've got as my arms snake around his neck, holding him to me and never wanting to let go.

His touch is like coming home, so pure and right. How could I have resisted him so long?

I moan into him, and he takes it as his cue to continue, deepening our kiss and making my knees go weak. Those strong hands trail down my body before gripping my ass and hoisting me up into his arms. I wrap my legs around his waist and hold on for dear life as he kisses me like a starved man, so damn hungry for a taste.

Without a doubt, no man will ever amount to the one before me. Every time I meet a guy, he will always be compared to Logan. I will never be kissed like this again, never have a man caress my body like this, never feel like I'm floating on air, not unless it's with Logan.

I just need to be prepared for him to pull away the second this is over. At some point, I'm going to drop my walls and let him in. When that happens, he's going to realize that I'm just like every other inexperienced, messed-up girl out there, and what we have is going to fade away, just like I've always known.

Just as I've always known that sooner or later, Logan Waters is going to break my heart.

Chapter Thirteen

LOGAN

Night has fallen, and we sit around the campfire as Coach Robinson does his best to keep the flames alive. After all, Elle and I didn't really do such a great job at collecting firewood. I was too busy with my tongue down her throat, but I wouldn't change it for the fucking world.

For weeks I've been craving that moment with her, and now that I've had a taste, I need so much more. But it's not just physical, I need her mind, her soul, her heart. I want it all, and I won't stop until I get it.

I have to admit, I was surprised she let me get that close. She sucked in a breath, and I could see the hesitation in her eyes, but the second she dropped those fucking twigs, I knew I had her. She's mine just as much as I am hers. She just needs to figure that out, and unfortunately for me, it's not something I can force on her. She needs to figure it out on her own. Until she does, I'll be right here waiting for her.

The second my lips touched hers, I was a fucking goner. I didn't want to stop. If I had my way, I'd still be in those trees with those perfectly toned legs wrapped around me as she moaned for more.

The majority of the team sits around the fire, soaking in the warmth of the flames while trying to avoid the cool breeze. Winter is still a while off, but these Denver nights can often be a bitch.

Max hasn't been able to keep his eyes off her, and I don't blame him. She's fucking gorgeous. There have been three separate times where he's gotten up and beelined for her, and each time, she's somehow slipped away, either to grab a drink or step into our tent for a blanket. Hell, I don't think she's aware of the attention she's getting from him, she's simply lost in conversation and enjoying her night. Though one thing is for sure, Max knows damn well that I'm aware of what has his attention. Each time he got up, his eyes landed on mine, and luckily for him, he decided to change his course of action.

Elle doesn't need Max in her life. Besides, if she insists on spending her time with a hockey player, it's gonna be me, not a loser like Max. I'll have to have a quiet word with him when I get a chance.

Elle sits next to me, and I want nothing more than to pull her into my lap and tangle my fingers into that silky brunette hair. She laughs as she listens intently to all the stories being told, and when a bag of marshmallows comes around the circle, she can't resist. Her face brightens as she leans back in her chair, reaching for one of her discarded twigs, and I have to latch onto the side of her chair to keep her from toppling over.

"Thanks," she laughs, beaming joy in her eyes as she squishes the marshmallow onto the end of her twig. "I've always wanted to do this."

"What? Roast marshmallows?" I question.

"Yeah."

"You never did this growing up?"

"No," she says, averting her eyes. "There were a lot of things I missed out on."

A sadness flickers in her eyes, and I desperately want to poke and prod until I have all the answers I need, but now isn't the time.

I find myself mesmerized, watching as she thrusts her marshmallow into the fire. She concentrates, making sure she's not burning it before pulling back her twig and blowing on the marshmallow to cool down. She peels the sticky goo off the end and pops it into her mouth, groaning in delight before licking her fingers and making me positively hard.

I adjust myself as she turns to Jax with that same curiosity that she looked at him with earlier in the day. "So, what's your story, Jax?" she asks.

Jax scoffs. "It's a good one, but it was hard for a few years."

Elle thrusts her hand back into the bag of marshmallows and claims another one before shoving it onto the end of her stick, then into the fire. "How so?"

Jax presses his lips into a hard line, and I don't doubt this is still difficult for him to talk about. "A few years ago, Cass and I broke up and she moved to New York for a while. Things got a bit rough after that, and when their parents died, the triplets went and brought her back, and the rest is history. I'm marrying her in a few months."

Elle nods slowly and gives him a smile that doesn't quite meet her eyes, making it clear she's deep in thought. She turns to me with sorrow shining through her big eyes. "Your parents are gone?" she asks quietly, a heaviness thick in her tone.

"Yeah, babe," I say.

A tear falls from her eye, and I reach across to wipe it away. I always hate talking about it, but maybe if I open up, it might encourage her to do the same. "It's okay. Mom passed a few years ago from breast cancer. She fought for as long as she could, but in the end, she couldn't hold on. And Dad was hit with a heart attack nearly three years ago."

"I'm sorry," she murmurs as her eyes fall back to her lap.

Elle silently sticks another marshmallow onto her stick and places it over the flames, only that same enthusiasm from her first two is long gone, and instead, she sits in silence, just watching the fire.

It's well past midnight when her yawns come in hard, and I get up and start heading over to the truck, only I hear light footfalls rushing behind me. I turn to find Elle dashing through the darkness, and I pause, waiting for her to catch up. "Where are you going?" she murmurs through the night.

"Come and see," I say.

She falls beside me, and I wrap my arm over her shoulder, the cover of darkness concealing us from the rest of the team. Being away from the fire, there's a nastier bite in the air, and that becomes evident as Elle's teeth begin to chatter. "Are you okay?" I ask through the silence.

She nods her head, but I know something is still heavy on her mind. I let it go as we reach the truck, and I open the back door to pull out one of the many air mattresses that lay across the back seat.

"Seriously?" she asks.

"What? You think management is going to let a shitload of professional athletes sleep on the ground?"

"No, I guess not," she chuckles. "But at least my job would be safe for a while."

"Stop stressing about your job so much. The fact that Tony even considered you for the senior position means you'll be around for as long as you want to be."

"You think?" she questions.

"I know."

We head down to the tents, and I see that most of the guys have already called it a night. Elle practically goes flying into the tent and dives for her bag before pulling on as many hoodies, socks, and sweatpants as possible.

She turns to me, looking like a snowman in all her clothes, and I have to turn away to avoid laughing at her, but the sound of her yawn gets me moving. I pull out the air mattress, shove the small pump into the side, and get it set up.

The second a blanket is thrown down, Elle collapses onto the bed and snuggles into the blanket, her teeth still chattering as she slowly begins to thaw out. She snuggles down into the air mattress, letting out a heavy breath before glancing up at me. "Where are you sleeping?" she questions.

I stare right back. "Where the fuck do you think? Move your ass over,"

She shakes her head. "Nu-uh. No freaking way, cowboy. That is not a good idea."

She couldn't be more wrong. "I'll be the perfect gentleman," I lie.

Elle narrows her gaze, not believing me for one second. "Fine," she finally says with a huff, giving in, knowing damn well she wants this just as much as I do. "But you better stay on your own side."

Unlikely.

Not hesitating for a damn second, I climb in beside her and make myself comfortable as Elle lays on her side, her arm squished under her pillow, propping her head up. I can't help but feel as though this is a glimpse right into my future. This very sight is what I want to wake up to every fucking morning for the rest of my life.

"What's on your mind?" I question after she remains quiet for way too long.

She lets out a breath as her eyes meet mine. "I . . ." she starts before hesitating and looking away. Her eyes grow watery, and I reach out to take her hand in mine, rubbing my thumb back and forth over her knuckles, hoping I'm helping to soothe whatever emotion is running rampant through her body.

"It's okay, you don't need to say anything," I tell her.

"I want to," she murmurs, those big eyes coming back to mine.

"It's just . . . apart from Jaz, I've never told anyone this."

"Come here," I say as I pull her into me.

Elle scoots across the bed and instantly folds into my arms, right where she belongs. She nuzzles her face into my chest, and I hold her a little tighter, but the fact that she's done it without commenting about it being wrong or that we shouldn't be doing it tells me that whatever she's about to say is a lot bigger than us.

"Eight years ago—it was the night before my seventeenth birthday—my parents had taken us out to dinner because I insisted that I spend my actual birthday with my friends. I remember Mom had been upset because she thought I was growing up too quickly, but I shrugged it off, saying she was being silly," she says as her voice begins to crack.

Elle takes a deep breath before slowly letting it out. "My whole family had gone to dinner, which for my parents, was a big deal because we weren't particularly well off. They insisted that as I was getting older, there would only be so many times left when we would all go out together. It was the middle of winter, and it had been raining for the past couple of days, which really pissed off my little sister because she'd been hoping for snow rather than rain. Dad kept telling her, 'Just a few more weeks,' and she absolutely hated it. She'd get this little crease between her eyebrows every time, but she never said anything, she was too sweet."

A sinking feeling comes over me as I take in her last comment and how she referred to her sister in past tense. I realize before she finishes her story that she has suffered great loss, and I start to understand why she asked about my parents earlier.

Speaking about my parents is hard, but I'll talk about them all day long if it helps to heal something buried deep within her.

"That night, after dinner, we all piled into the car," she continues. "It was super late because we stayed to have second and third helpings of dessert. It was pouring, and with how cold it had been, the roads were practically ice. We were just about home when some stupid animal darted out onto the road. It could have been a squirrel or a cat, I have no idea, but my dad swerved to avoid hitting it and lost control of the car."

Elle stops there as she brings her hand up to rub her eyes and take a breath. "It happened so fast," she breathes. "I remember screaming and looking at Sammy while Brendan tried to force me back into my seat, then I blacked out. I must have only been out for a minute or two, but the first thing I saw was Brendan. He was sitting next to me. He was unconscious, but he was fine. Next was my parents. Mom wasn't wearing a seatbelt and was sent flying out the windshield, while Dad hit his head against the steering wheel. Both of them died on impact."

Fuck.

"Me, Brendan, and Sammy were pulled out of the car. Bren and I seemed fine, but Sammy was bleeding too much. She died in my arms while we waited for the ambulance."

"Babe," I say before we both fall into silence. I feel the front of my shirt becoming wet, and there's no doubt she has tears streaming down her face as she thinks about the worst day of her life.

"I came out of it unscathed, but Brendan suffered damage to his spinal cord and was paralyzed. He's been in a wheelchair ever since," she explains as her voice cracks once again. "I've never forgiven myself. If we hadn't gone out for my birthday . . ."

"Don't, Elle," I whisper. "You can't put the blame on yourself like that. It was an accident and could have happened to anyone."

"I know," she sighs, "But no matter how much logic there is, it doesn't change the fact that I'm here and they're not."

"It's called survivor's guilt," I explain. "I got it after my dad died. I kept telling myself that I should have been around more and looked out for him. If I had known his heart wasn't doing so great, I could have helped. We all would have."

"Did it go away?" she questions.

"No," I tell her. "I don't think it ever will."

She lets out a sigh, and I know her mind is going straight back to her lost family, so I do what I can to keep her talking. "Tell me about Brendan."

"He's a survivor. One of the toughest guys I know," she says, her tone filling with pride before going on to tell me about the rehabilitation program he's in and the possibility of him being able to walk again. She explains how going to his appointments was where she first discovered her passion for physiotherapy, which also explains why she didn't want to answer my question the first time we met.

It becomes clear that for the past eight years, Elle has been a parent to Brendan. She went through the worst thing any seventeen-year-old could go through, then she took on the responsibility of caring for her brother. The medical bills and grief had to have been endless, and the fact she's been able to put herself through college as well tells me just how hard she's had to work to get here.

And just like that, it finally makes sense. She said that she can't risk her job, and I got that, but I didn't understand just how serious she was or what was on the line. But knowing just how far she's come and what a strong woman she is only makes me want her more.

Now I just have to prove to her that being with me isn't going to be a risk. There's nothing for her to lose here, only something incredible for us both to gain, but that's something she's going to have to work out on her own.

The second she started talking about Brendan, she couldn't stop, and it was clear just how much she loves him. I could stay right here and listen to her talk for hours, but when she finally runs out of things to say, she snuggles in deeper and looks up to meet my eyes. "Thank you," she murmurs. "I really needed that."

My heart swells as I look down into those beautiful blue eyes, and I press a kiss to her forehead, wishing it was her lips. "Go to sleep, Elle. I've got you."

With that, she closes her eyes and drifts off into a peaceful sleep, wrapped in my arms, right where she will always belong.

Chapter Fourteen

ELLE

The sound of birds chirping seeps into my unconscious mind and has me waking from the best sleep I've had in over eight years.

Warmth consumes me as my eyes open to find myself tucked safely in the arms of the most amazing man I have ever met. My mind flashes back to last night, how he was able to give me the courage to open up and talk about my family. No one has ever been able to give me that strength before. Perhaps it was knowing that he had suffered his own loss and would better understand. I don't know, but whatever it was, it has taken a weight off my chest and somehow made it easier to breathe.

I've spoken with therapists in the past. All of them looked at me like some kind of messy pet project, thinking they could break me out of my depression. I couldn't handle it. Their poking and prodding into my head only broke me more. I doubt they had ever lost their family in the same way I had, and I doubt they could even begin to understand my pain.

Of course, I'd spoken with Brendan at length because he was suffering the same loss. We so effortlessly could share stories about Sammy and our parents, reflect on the best times of our lives, but he's my brother, and while I love him with everything I've got, I've always needed someone outside of my inner circle to talk to. It helped when I found Jaz. We cried and cuddled, but there was something different about opening up to Logan.

At least now he'll understand why I've been so standoffish with him. Well . . . mostly. I don't think he could possibly realize the kind of debt I'm in after having to support my brother through his continuous rehabilitation, put myself through seven years of college, pay rent, and still live.

I was able to sell my parents' house and claim insurance, which helped a lot, but that money only went so far.

I lived with my aunt and uncle for a little while to be close to Brendan and finish high school, but then I went to college. Things got so much harder, but we were strong and made it work.

Now we've come out the other end. I've got this amazing job with a promotion on the horizon, and Brendan is back in rehab with the possibility of walking again. The weight of college and finding a good job is off my shoulders, and now all I have to focus on is getting Brendan better—and somehow keeping Logan at arm's length. But something tells me that's not possible, not now, not after tasting him on my lips.

He said last night that he believes my job is safe, but how could he possibly know that? It's a nice thought and would mean that I could maybe give this thing with Logan a go. It's becoming startlingly clear that he isn't the player I thought he was. I mean, sure, I bet he's had his moments in the past, but he's serious when he says this is different, but doesn't every guy say that?

Logan's arms pulling tighter around my waist break me from my thoughts. I'm pulled right in beside him, my back pressed against his warm chest, his heavenly scent wrapping around me. His lips graze the side of my neck, breathing me in. "How'd you sleep?" he murmurs, that sleepy tone taking grip of my soul and refusing to let go.

I turn in his arms and look up at him, his hooded eyes already locked on mine. "Better than I have in eight years," I admit.

His eyes shimmer with happiness, and I immediately become addicted, undeniably falling for his wicked charm. "You don't know how happy that makes me," he murmurs. Then in a flash, he shifts his weight until he's hovering over me, his strong arms caging me in and his lips firmly against mine.

My traitorous body comes alive beneath his touch as a needy groan slips from my lips. My knees hook around his hips, and I feel him right there, his hardness pressed firmly against my core. My hands trail down his hard body, exploring every inch of him before finding the hem of his shirt and pressing my fingers to his bare skin. My fingers skim back up his waist and around to explore the sculpted, strong muscles of his back.

Moaning like a needy bitch, I push up harder, pressing against him, needing so much more, and as if reading my body, Logan grinds down, making my eyes roll in the back of my head. Every last thought escapes me, and while I know the second I allow us to cross this line, I'll never be able to go back, but I can't possibly stop. I need him more than I need air.

Logan's lips move down to the soft skin of my neck, and once again, I find myself arching up into his touch, even more so when his hand pushes up beneath my hoodie to caress my skin. His thumb brushes over my nipple, and it pebbles instantly, so damn sensitive to his touch. I've never felt anything quite so intense.

Needing to feel him, my greedy fingers grasp onto the fabric of his shirt, and I pull it up. He helps me out, ripping it over his head, and the second it's gone, my eyes begin roaming. I've seen him like this once before, but I'll never get used to it. His body is perfection, clearly one that comes from years of intense training, and I can't help but feel like the luckiest girl in the world. He's simply gorgeous.

Desperate to feel his skin on mine, I reach for the hem of my hoodie, but Logan beats me to it, clearly wanting to be the one to unwrap me like his most anticipated gift on Christmas morning. He pulls my hoodie right over my head, discarding it on the ground beside the air mattress before diving for my shirt. It's gone in record time, and I watch the way Logan devours my body, taking in every last curve, his eyes hooded and filled with the most intense desire.

His gaze lifts to mine, the hunger like nothing I've ever experienced. He kisses me fiercely before his lips work their way down until they close over my pebbled nipple. My head tips back, pleasure rocking through my body, an electric pulse shooting straight to my core. "Oh, God," I groan, my fingers knotting into his hair.

His hands work down my body, and as he reaches the waistband of my sweatpants, my eyes start rolling again, the desperation for this man like nothing I've ever known.

"You're fucking perfect," Logan murmurs as his hand pushes down between my legs, his fingers brushing over my clit and making my whole body jolt. He pushes up onto his elbow to watch the way my body reacts to his touch. As his fingers press harder against my clit, he rubs tight circles, making my head tip back. I suck in a deep, needy breath, digging my nails into his strong arm.

I can't resist him a second longer, and I reach down between us, slipping my hand into the front of his pants. My fingers curl around the base of his thick, veiny cock, and the soft groan that pulls from deep within his chest is the most addictive sound I've ever heard. I need more. So much more.

I start moving, exploring his velvety cock, moving right up to his tip and roaming my thumb over the top, loving the way his body stiffens beneath my touch. His head drops to the curve of my neck, and I feel like a fucking queen holding him hostage to my touch.

"Logan," I pant as I get closer and closer to the edge, but he's not nearly finished with me.

"That's right, babe," he murmurs, his hungry kiss coming back to my lips just as his fingers push lower to my entrance. I gasp into his mouth, and as he pushes them inside of me, massaging my walls, it's all I can do not to fall apart right here in his arms.

His thumb stretches up and works my clit as his skilled fingers take me right to the edge. His mouth drops back to my nipple, his tongue flicking over the sensitive bud and forcing my back to arch up off the air mattress. Desperation pounds through my body like a million electric pulses, all heading straight for my core.

My grip tightens on his cock as my orgasm quickly builds, and as those skilled fingers split apart, scissoring inside of me, my world explodes. I come hard, my head thrown back as my walls start to convulse, spasming with the intensity of my orgasm.

Logan doesn't hold back. He keeps working my body, his thumb rolling over my clit in tight, addictive circles, only making everything all the more intense. But that need for him is far from gone. I want to hear him groan, want to hear him whisper my name as he comes, and the second I'm freed from the intensity of my orgasm, I push Logan back to the mattress, that hunger only getting worse.

I crawl on top of him, moving down his body and completely freeing his cock from the confines of his pants, my mouth watering as I take him in, in all his glory. When I first saw him on my table, I knew he was big, but seeing him like this, every last bit of him standing tall and proud, I fear I'll never be able to handle it. But I'm gonna damn well try.

Scooching down, my heavy gaze locks onto his, my mouth watering. My tongue rolls out across my bottom lip, and I watch as the anticipation builds in his eyes, knowing exactly what I'm about to do.

I can't wait another second.

Keeping my eyes locked on his, I lean down and bring my lips to the tip of his cock. My tongue peeks out first, stealing just the slightest taste before opening wide and taking him deep. My lips close around him, and as my grip tightens at the base of his thick cock, I start moving up and down, my tongue roaming over every inch of him.

Logan groans and reaches out, pushing his fingers through my hair and gripping tight as I hollow out my cheeks. I give it my all, moving up and down and following the cues he's giving me. "Fuck, Elle," he grunts, making a wicked grin pull at the corner of my lips, only it doesn't get the chance to spread as my lips are far too busy. "I could fuck this sweet little mouth for the rest of my life and still not have enough."

A thrill pulses through me, desperate to see how he comes undone, and as his grip tightens in my hair, I know he's close. So fucking close.

I work him harder, taking him right to the back of my throat, desperate to impress him. His body jolts, his hips pushing up. His other hand comes to my face, pushing the loose strands of hair back as a deep growl rumbles through his chest. "I'm gonna fucking blow, babe. If you don't want it . . ."

Oh, God. Stopping would be a tragedy.

Instead, I meet his wild stare and grin around his thick cock, not daring to stop. My fist moves up and down at his base, and I watch as his chest rises and falls with panting breaths. His eyes roll, a smirk pulling at the corner of his full lips, and as that grip tightens in my hair, he comes hard, shooting hot spurts of cum sailing down the back of my throat. "Fuck, Elle," he groans, keeping his tone low so that the players in the tents around us don't know what the fuck is going down in here.

After devouring every last drop, I gently release him from my clutches, and the way he's looking at me has me feeling more woman than I ever have in my life.

I start crawling back up to him, but he's far too impatient and grabs me, hauling me back up his body until I'm settled right back on the mattress, his big body hovering over me again. Logan's lips find mine, but rather than the intense, needy deep kisses from before, it's now slow and full of wild passion.

My arms twine around his neck, never feeling so right, and when he pulls back to catch his breath, his forehead drops against mine, his gentle caress making me feel like his most precious possession. "When are you going to realize we're perfect together?" he murmurs with his lips gently brushing over mine as he speaks.

Undeniable warmth spreads through my veins, each one leading directly to my heart, filling it with the sweetest kind of bliss. Taking his face in my hands, I slowly lift his head to meet my eyes. "I already have," I whisper.

His gaze softens as he looks down at me before sadness flickers in his eyes, a sadness that tears me to shreds. "It doesn't change anything, does it?"

I shake my head ever so slightly, hating that my need to keep him at arm's length is hurting him. "I'm sorry," I tell him, the weight of my rejection so heavy on my heart. "I just . . . I can't."

He nods, understanding me perfectly. "I'm not about to back down."

A small smile settles across my lips, and I raise my chin to kiss him again. "Is it selfish of me to not want you to?"

"No, it's not," he tells me. "You'll be mine sooner or later."

"You're so sure of yourself," I laugh.

"I am, because you and I both know this right here," he says, indicating between us, "is so fucking right that to ignore it would be a crime. I get it, though. You need time to be okay with that and find the courage to take that leap while still learning how you fit into this world. But just for the record, soon enough you're going to realize that all your excuses are bullshit."

"What?" I grunt, pressing against his sculpted chest and pushing him up off me. I sit up in front of him waiting for an explanation, and I have to scramble for my hoodie since he's instantly distracted by my exposed tits.

Logan's gaze lifts back to mine. "You're scared I'm going to hurt you," he declares.

My brows furrow. "Aren't you?"

"No. I've already told you, Elle, you're mine, and I don't intend on ever letting you go. So, considering we have the rest of our lives, I have more than enough time to wait for you. Though just between you and me, I don't think that's going to be very long. So, with that being said, could you please stop putting your hoodie back on?"

"Logan," I groan.

I don't get a chance to finish dressing before he tackles me back to the air mattress. "Look," he says, caging me in and holding my stare to make sure I truly hear what he has to say. "You've had a lot to deal with over the past few years, that much is clear, and I get your reasons for not wanting to lose your job. You haven't had it easy, and you've worked your ass off to make it this far, but I don't believe that our being together is going to compromise that. You already know I want to be with you, and it's pretty damn clear you feel the same way."

"I don't know, Logan," I say as my eyes begin to water. He's completely right. I do want to be with him, so freaking bad it hurts, but I have too much riding on this job. "I need to think about Brendan. If I lose this job because I was too busy screwing around with the captain, Brendan loses his chance of walking again. I can't let him down like that. He's all I've got left."

He lets out a sigh as he drops his forehead to mine. "It's okay," he soothes as he wipes away a tear. "I get it. I'm not going to push you on this, but just so you know, Brendan isn't the only one you've got now."

It goes against everything I'm telling him, but my need for him is too hard to resist, and I reach up, lock my arms around his neck, and pull him down to me, letting his lips meet mine in the sweetest kiss. I close my eyes, reveling in his touch, but it's different now. I can feel the disappointment radiating out of him, and I want to hate myself for bringing this incredible man down.

Why do I have to ruin everything good in my life?

Logan pulls back and gently rests his head against mine before getting up from the bed. "Where are you going?" I ask as I sit up.

"I just need . . . a few minutes," he tells me as he reaches down and grabs his shirt before turning and facing me with fire in his eyes. "I've seen the way you look when you come, and I want to see it again. So, if you keep kissing me like that, I'm going to fuck you so hard that you won't be able to walk for a week."

Holy shit.

Maybe I do want that.

My breath catches as I pull my bottom lip between my teeth, hunger crashing through me like a fucking tsunami.

Goddamn.

I can only imagine the pure ecstasy of getting fucked by a man like Logan Waters. Shit, I'm supposed to be a good girl with values, not a skanky whore who's excited about the possibility of being fucked by the man who could potentially ruin everything.

But . . . it would be so good.

"Don't look at me like that, Elle," he warns, that deep growl in his tone making me wet. "You're making it too hard to walk away right now."

Knowing I need to chill, I lay back on the air mattress and pull the blanket right up to my chin before watching Logan slowly back away. He reaches the door of our tent, still with those wicked eyes trained heavily on me. Then letting out a breath, he finally steps out of the tent, letting the tension between us dissipate and giving me the chance to think straight.

Shit. What kind of mess am I getting myself into?

Needing some time to myself, I slowly get presentable before running my fingers through my hair so it doesn't look like I was just fooling around with the star player. After putting my shoes on, I head out of the tent with my toothbrush and toothpaste in hand and find a bottle of water before disappearing into the trees.

Desperately needing to pee, I head deeper into the woods and stare down a tree before making it my bitch. Hearing voices close by, I quickly finish and pull my pants back up before I get caught by a bunch of extremely hot guys with my pants around my ankles. Satisfied that I haven't been caught, I double check my shoes just to make sure I didn't pee all over myself then start getting myself ready for the day.

I take all the time in the world brushing my teeth and stroll back to the campsite feeling like a million dollars . . . Well, apart from the fact I haven't showered. But waking up in Logan's arms and having a ground-breaking orgasm would make any woman feel on cloud nine.

I find the guys inhaling their breakfast and take a seat beside Logan. "Where'd you take off to?" he asks, handing me a plate that's filled to the brim.

"I was brushing my teeth if you really must know," I say with a smirk before digging into my breakfast, knowing there's no way in hell I'll be able to eat all of this, but I'm gonna try anyway.

"What are your plans for the day?" he asks.

"I don't know," I say with a shrug. "Probably washing and cleaning

Louie's cage, to be honest."

"Wow, living the high life," Jax murmurs as he tries to smother a smirk.

"Tell me about it," I grunt.

"You can do it tomorrow," Logan says. "You're coming to my place."

"Um. No, I'm not," I grunt, baffled at how he can possibly think that's a good idea. "Besides, I work every other day, and Louie isn't going to clean his cage himself."

"Fine," Logan says, his eyes sparkling, making me realize I'm quickly walking into a Logan-sized trap. "Spend the day with me and then I'll come back to your place and help you clean Louie's cage."

I narrow my eyes on him. "You wouldn't have the first clue how to clean a bird's cage."

"This is true," he says with a sexy glimmer in his eye. "But it couldn't possibly be that hard, and if I'm really fucking it up that bad, I can look after Louie while you do it."

"Louie is more than capable of looking after himself," I shoot back.

The wicked smirk I've become so addicted to spreads across his face, his gaze practically eating me up. "Ahh, if that were true, he wouldn't need you to clean his cage for him, would he?"

Fuck. He's got me there.

"You're such an idiot," I laugh.

"So, that's a yes?"

Rolling my eyes, I realize there's no way in hell I'm about to win this one, so I might as well give up while I'm still ahead. Though I'm pretty damn sure where Logan Waters is concerned, I've not been ahead once. "Fine," I tell him. "But you better make it worth my while."

Chapter Fifteen

LOGAN

Concentrating on the road has never been so fucking hard. Elle sits beside me, her gaze trained out the open window, watching the world pass us by. But all I can think about is that beautiful curve of her neck and how fucking good it feels to have my lips roaming all over it.

If only she weren't so damn stubborn. I get where she's coming from. Sleeping around with the guys is a risky move and one she would suffer consequences for, but this is different. I don't want to just get between her legs, I want the fucking world with her. Surely management wouldn't have a problem with it if we were in a committed relationship, especially if we were open and upfront with them about it.

This is all new to me. I've never felt this way about a woman before. It's always been about sex, and if the girl was good, I'd keep her around for a week or two, but the second she started to think there was even a shot at a future with me, I'd cut her loose. But not with Elle. The moment I saw her, I knew I wanted something more, and sure, I hadn't figured out what that was, but now I know for sure. I'm going to fall in love with this woman, and I can't fucking wait.

Turning into my driveway, I watch as her eyes widen in surprise. My place isn't really what people expect from me. Most people assume I have a killer bachelor pad in the city, which don't get me wrong, I do, I own a few of them actually, but they're not for me.

My home is situated on a huge piece of beautifully landscaped property, very similar to my parents' place with the tree-lined driveway leading right up to the house—a house that is most definitely bigger than any single person could ever need. When I built it, I wanted this to be my forever home, the home I would raise a family in. I just hadn't expected to find the woman of my dreams quite so soon, but now that I have, I can't wait to see her barefoot and pregnant in my home, dancing over the stove on a Sunday morning, making pancakes together.

Fuck. The visual only makes resisting her harder.

"What the hell is this place?" Elle questions from beside me, gaping out the window at the property and taking in the landscaped gardens, the high arches of the tree-lined driveway, and the mansion sitting at the end.

"This," I say, pride surging through my chest, "is my place."

"What the actual fuck, Logan?" she breathes, staring at me in disbelief. "How many people do you have living in there?"

"Just me."

"What could you possibly need a place so big for?"

I try to keep from laughing. "Well, first, I needed land big enough that I could skate on. And second, I wanted to build something big enough so there was room for my whole family. When my brothers and Cass get married and have kids, I want there to be enough space for them all to come and stay here. And of course, when we have a family of our own. It seems big and lonely now, but it's not always going to be this way."

Elle's cheeks flush, and I don't miss how she skips straight over my comments, not ready to entertain the idea of our future together, even after seeing the perfect glimpse into what that's going to look like. I bring my truck to a stop at the top of the circle driveway before getting out and meeting her by the stairs that lead up to the front door.

"Hold on," she says, starting her way up the stairs. "What do you mean you wanted space to skate?"

"Oh," I smile, pointing out my thigh, the very reason why all this shit started in the first place. "You know how I fell while skating? It kinda happened here. Last summer, I had a pond put in the back, big enough to skate on in the winter."

Her jaw drops. "You're shitting me, right?"

"Nope."

"I've got to see this," she says as she meets me around the front of my truck.

The pride that soars through my chest is unbelievable and has me holding my head just a little higher. "No problem," I laugh as we climb the stairs to the front door. "It's not frozen anymore, but it's just as beautiful. I think I'll find some geese or some shit like that to have here during the spring. My mom would have loved that."

Not wanting to get emotional, I quickly shake it off before I unlock the door and welcome her into my home. Elle gets one foot inside the front door before pausing, her eyes widening as her gaze lifts, following the pillars right up to the high ceilings. "Holy shit," she breathes. "Your foyer is bigger than my apartment."

"It is not," I smirk, but yeah . . . it kind of is.

"Bullshit," she scoffs under her breath. I lead her through the house and watch as she takes it all in. "I'm in the wrong profession," she murmurs as we hit the kitchen.

"Yeah, it pays to be a professional athlete," I tell her, but truth be told, this place cost a fortune, which I paid for by using a portion of my inheritance from my parents, and my trust fund. I use the money from hockey to pay bills and whatever is left goes straight to charity. I don't need all that.

I show her around the rest of the house before coming out back and leading her down to the pond. "This place is incredible," she says as she takes it all in.

"Thanks, I had Carter design and build it," I tell her, picturing her standing right here, watching our kids out on the ice.

"Carter did?" she questions.

"He's an architect," I explain. "Just like Dad was. He built Waters Construction from the ground up, and when he passed, Carter took the reins."

"Wait . . . you're *that* Waters?" she breathes, her eyes widening. "That's one of the biggest construction companies in the US."

"Correction. It is the biggest," I tell her proudly. "It was right up there when Dad was running it. But with Carter's new designs, it's taken off. Everybody wants a home built by Waters Construction."

"That's amazing," she says. "I never would have guessed that, especially after meeting him."

"What do you mean?"

"It's just, he's so . . . carefree. I never would have expected him to be this crazy good architect businessman."

"Yeah, no one ever does," I say with a smirk, knowing all too well. "He's the best at what he does and is a fucking killer in the boardroom, but the second he steps out of the office, he's back to being that fucking idiot I grew up with."

"What about Sean? What does he do?" she questions.

"He's a lawyer," I murmur.

"A good one?" she asks.

"Yeah," I scoff. "You could murder a hundred people and be caught with the gun in your hand and Sean would still be able to get you off."

"Really?"

"Well . . . that might be a slight exaggeration."

Elle laughs, but it doesn't reach her eyes, and I realize that all this talk of my family must have her thinking about her own. "You're thinking about your family?" I question as I slide my hand into hers.

She looks up at me as she laces her fingers through mine. "Always," she says. "You're so lucky to have such a big family. I'd do anything to get mine back."

"I know," I say as I give her hand a tug and pull her into me. I wrap my arms around her and take pleasure in the way her head rests against my chest. "I can't give you your family back, but you're welcome to share mine until I can give you a family of our own."

Elle buries her face into my chest and remains silent, but I know my comments are heavy on her mind. We stay this way, wrapped in each other's arms as we look out at my property, taking in the beauty of it. "Come on," I murmur, not wanting her to get sick in the chill. "It's way too cold out here."

We walk up to the house together, but my phone buzzing in my pocket steals my attention, and I pull it out to find a message from Sean.

Sean – Lunch at my place. Be there. 2 pm.

With a grin, I start typing out my reply.

Logan – Sure. I'm bringing Elle.
Sean – Does she know that? I'm not bailing you out on kidnapping charges.

I roll my eyes as I turn to Elle. "I was going to say we can chill here for the day, but how do you feel about meeting my brother for lunch?"

"Not great," she mutters. "You're lucky you even got me here. I'm not meeting your brother for lunch after I've spent the night in a tent, peed in the bushes, and haven't showered. Besides, I have nothing nice to wear."

I can't help but smile at the little vixen. "You can shower here, and as for sleeping in a tent, I recall you saying something about it being the best sleep you'd had in years."

"Shut up," Elle groans, averting her gaze as those cheeks flush with the most gorgeous shade of red. "I'm not going."

"Yes, you are." I take her hand and lead her up the stairs. "Cass has a whole heap of clothes here for when she stays. I'm sure you'll find something you like in there."

"You're impossible."

With that settled, I lead her back into my home and show her up to the room Cassie has claimed as her own before heading straight for her closet. Elle grumbles the whole way upstairs, but the moment I open Cassie's closet, her jaw drops. She starts searching through Cassie's clothes, pulling out a pair of tight jeans, a black top, thigh-high boots, and a leather jacket that I know I'm not going to be able to resist her in.

After finding her a towel and showing her to the bathroom, I make sure it's fully stocked with shampoo, conditioner, and all that girly shit. I lean against the open door frame, watching as she dumps the clothes on the vanity before noticing me here. "Uhh . . . this is the part where you leave," she says, watching me through the mirror.

Stepping deeper into the bathroom, I walk straight up behind her and grab her waist. A beaming smile tears across her face, and I can't resist pulling her right into my chest and dropping my lips to her neck. "I thought you could use some help in here."

Elle groans, her hand sliding up around the back of my neck as she closes her eyes, reveling in the feel of my lips moving against her sensitive skin. That juicy bottom lip gets caught between her teeth and as she presses her ass back into me, my hand starts moving around her waist, dropping down to the waistband of her sweats.

Pleasure flickers across her face, and just as I'm about to push my hand down between her glorious legs, she captures my wrist between her fingers, stopping me, disappointment in her eyes. "No," she breathes as her eyes meet mine in the mirror. "I'm not about to have my first time in a . . ."

Her eyes widen, cutting herself off as my other hand tightens on her waist, both of us freezing to the spot. Did she just say first time? Fuck. Don't tell me this woman has never been touched by another man. God, I'm pretty sure I just came in my fucking pants.

Elle cringes and averts her stare, but I spin her around and grip her chin, holding her blazing blue stare. "Did you just say what I think you just said?"

"No," she rushes out, the pulse in the base of her neck racing.

Fuck me. I knew there was something special about this girl.

Undeniable warmth spreads through me as I smile down at her, lowering my face to hers. "You're so fucking perfect," I murmur before closing the gap and settling my lips on hers, kissing her deeply. "I'm going to be the only fucking man you will ever need or want."

Elle falls victim to my kiss as she melts around me, her body so effortlessly folding against mine, right where she's always belonged. Her hands slide up and around my neck as she moans into my mouth, making me want her more, and I can't resist lifting her onto the counter.

Elle's legs wrap around my waist, holding me close against her. As she pulls back to catch her breath, my lips drop to her neck once again, devouring her as her fingers roam up into my hair. "I guess you could use a shower too," she murmurs as quietly as ever.

I pull back to meet those big blue eyes, making sure she truly means what she's saying. "Are you sure?" I question, my hands dropping to her thighs and squeezing. "What happened to us not being a thing?"

"I just . . . I can't help myself around you," she whispers, meaning every damn word.

Goddamn. This woman will be the death of me, and better yet, I'll let her destroy me over and over again.

Unable to resist, I pick her up off the counter, and she clings to me as I walk us right into the shower. Pressing her back against the wall, I reach for the tap and let the cold water rain down over us. "What are you doing?" she screeches, pulling away from the water as it quickly starts to warm. "My clothes are getting all wet."

"You don't need them," I say.

Elle grips the hem of my shirt before tugging it up between our bodies and letting it fall to the ground, the wet, heavy fabric slapping against the tiles. Then with both her hands free, she puts them right on my body, her fingers digging into my muscles as though she can't quite get enough.

I do my best to rid her of her clothes while she's pressed against the wall, the desperation and hunger pulsing between us. It's a race to strip out of our clothes, and before I know it, that beautiful naked body of hers is pressed right up against mine, begging me to ease the ache between those gorgeous thighs.

What can I say? I'm a fucking gentleman and get straight to work. No woman of mine is going to be made to wait. Keeping her pinned with my body, I reach down between us, my fingers grazing over her needy clit. She groans at the touch, and I do it again, loving how she comes alive for me, but it's not enough. Ever since I touched her this morning, I've needed more. So much more.

I need to fucking taste her.

Working my way down her body, I drop to my knees and watch the way her eyes flutter with anticipation. She lets her head fall back against the wall, and a low groan rumbles through her chest. "Oh, God."

Damn fucking right, baby!

Taking her thigh, I hook it over my shoulder, and I can't wait a second longer before diving in and closing my mouth over her needy clit. My tongue flicks over the sensitive bundle of nerves and Elle gasps, her fingers knotting into my hair.

I suck, nip, and tease, and as I continue working her body, I push my fingers up into her sweet pussy, working her from inside. Her knees weaken, and she's forced to use me to keep herself up. I can't help the smile that tears across my face. I've been craving this moment, desperate to see how she tastes, and she's fucking perfect.

With my spare hand, I grip the base of my cock, slowly working up and down. As I glance up, I find her gaze already locked on the way I work myself, those gorgeous blue eyes filled with intense desire and lust, and goddamn, that fire has me ready to blow.

I don't dare stop, giving her everything she needs until I feel her tight little cunt convulsing around my fingers. She comes hard, reaching that high and crying out, her whole body weakening as she desperately tries to catch herself against the wall. I come right along with her, spilling hot spurts of cum over the fucking tiles.

As she pants for air, I get back to my feet and crowd her against the wall. Her forehead drops to my shoulder, needing a minute to catch her breath. "Holy shit," Elle pants, barely able to keep herself up. "Why does it have to be so good with you?"

"Baby, we haven't even gotten close to the good shit yet," I tease. Elle lifts her head and her cheeks flush the most brilliant shade of pink. She doesn't respond, and I know it's heavy on her mind. But I'm not going to push it. Not until she tells me she's ready, and fuck, the second she does, I'm going to make sure I blow her mind.

With a lunch date to get to, I soap her up, my hands roaming all over her body, making me hard all over again. I make sure to be thorough, my hands sliding between her legs, making her gasp and groan with every little touch, keeping her wound up and ready for more. Then as I lather up her waist and tits, I pull her back hard against my chest and make her come all over again.

We spend way too long in the shower, and by the time we're out, dressed, and back in my truck, we're late, but it was worth every fucking second. Just as I knew she would, Elle looks amazing, and the whole drive over to Sean's house, I have to force myself to keep my hands off her.

"Are you ready for this?" I ask as I pull up to Sean's place.

"What do you mean?" she questions through a narrowed stare, not sure if she should be nervous or excited.

"The second I told Sean I was bringing you, the lot of them would have been on a group call, trying to figure out what the fuck is going on here. They're going to drill you, ask every question under the sun until they inevitably decide you're too good for me."

Her eyes widen. "And what the hell am I supposed to say?" she asks. "I don't even know what's going on here."

I shake my head, a smile playing on my lips. "Come on, babe. You know damn well what's going on here. You're just too fucking stubborn to admit it."

Elle rolls her eyes, but her smile quickly fades, something on her mind. "I'm not too stubborn to admit it. I know damn well that this thing between us is . . . I don't know. I just . . . I'm sorry I have to keep denying you. The thought of hurting you makes me sick, and every time I tell you no, I know that must sting."

"What? No," I scoff. "I fucking love it. I live for your rejection."

"Oh, in that case, I might just do it some more."

"No, no, no," I rush out.

Elle laughs, a spark lighting up her eyes and making my chest ache with happiness. "What I was trying to say is that maybe you're not the douchebag I thought you were."

I stare at her, my brows furrowed. "How is that what you were trying to say?" I laugh, having no idea how she possibly connected the dots between hating the idea of rejecting me to me being a douchebag. "But really, I'm touched. It's always been my dream to have a beautiful woman declare me an anti-douchebag."

Elle lets out a heavy sigh before fixing me with a hard stare. "Is it possible for you to have a conversation without being a sarcastic jackass?"

"Sorry, babe, but that would be a firm no."

Elle lets out a groan as she unbuckles her seatbelt and climbs across my truck to straddle my lap, her hand fisting in the material of my shirt. She pulls her bottom lip between her teeth and looks as if she might be sick, a nervousness flickering in her big blue eyes. "Maybe we could . . . I don't know . . . try," she says.

My brows shoot up, staring at her as though she just spoke another language. "You're fucking with me, right?" I question, sitting up a little straighter. "Because the Elle I know would be fighting tooth and nail, telling me I'd have better luck fucking a nail gun than getting her to be my girl."

She rolls her eyes again, a soft smile kicking up the corners of her lips, still nervously fidgeting with my shirt. "I'm serious," she tells me. "But I'm also serious about protecting my job. I don't want to go flaunting this just yet. I don't particularly like the whole keeping you as a dirty little secret thing, but we would have to keep it on the down low from the team. You know, if it doesn't work out. I just . . . it's too important."

I pull her into me, my lips barely a breath away from hers. "It's going to work."

"How can you be so sure?"

"Because I know how I feel about you, and something so strong, so fucking pure could never be wrong." Her eyes shimmer with happiness, and I grip her chin, making sure she really hears me. "We're going to make this work, Elle. You're it for me, and I'm not about to let you go."

Tears well in her eyes, and I don't let her say another word before I close the gap between us, pulling her back into me and kissing her deeply, letting her feel everything in this one touch. My hand grips the back of her neck, and as my fingers move up into her hair, a knock sounds on the window and Elle springs away from me. Her eyes widen as if she were just caught doing something she shouldn't be doing.

I groan as Carter grins back at me. "Am I interrupting something?" he calls with a stupid fucking grin, his voice muffled through the closed door.

"Fuck off, dickhead," I say, but Elle is mortified. Her cheeks glow a bright red as she quickly scrambles off my lap and out of the truck, all while I laugh, more than amused. But hell, if she's embarrassed about this, she's got another thing coming. The PDA she's about to walk in on inside Sean's place with three other couples is about to blow her mind.

Joining her in front of my truck, Carter and Brianna all but pounce on her, saying quick hellos before I take her hand and lead her inside. "Wow, it's nice to see your brother understands what a normal house is supposed to look like," Elle murmurs as she looks up at Sean's house. Though there's no denying it's significantly smaller than mine, this is no normal home. It's still huge by any standard.

"Trust me, he doesn't," I tell her. "He wanted one like mine, but Sara made him dial it down."

She shakes her head in exasperation, and as we make our way through the foyer, the sound of my sister's singing fills our ears. "Holy crap," Elle whispers beside me. "Is that Sara?"

"Nah," I grin. "That's Cass."

"That's right. I remember the girls at college talking about her singing, but I never got the chance to hear her," she says in awe. "She's incredible."

"Sure is," Carter throws over his shoulder.

We make our way through the house and find the kitchen in an array of activities. Sara is busy putting a salad together while Sean is getting something out of the oven. Jax is setting the table like a little bitch and Cassie . . . Well, I don't know what the fuck she's doing.

"Cass?" I question as she walks from one end of the kitchen to the other, singing to herself while doing lunges. "What the hell are you doing?"

"I'm lunging," she informs me as if I couldn't work that part out.

"Yeah, I got that, but why?"

"My wedding is in two months, and I want one of those asses the gym girls have," she explains as she gives Elle a brilliant smile and lunges toward her to give her a welcoming hug. "Plus, it wouldn't hurt to lose a pound or two. My dress was a bit tight at my last fitting."

"Can you just let the dress out?"

Every pair of female eyes turn to me in horror. Crap. Clearly, I've said something wrong. "You don't alter a designer dress. You alter yourself," Sara scolds, definitely not one to care about this shit, but right now, I really can't tell if she's joking or not. Either way, I'm way out of my depth here.

At that, Jax rolls his eyes at his fiancé. "Babe, you're fucking perfect the way you are. You don't need to lose weight."

"Jax," Cassie says, holding her hand up to stop him. "We are not getting into this again. I wanna be thick—a nice juicy fat ass with a tiny little waist. God, just imagine how good my twerking game would be. This ass here," she says, pointing to her behind, "not even a little jiggle."

Jax lets out a groan and gets back to setting the table only to have Brianna shove him out of the way and start again, but I must admit, she does a much better job. Elle jumps straight in and helps with whatever she can, and watching her fall in so easily with my family does something to me that I can't quite understand.

Twenty minutes later, we're sitting around Sean and Sara's massive table with the conversation flowing. As expected, they've all drilled Elle on our relationship, given me shit about bringing a girl around for the first time, and asked how my broken dick is going. And despite Elle's shy nature, she has absolutely no problems letting every last asshole here know just how not broken my dick is.

We're having an amazing time when Sara and Sean finally get to the reason we're all here. Sean proudly stands at the head of the table and looks at his wife with love in his eyes—a look that has caused him a lot of shit over the years—but now I feel like I'm starting to understand it.

"So, you all know I'm not one for speeches, so let's make this short and sweet," he starts. "As you know, Sara and I have been together for a while . . ."

"Holy crap," Cassie shrieks, cutting off Sean's speech as she looks at Sara with a wide, hopeful stare. "You're pregnant?"

What? Pregnant? I turn to Sara along with everyone else in the room, eagerly anticipating her response. How the fuck did Cassie come to that conclusion? Sean's barely said a word yet.

Sara looks up at Sean with a cheesy grin before turning back to the rest of us. "Yes, I'm pregnant. You'll all have a little niece or nephew in seven months."

Holy fuck.

The whole room turns into chaos. We jump out of our chairs and crowd Sara and Sean with our hugs and congratulations. We couldn't be more excited for the first Waters baby to come along. Though to be honest, between me and Carter, I'm surprised we haven't accidentally knocked anyone up yet. We did well for ourselves.

It takes at least ten minutes for everyone to settle down and get back to the table to finish our lunch, and even then, I can hardly believe it. These two are going to make amazing parents. There's nobody more deserving. I couldn't be happier for them. The only thing missing is Mom and Dad, but I know they're looking down on us and are just as happy as the rest of us.

Chapter Sixteen

ELLE

It's well into the night when Logan and I get back to my tiny shithole apartment, and after spending the day in two different mansions, I've realized just how far I have to go before finally making it big in this world, but I'm on my way. I'm going to show management that I deserve the senior position next season, and I'm going to finally start living.

I can just see it now. I'll be able to buy myself a proper home. It will probably still be small, but it will be decent—just big enough for me, Brendan, and Louie. Though I'll have to figure out a way to get Jaz to stay close to me too, but I'm sure it will all work out. You know, assuming Logan doesn't kidnap me and force me to live in his home for all eternity.

After getting through the door, I dump my bag on the ground before collapsing in an exhausted heap on my couch as Logan beelines for my foul-mouthed bird. He gathers Louie out of his cage, props him up on his shoulder, and looks over the cage as though it's some sort of puzzle.

I'm exhausted. It's been a crazy weekend filled with all sorts of emotions, some high and some very low, but mostly, I've just been enjoying being in Logan's company. I've never felt that way with a man before. Usually, I can't wait to get away, but with Logan, I keep needing more.

I'm starting to wonder if I'm being ridiculous thinking management will fire me. I mean, it's not like I'm getting around sleeping with half the team, we'll be in a real relationship. Logan will be my partner, my forever.

But God, that shower was so amazing. It's got me wondering about what it might be like if I were to go the distance with Logan. It's clear he knows what he's doing. Not to mention, I opened my big mouth, and now he knows I'm a virgin, but he would take care of me . . . Well, I'm assuming he would take care of me. He seems like that kind of guy.

Shit. I can't believe I let that slip out. I'm such a fucking moron. It just came tumbling out of my mouth like word vomit. I haven't even told Jaz, but watching Logan's eyes light up like Christmas was kind of worth it. The way he told me that he'd be the only man I'd ever need or want . . . good God!

"Come on," Logan says, reaching over the top of the couch and hauling me to my feet. "We need to clean the birdcage."

"I don't want to clean it," I groan. "Can't I do it in the morning?"

"Nope," Logan says, rubbing Louie's chest. "I wouldn't let you sleep in your own shit, so why should Louie?"

Damn it. He has a really good point.

"Fine," I grunt before heading off to get my cleaning supplies.

Coming back with my arms loaded up, I get straight into it, changing the paper in the bottom while Logan rearranges all the toys and perches within the cage. After making it all shiny and new, I refill his food bowl and give him fresh water before chopping up some fruit snacks like a good bird mommy should.

"That's it?" Logan asks stumped, clearly thinking it was going to be a much bigger job than he thought.

"Yep. I'm not one for high-maintenance pets," I explain as I make myself comfortable on the floor and go through some stretches.

"What are you doing?" he questions.

"Stretching. I mean, if you paid attention to anything I've said since we met, you'd know it's good for you," I say, bluntly. "You should probably be doing yours too," I remind him. "The start of the season is getting closer, and you still have a bit to go before you're completely back to normal."

He lets out a sigh and comes to join me on the floor. Logan stretches out his legs, and I crawl across to help him loosen up the muscle a bit more, loving the way his face scrunches with the pain. The second he has deemed himself fully stretched, he grabs me around the waist and lifts me onto his lap.

Logan gives me the sweetest kiss before pulling back and really looking at me. "I had a good day," he says.

A smile spreads over my face, and I feel like the biggest dork, even more so when my cheeks start to flush bright red. I'm so crazy in love with the way he looks at me. "Me too," I say just as someone barges through my front door.

I whip around to face the door before realizing it's just Jaz. "What's up, whorebag?" she booms through my apartment, her hands filled with wine and Thai food. She gets three steps in the door before coming to a standstill, her eyes widening in surprise. "Oh," she says as a slow grin stretches across her face. "Do I need to leave?"

"No. Stay," Logan says as he lifts us both off the floor. "I need to get going, but I'll see you tomorrow."

"What?" I question. "We don't have an appointment tomorrow."

"No, but I get to go back to training tomorrow," he reminds me with a massive smile on his face, looking like a kid in a candy store.

"Oh, yeah," I say, feeling like a complete idiot for not remembering. After all, I was the one who approved his training schedule. Despite knowing he's doing amazing in his recovery, I'm terrified that he'll push it too hard too soon and ruin all of his progress. "I suppose I'll see you then."

Logan leans in and gives me the kind of kiss that has my knees buckling under me, then all too soon, he's gone, closing my door behind him and leaving me with a gaping Jaz.

"You've got a lot of explaining to do," Jaz says as she walks straight past me and into the kitchen where she pours two glasses of wine. I get our usual blanket out of my cupboard and get comfortable on the couch as Jaz comes over with the food, two forks, and the wine glasses. And then I hit shuffle on my playlist before getting stuck into my extremely detailed recap of the past two days.

Jaz's fork hovers in the air, food hanging off the edge. "Holy shit," she breathes. "I've known you for four years and never have you been so wild and spontaneous with a man. It's always carefully thought out and only ever lasts one night, but this, this is not the Elle I know. I mean, did he give you something to, you know . . . relax?"

"No," I laugh. "I'm not that much of a prude."

"Uh, yeah. You are."

"Oh, stop," I say, rolling my eyes. "He's just . . . different. He's fun and charming and sexy and . . . I mean, could you say no to that?"

"Well, no, but there isn't a lot I'd say no to," she laughs.

"Skank," I grunt into my food.

Jaz grins at me from across the couch, accepting my insult. "What's so different about him?" she questions, getting back on track.

"I told him about my family," I tell her.

She sobers, her brow raising as she lifts her gaze back to mine. "Really?" she murmurs. "You told him?"

"Yeah, I don't know what happened. We were sitting around the campfire talking and Jax mentioned that Logan lost his parents, and I don't know. I guess I found some common ground with him and realized that he would have a real understanding of my grief. So when we were alone, it just came out."

"Wow, then what happened?"

"We cuddled," I say.

Her face falls and she looks at me in disgust. "You cuddled?"

"Yes," I laugh. "We cuddled. It was nice."

She rolls her eyes as she gets back into her dinner. "You and I have very different definitions of the word nice."

I get back on track with my story and tell her all about this morning's air mattress activities before following it up with our shower activities as we finish off the bottle of wine. Then before we know it, it's past midnight. After shoving Jaz out the door, all too aware that we're both supposed to be working like mature adults tomorrow, I tuck Louie in like a good bird mommy and get my ass in bed, more than excited to see Logan again tomorrow.

I wake with a start, my eyes springing open before I scramble across my bed, reaching for my phone. I hastily light up the screen, my eyes widening with horror.

Oh no. It's already past 8:30 a.m.

Fuck, fuck, fuckity, fuck.

Throwing the blankets back, I scramble out of bed, rushing through my morning routine while trying not to think about the way Logan had me up against the wall in his shower. Shit, why is my head hurting so bad? I only had half a bottle of wine last night. This isn't fair. I should be rewarded for sharing it, not punished.

I rush around my apartment and quickly say good morning to Louie, who looks as happy as a pig in mud in his newly decorated cage. "Morning, fucker," I call out before disappearing back down the hallway.

"Fucker, Fucker," Louie squawks in the screechiest tone known to man, probably pissed off that I didn't let him out for his morning play.

"Sorry, Louie," I yell back to him from my bedroom as I grab my phone and keys off my bedside table and start searching for my handbag. I head up to the kitchen, bypassing the coffee machine in my attempt to find something to eat, but not being home all weekend means I skipped out on going to the store.

Shit. I'm gonna have to figure out lunch later. I don't have the time right now.

Finding my handbag laying haphazardly across my dining table, I grab it and run, flying out the door and barely remembering to lock up behind me. "Shit," I curse as I rush out the main door of the apartment complex and almost fall right into the overgrown garden before continuing to my car.

It's barely nine in the morning and today is already shaping up to be a pain in my ass. Getting in the car, I have to kick it over three times before the bastard decides to turn on. Frustration burns through me, but at the same time, I've never been so thrilled to hear this old engine run.

Hitting the gas, I take off down the street when a text comes through on my phone. I really don't have time to check my messages, but if it was an emergency with Brendan, I'd never forgive myself.

I pull over and reach for my bag on the passenger side and drag it into my lap before scrambling through the mess to find my phone.

Unknown – Are you planning on actually showing up to work today?

Ahh shit. I really hope this isn't someone in management.

Elle – On my way. Who is this?
Unknown – The man who's been dying to tie you down, spread those pretty thighs, and fuck you until you're seeing stars.

Holy shit. Logan Fucking Waters is going to be the death of me.

Elle – Wow. Chris Hemsworth? I'm flattered, but I think I might be seeing someone…
Logan – Think? What the fuck is that supposed to mean? You're my fucking girl. Call it what it is. I'm your boyfriend.

Butterflies swirl through the pit of my stomach, and I find myself grinning like an idiot, but seeing the time on the dashboard, I toss my phone back down and pull out into traffic. As much as I want to respond to that text, it's going to have to wait.

Twenty minutes later, I pull up at the Colorado Thunder training facility to find the parking lot packed with cars and trucks, and before I rush inside, I quickly check my phone once again and can't help but grin manically as Logan's latest message shows up.

Logan – Don't leave me hanging, babe.

Laughing to myself, I throw my phone back into my bag and rush inside before I miss the start of my first appointment.

How is it something so simple as a text message can make my already shitty morning turn into something so good?

Speed-walking through the foyer and into the main part of the arena, I hear the familiar sound of hockey pucks slamming into the boards. I look up at the guys training as I walk around to the hallway leading to my office, and I stop in my tracks, seeing the star player in action for the very first time.

Wow, just wow. He's incredible.

Logan moves across the ice so naturally, it's as effortless as walking and has me gaping like an idiot. I'd like to be that girl who can say she'd seen some of her man's games online, but let's face it, before taking this job, ice hockey wasn't an interest of mine.

Logan races up the ice, dominating the puck as Max attempts to step in and steal it out from under him, but Logan is too fast. He rears back before shooting, and the puck flies across the slick ice, straight past the goalie, and crashes into the nets behind.

Logan smirks, all too fucking proud of himself, and I want to scold him for training so hard. He knows damn well he's pushing the limits, but something tells me there's no stopping Logan Waters when he's on a roll. Logan flies around the back of the net, and I watch as Max scowls at his back before taking off. I have to wonder if there's something going on there . . . until Max's gaze flicks to me, deep jealousy shining in his eyes, and it becomes startlingly clear—he's into me.

Ugh. How the hell did I miss that? It makes sense now. The way he would keep trying to get my attention on the camping trip and how he's been so short with Logan. He knows there's something going on between us, so we're gonna have to be careful.

As Logan takes off again, thoughts of Max fade from my mind as easily as though they were never there to begin with. Logan is so fast and strong on the ice, right in his element. It's the hottest thing I've ever seen.

As if sensing my stare, his dark gaze locks on mine, and with a smug-as-fuck grin, he gives me a wink that has my knees buckling and my stupid ass nearly falling to the floor. My face flames, and I want to hate myself for how obvious I am, but when Logan is around, there's simply no telling what my body might do.

Logan skates by, and I find myself desperately wanting him to stop, but that's not possible, not while we're trying to keep this on the low down.

A throat clears at my side, and my eyes widen, not having noticed anyone creeping in. My head whips up, and I force a smile across my face as I find Tony looking down at me with a curious stare.

"He's good, isn't he?" Tony questions, deep suspicion in his tone.

"I'm sorry?"

"Logan," he states.

"Oh, yes. I guess you can't get this far in the NHL if you're not good," I say.

"Very true," he laughs, pausing a moment to watch his star player. "I couldn't help but notice on our camping trip that you and Logan seem to be getting along quite well."

"I suppose," I say, cutting myself off before I dig a hole I can't claw my way out of. My hands start to sweat as my heart rate picks up. Crap. This is exactly what I didn't want to happen.

Tony looks over me with curiosity, and I realize it's too late. He knows. "I don't want to have to ask you this twice, so be honest with me, Elle. Is there something going on between the two of you, something that would be best brought to management's attention?"

Letting out a heavy breath, I watch the way Logan watches me and Tony, clearly able to see how uncomfortable I am, but I can't lie, even if I wanted to. People usually see right through me, and I'm not about to risk that now. Looking up at Tony, my hands shake at my sides. "Would it be an issue if there were?" I question, feeling sick to my stomach. "I don't want to risk my position here, nor Logan's. So if I have to, I will distance myself from him, but just know that it would kill me to do so."

He looks me over once again, clearly deep in thought. A few moments pass, and as the silence gets heavier, my heart begins to race. "No, there's no issue," he finally says. "I've known Logan for a few years and believe myself to be a good judge of character. He has never crossed business with pleasure before and has great respect for his career. I don't believe he would intentionally cross that line if it weren't something serious. So, by all means, you have my approval."

My eyes widen as a stupid grin starts spreading across my lips. "Really?" I question, the weight of the world beginning to drop off my shoulders.

"Yes," he smiles as if he has just gifted me a million dollars, "as long as your relationship remains strictly professional while in the confines of our training facility and at away games."

"Of course," I rush out, the smile impossible to wipe off my face.

All this time I've been so scared to give this a go, but with management's blessing, Logan and I will really be able to give this a real try. There's nothing stopping me from falling madly in love with him now. I just hope to God that Logan is as serious about me as I am about him because if I turn out to be just another notch on his belt . . . Well, shit. I don't think I'll survive a heartbreak like that.

Tony disappears just as discreetly as he's arrived, and just as I go to make my way to my office, Logan skates past again. He gives me a curious stare, silently asking if I'm alright, but I don't give anything away. Instead, I pull my phone out and start replying to his earlier message, more than ready to start the rest of our lives.

Elle – Alright, Captain, I'll give you the satisfaction of being able to call yourself my boyfriend.

Chapter Seventeen

LOGAN

I get off the ice around lunchtime, covered in sweat and on the brink of exhaustion. After having the past few weeks off, plus being in the off-season, my fitness levels have severely dropped. I've got a lot of work to do to get back to where I was, which is going to be hard, seeing as though my leg is killing me right now. Not to mention, Max has been riding my ass all day trying to assert some type of dominance over me, which I had to shut down real fucking quick. He wasn't thrilled about it, but I don't really give a shit.

I'm only supposed to be doing basic training, but being back on the ice and actually able to skate felt way too good to limit myself.

Heading into the locker room, I collapse onto the bench, needing a break before heading into the gym after lunch. I strip off my gear and decide to hit the showers early, needing the warmth of the water to perk me up. Grabbing my things, I rush through a shower, which has me feeling a million times better, but it does nothing to soothe the ache building in my thigh.

Hmm, I wonder if Elle is busy right now. Better yet, I wonder if she's had her lunch.

I get dressed and head back to my locker to grab my phone and wallet and find a text waiting on my phone, one that has a stupid grin spreading across my face.

Elle – Alright, Captain, I'll give you the satisfaction of being able to call yourself my boyfriend.

Fuck yeah, that answers that question. There's no doubt about it now. Elle is mine. My girl to fall in love with, my girl to pamper and spoil, my girl to build a life with.

I walk the familiar path that leads to her office and push my way through her open door to find her hunched over her desk with her head resting on her arms, half asleep. I can't help but grin at the sight before taking pity on her. "Am I interrupting something?" I ask.

Elle gasps as she flies up from her desk and turns to find me standing in her doorway. "Holy shit, Logan, you scared me."

"Sorry," I laugh as I walk in with a limp, closing the door behind me. "You busy?"

"Oh, yeah," she says sarcastically, her gaze narrowing on my thigh. "Super busy. Why the hell are you limping again?"

"I might have overdone it this morning," I tell her.

"I freaking knew it." She crosses her arms over her chest, and I have to grin as the action pushes her tits up. "The second I saw you this morning, I knew you were pushing yourself too hard, but you were too caught up in your pissing contest with Max to care."

"Guilty," I admit. "But for what it's worth, I won."

Elle rolls her eyes. "I know."

I walk over to her, my hand on her waist as my lips drop to the curve of her neck. "Sooo . . . are you going to fix me?"

Elle ignores my question as her arm loops around my neck. "What I should be doing is bitching you out for being such a moron."

I groan as I grab her and lift her onto the edge of the massage table. "You're lucky I like you," I tell her before pressing my lips to hers. "You can't resist it though. The thought of getting your hands on me is eating you alive."

She grins, her smile pulling against my lips. "I'll make you a deal, Captain. If I fix you, you buy me lunch. And a good lunch too. Not some shitty to-go meal from a random corner store."

"Oh, I don't know about that," I tease. "You're asking a lot."

"Come on," she begs. "I skipped breakfast and ate my lunch before I even made it through the door."

I can't help but laugh, not surprised in the least. "Well, you're lucky that was my plan when I came up here."

Elle pauses as she narrows her eyes on me once again. "Why do I sense a but coming along?"

"Tell me what I want to hear," I demand, stepping closer as her legs lock around my waist.

She presses her lips together and looks up at me with those beautiful big eyes, making everything in my chest ache for her. "I don't know what you're talking about."

"You're a terrible liar."

She smiles, confirming what I knew was true. "And if I don't?" she questions, the challenge thick in her tone.

"No lunch for you," I tell her.

She rests her hand against my chest and splays her fingers, making herself look like a seductive little vixen in the process. "You wouldn't be bribing me, would you, Captain?" she murmurs, her hand slowly trailing down to the waistband of my gym shorts.

"You wouldn't be trying to distract me with your wicked charm, would you?" I counter.

Elle smirks, leaning in and closing the gap between us, kissing me deeply. I devour her, kissing her back and feeling the way she melts in my arms. "Tell me what I want to hear," I murmur against her soft lips.

She smiles, and I see her becoming shy right in front of my face. "I'm ready, Logan. I know we talked about it in your car yesterday, but I'm really ready to make something of this. I want to be yours, every part of me, and I don't want you to ever let me go."

"Never," I whisper, meaning it with everything that I am.

She smiles wide, and I can't help but sense a weight lifting off her shoulders. She looks so happy and carefree, it's addictive. This right here is how I want to see her every day for the rest of our lives. You know, apart from seeing her bent over in my bed, taking me deep and screaming my name.

Stepping away before this goes somewhere it shouldn't, I get ready to take her to lunch, but she remains glued to the spot. "What's up?" I ask as I turn back to her, my brows furrowed, the thought of something bothering her eating at me.

Elle looks up at me with fear in her eyes, a look that I would do anything to take away. "Don't break my heart," she whispers.

My chest cracks wide open, and I rush back into her, pulling her into my arms. I look her deep in the eyes, allowing her to truly see me, the real man hidden beneath the persona. "To break your heart would be to break my own," I say, letting her know just how serious I am about making this thing between us work. "Trust me when I tell you, I'm never going to do that. I want this. I want a whole fucking life with you, Elle."

She nods as she accepts my declaration, a wide grin slowly stretching across her face. "Wow, I should have made you get on your knees before you started begging for me."

I give her a blank stare, and she bursts into laughter. "I'm glad you think this is funny."

"I'm sorry," she laughs, tears filling her eyes. "It's not. I just get awkward when things get intense. It's a coping mechanism."

Oh, God. I can only imagine.

Letting out a heavy sigh, I step back and meet her stare. "Can I please feed you now?"

A brilliant smile stretches across her face as she jumps down from the massage table and slips her hand into mine. "I thought you'd never ask."

With that, Elle takes off to the door, and I stumble as I try to keep up with her, momentarily forgetting that I can't fucking walk. "Slow down, babe. Are you trying to kill me here? I can barely walk."

"And whose fault is that?" she grins back at me.

Fuck, I love her smart mouth. Usually when a girl is sarcastic and tries to play cute, I can't stand it, but on Elle, I just want more. Though our first fight is going to be interesting, seeing as though we're both sarcastic, stubborn, and need to be right. "What was Tony saying this morning?" I question as she basically drags me out the door.

"He told me if I wanted to screw your brains out, that I should just go right ahead and do it."

"Seriously?" I ask.

"Well . . . I might be paraphrasing," she says with a cheesy grin. "Moral of the story is we have management's approval, so I don't have to worry about losing my job or the other guys assuming I'm a skanky whore who gets around fucking the players."

"If any of them even think that, they'll have to deal with me," I promise her.

She turns to me. "I know it's in your nature, but I don't need saving."

"Not negotiable, babe," I tell her. "It's part of the package. I know you can handle yourself and you have done so for a long time now, but now you're mine, and I intend to treat you that way whether you like it or not." She presses her lips together and gives me one of those stubborn looks that have me ready to throw her down and make sweet, sweet love to her. "Don't tell me you're going to fight me on this."

She thinks about it for a little while. "I have a feeling I won't win this one," she says.

"Not a chance."

We return from lunch an hour later and Elle instantly orders me to drop my pants and climb on her massage table, but somehow it doesn't come across creepy like it did with Dave. I'm too busy smirking at her, so she comes and does it for me, and I must say, watching her unbuckle my belt and pop the button on my jeans has me turned the fuck on.

I jump on the table, and as expected, the second she has a patient to work on, that laughter fades away as a seriousness comes over her. I can't help but cringe as she presses down into the sore muscle, though anyone would think I'd be used to it by now. "Fuck, babe," I groan sounding like a little bitch, not the captain of the best NHL team in the country.

"It's not my fault you decided to be a dumbass during training."

Back and forth we go with the banter. It's the most frustrating but satisfying thing I've ever experienced. She constantly keeps me on my toes, and I absolutely love it.

My muscle starts to loosen up, and I want nothing more than to pull her on top of me, but she demands that I do some exercises instead, promising that I can take her on a date and fool around afterward. And honestly, I'm really looking forward to it.

We're wrapping things up when Elle's phone starts vibrating on the desk. She disappears to check it and a crease instantly comes between her brows as she reads the caller ID. She answers it instantly. "Hello," she breathes, fear thick in her tone. "Yes, this is Elle."

I watch as her face continues to turn from fearful into complete horror. Her eyes meet mine across the room, and I see the very moment her world comes crashing down around her. Her eyes widen and her beautiful face falls.

She starts scrambling for her things before throwing her bag over her shoulder, and I start pulling my pants back on, feeling as though I'm about to be running out of here after her. "I'll be there in ten minutes," she rushes out before ending up the call.

"What's wrong?" I ask as I rush out the door behind her.

"It's Brendan," she says, her voice breaking. "He's had a fall."

"Shit," I grunt as I catch up to her. I look at her and see the tears falling down her beautiful face and realize she's caught up in her thoughts, thinking the worst-case scenario. But goddamn, I know without a doubt that I will do everything in my power to ensure I never have to see those tears again.

Taking her hand in mine, I pull her into my side. "Come on," I tell her. "I'll drive."

"No, no," she says, wiping her eyes. "I'll be okay. You have training."

"Babe, you know that whole you're not a damsel who needs saving bullshit? This is me swooping in and saving you. I don't care who you are, you're not driving like this, now get your ass out the door and in my truck so we can check on your brother."

Elle zips her lips and wipes her eyes again. "Yeah . . . okay," she says before allowing me to lead her to my truck.

I help her in, and she gives me directions on where to go as we fly down the road. I watch her out of the corner of my eye as I rush toward the rehab facility and notice her constant fidgeting. I reach out and take her hand in mine, putting a stop to the fidgety hands. "He's going to be alright," I soothe.

She doesn't respond, just nods her head and looks out the window.

"Babe," I say, pulling her attention back to me. "From everything you have told me about him, the one thing I've realized is that he's strong, just like you. He has survived every hurdle life has thrown at him and has come out the other end. He's going to be okay."

"How do you know that?" she questions, tears brimming in her eyes.

"Because he has you and if for some godforsaken reason you're not coping, you have me."

Elle squeezes my hand. "Thanks," she whispers as we pull up at the facility.

We get out of my truck and I meet her at the front, wrapping my arm around her shoulder and holding her to me. "Are you ready?"

"Yeah," she breathes, her whole body shaking. I take a step forward, but she pulls me back. "Wait," she says. I turn back with a questioning look and wait for her to continue. "Brendan's very protective, so he's most likely going to be a dickhead, especially if he's done any damage in the fall. And . . . Well, he thinks you're a manwhore, so there's that too."

"Don't worry about me. I can handle it," I tell her.

She nods as we make our way inside. "I didn't want you to meet him like this."

"Really?" I question. "I was under the impression you hadn't thought about me meeting him at all."

At that, she finally cracks a smile. It's small, but it's enough to give her that little bit of strength she needs to keep going.

Elle rolls her eyes as she leads me down the hallway. "Brendan was actually a great hockey player before the accident. He stopped watching it after that, but in the past two years, he's picked it up again. I think it's helped him find motivation, and I fear his end game is getting back on the ice. But don't be fooled, he knows exactly who you are, and no matter how much he may look up to you as a player, he doesn't approve of you as a boyfriend. In fact, he doesn't approve of anyone as a boyfriend."

"He wouldn't be your brother if he did," I tell her, all too aware of how hard it was for me to accept Jaxon dating my sister when they were barely teenagers. "I'm just going to have to prove to him that I'm not going to break your heart."

"Challenge accepted," she agrees before taking a deep breath and stopping at a door.

She knocks gently before pushing her head into the room. "Brendan?" she says softly.

"Come in," I hear her brother say from within the room.

Elle pushes the door open and we both walk in to see Brendan lying in his bed. His eyes flick to me before he even takes a second to greet his sister. "What the fuck, Elle?" he scolds, disapproval wafting off him in waves. "You said nothing was going on between you two."

From the tone of his voice, it's pretty damn clear the kid is angry, but I don't know if that's my doing or if he's upset about the predicament he's gotten himself into.

Elle lets out a sigh as she goes and sits on the edge of his bed. She places a soothing hand on his leg, but from her explanation of his injuries, he probably can't feel it, telling me this is a gesture for herself. "Logan, this is my brother, Brendan," she introduces.

"How's it going, man?" I say with a nod rather than offering him my hand—just in case he decides to break it. My father would be rolling in his grave if he knew I hadn't offered the brother of my girlfriend a handshake, but if I return to the Thunder's arena with a broken bone, I'd never hear the end of it from management, especially after my leg injury.

Brendan presses his lips together and narrows his eyes, reminding me of his big sister. He doesn't answer, but the look tells me that we're going to have words the moment Elle is gone.

Elle doesn't put up with his shit as she gets stuck straight into him. "What the hell happened?" she questions, unable to wait any longer for the answers she desperately needs.

Apparently, Brendan's bad attitude isn't just reserved for me because he turns it on for Elle. "Nothing," he snaps. "They shouldn't have called you."

"Hey," I snap back. "I know she's your sister, but she's here because she loves you and has just spent the last twenty minutes terrified that you were hurt. Don't speak to her like that."

Brendan watches me through narrowed eyes, and it's clear the kid has a lot on his mind right now. Maybe he hates me because I'm dating his sister, or maybe it's because I'm currently living the life he would have loved for himself, either way, it does not permit him to talk to my woman like that.

He lets out a breath and reaches for Elle's hand. "Sorry," he murmurs before looking down at his lap. The anger in his eyes turns to sadness, and I listen as he explains it all to Elle. "I got movement in both feet," he says.

"Shit," Elle says, cutting him off, her eyes wide. "That's amazing."

"Just . . . listen," he says, stopping her before she gets too excited. "I . . . I could see my feet moving, but I couldn't feel it, so when the nurse left, I tried to stand."

"What?" Elle shrieks as she throws herself to her feet and looks at her brother in outrage. "Do you have any idea how fucking stupid that was? You could have ruined everything," she yells. "Is that what you want?"

Brendan sits silently, listening to his sister as she loses her mind. "Answer me, Brendan," Elle demands. "I'm not sending myself broke for you to fuck around like this. I love you, and I want nothing more than to see you walk again, but if you're not going to take this seriously, why the fuck have I busted my ass for you for the past eight years?"

I walk up behind Elle and place my hands on her shoulders before giving them a gentle squeeze. She instantly calms and takes a deep breath. "Sorry," she says to her brother who looks as though he's about to break.

"No, I'm sorry," he says. "I shouldn't have been so stupid. It's just so frustrating not being able to just do it. I should be stronger than this. I know I can do it," he insists.

"No, Brendan. You can't," she says, giving him the tough love he desperately needs. "What part of spinal cord injury do you not understand? You can't just get up and walk. If it's ever going to happen, it's going to be from a shitload of time and hard work, not from being impulsive."

A doctor makes his presence known at the door. "Is now a bad time?" he asks.

"No, come on in," Elle says as she lets out a calming breath. "Logan, this is Brendan's doctor, Dr. Ellis."

"Nice to meet you," I say, offering my hand. He gives it a firm shake, and I excuse myself to let them talk.

"What's the damage?" I hear Elle ask as I close the door behind me. Then allowing them the privacy they need, I head over to the reception desk and do the one thing I can to help.

Chapter Eighteen

ELLE

It's been a week since Brendan's fall, and I've spent nearly every spare minute with him. He has been stuck in this little ball of depression, but I don't blame him after the ass-whooping I gave him. To say he feels like shit is a major understatement, but I don't regret it. He needed a little reality check, and I'm pretty sure it worked.

The fall set him back a few weeks, and he has had to have more therapy sessions added to his rehabilitation, which is going to cost me a bomb. I've not been blind to realize that the nurses are spending a lot more time with him, probably to make sure he doesn't try a stunt like standing again, but I don't believe he will. He understands what's at risk, and I don't blame him. It must be incredibly frustrating being so close to something but not being able to grasp it.

I've been able to attend a few of his sessions this past week, and it's been amazing watching his progress. He was lucky enough not to cause any extra damage after the fall, and I think having me in the room during his therapy motivates him just that bit more. Either that, or he's terrified of letting me down again in case I lose my shit.

The cost of all this added therapy has been weighing on my mind. I know things have been easier with this new job, so I've been able to slowly start catching up, but I'm just so far behind that the thought of getting further into debt makes me sick. I mean, I'm only twenty-five, I'm not supposed to be in so much debt. I'm pretty damn lucky I've been able to feed myself the past few years.

I wait until Doctor Ellis has left the room before also excusing myself. I head down to the reception desk and press the little bell, letting the nurses know I'm here. I wait a few moments and give Nurse Kelly a bright smile as she appears from down the hallway.

"Hi, Elle. How can I help you?" she asks as she makes her way behind the desk.

"I just wanted to pay off some of Brendan's therapy and check how much the extra sessions are costing," I tell her.

"Okay, no problem," she says as she takes a seat at the computer and goes about bringing up Brendan's file. A crease appears between her brows and she leans closer to the screen. "Hmm, that can't be right," she murmurs to herself as she continues clicking away.

"What's wrong?" I ask, resting my elbows on the desk.

"It's showing that there's nothing owing on your account," she tells me as she turns the screen to face me. "You're actually in credit."

"Huh," I grunt, leaning in and getting a closer look. "Yeah . . . no. That's definitely not right," I mumble before looking up. "Don't get me wrong, I like the way that looks, but this isn't right."

This is the last thing I need to be dealing with right now.

Kelly turns the computer back to investigate a little further. Her brows remain creased as the sound of her keypad and mouse become extremely loud. "Let me look into it," she says as I do everything in my power not to tap my fingernails on the desk as I wait. "So," she finally says. "It looks as though the account was paid in full last Monday."

"I didn't make any payments on Monday," I inform her.

Hold on, that's the day I was here with . . .

Fucking hell.

"The payment was made by an L. Waters," she informs me, breaking into my thoughts.

"Shit," I sigh.

That freaking big bastard. I could scream right now. Why the hell did he go and do that?

Anger blooms through my chest. I know he has a God complex, desperate to play the role of the hero, but I don't need his help. All I ever needed from him was to stand at my side. Does he think I'm some kind of damsel screaming out for help? Some kind of dimwit who can't possibly look after herself and her brother? I've been doing just fine for the past eight years. I don't need his charity.

"Is there any way you can undo it?" I ask. "That payment was made by mistake."

"Sorry," Kelly cringes, clearly picking up on something. "Once an account has been settled, we can't really return it."

"Of course, sorry," I say, shaking my head in exasperation. That was a stupid question to ask. Of course, they aren't going to refund an overdue account. How stupid was that? God, this man has me making an absolute fool out of myself. "I'll, um . . . see you next week," I tell her before heading back to Brendan's room.

I say a quick goodbye, but my head isn't in it, and I get my ass out the door before Brendan has a chance to pick up on the fact that I'm about to absolutely lose my shit . . . again. I get in my beat-up little shit box, and before I know it, I'm driving up the longest driveway known to man.

Pulling up outside the over-the-top mansion, I get out and slam the door of my car before storming up the elaborate stairs. Reaching the top, I don't hold back, my fist slamming into the wooden door over and over again. "Open the door, you big bastard," I scream, tears springing to my eyes.

I scream and bang until my hands are aching, and then finally the door opens and a wary Logan stands before me. "What's wrong?" he asks in alarm as he takes in the tears streaming down my face.

I storm into him and slam my aching fists into his chest. "You had no right," I yell. "I'm not some charity case who needs to be saved."

"Shit," he curses. "You know then?"

"Of course, I fucking know," I scoff. "Did you really expect me not to find out?"

"I was hoping," he murmurs under his breath.

"Are you kidding me?" I question, shoving my hands against his chest again, pushing him back. "Is this some kind of game to you?"

"No," he demands as he grabs my hands and slams me against the back of the door, caging me in. His dark eyes are fuming, but they hold me hostage making it impossible to look away. "It's not a game to me. I don't see you as a charity, and I know for damn sure you don't need saving. You're doing pretty fucking good on your own, so for once in your life, just suck it up and accept it. You deserve the fucking world, and I'm not about to let the woman I'm falling in love with go through that shit when I can do something about it."

My breath comes hard as the tears continue to fall, but the fight slowly starts to leave. "I'm so mad at you," I tell him.

"I know," he says as he fights for the same control. "I can live with that."

Logan's forehead drops to mine as his thumbs come up to wipe away my tears. "You need to undo what you did," I tell him.

"I'm not going to do that," he replies softly.

"But . . ."

"No," he says more firmly. "You're an amazing woman, Elle, and I am so damn lucky to be able to call you mine, but you need to learn to accept help when it's staring you in the face. I know you would have managed on your own and you would have done an incredible job of it, but I'm not going to sit back and watch you bust your ass when I can easily take your troubles away."

Logan presses his lips to mine, and I instantly melt into him. My hands come up a moment later, and I gently pull myself away, looking up into those intense eyes. "I don't know how, but I'll pay you back," I promise him.

"I don't want you to," he tells me in that smooth, dream-inducing tone. "I just want you to get your brother on his feet."

Realizing there's no way he's going to cave on this, I wrap my arms around him and pull him closer before pressing my face into his chest, needing to find a way to be okay with this.

Logan's arms wrap around me, holding me to him, both of us falling silent as the heaviness rests on my chest. "Thank you," I whisper as I slowly come to terms with it.

"When will you realize that I'd do anything for you?" he questions.

"I'm starting to see that," I tell him. I stand for a moment in his arms, and the weight of the world begins to fade away, taking my troubles, doubts, and fears along with it. "I've never had anyone want to help me before." Looking up at Logan, I finally get it. He truly is the man he keeps trying to convince me of, and I realize I was wrong to doubt him. This right here is as real as it's ever going to get. "You're falling in love with me."

"Yeah," he says with a soft smile. "I'm pretty sure I'm already there."

"I'm not too far behind," I breathe.

His lips come down on mine, and I take him in eagerly. His arms somehow manage to pull me in even tighter, and I revel in the joy of being in his arms. "Logan?" I ask as I pull back and meet those dark eyes.

"Yeah, babe?"

I focus on his stare and let him see right down into my soul, and my hands shake with nervousness. "I'm ready," I tell him softly.

His deep gaze searches mine, making sure I understand exactly what I'm asking of him. "Are you sure?" he questions.

I nod as my fingers run up his back and into his hair. "Yeah," I whisper. "I've never been so ready in my life."

Logan's lips find mine as his hands come down and scoop me into his strong arms. Without breaking his kiss, he walks us up the stairs before kicking open the bedroom door and lowering me back to my feet. His hand comes up, and he runs his fingers down the side of my face, making sure to push my hair back, his intense stare boring into mine. "You are so fucking beautiful."

His voice is thick and husky, and I see that this means just as much to him as it does to me. My cheeks flush under his intense stare, and before I get a chance to respond, his hands are back on my body. They come to a stop at my waist before finding the hem of my shirt, and he slowly draws it up my body, his fingers lightly brushing my skin and sending a wave of goosebumps sailing across my waist. Logan takes it slow, pulling my shirt up over my head before dropping it to the floor behind me, his lust-filled gaze lingering on my body.

My gaze drops down his chest, and I reach for the buttons of his shirt, taking my time as I undo each one, wanting to savor every moment of this. When his shirt falls open, I press my hands to his warm chest and push up to his shoulders, letting his shirt fall off his arms. With his beautiful, strong body on display, I suddenly can't wait for what he has in store for me.

Logan rids me of my jeans before lifting me into his strong arms and carrying me across his room. His lips fuse to mine as he lays me on his bed and comes down on top of me.

It's everything.

He kisses me deeply, his lips moving against mine as though they were always meant to be there. And without warning, a subtle moan slips from my lips as butterflies run rampant through my stomach.

Logan breaks our kiss and works his way down my body, and I suck in a gasp, his intentions clear in his dark, intense stare. His thumb hooks into the waistband of my underwear, and as his lips brush over my waist, he drags them slowly down my legs—so damn slowly the anticipation could kill me.

The second my panties fall to the floor, Logan takes my knees and spreads them apart, and while I know he's already seen me, there's nothing quite so erotic about being exposed and vulnerable in this way. I'm already addicted, and I need so much more.

His hungry gaze blazes with intense desire, sending a thrill blasting through my body as he settles between my legs. Then not being able to wait even a second longer, he dives right in, that warm mouth closing over my clit.

My body jolts with pleasure, and I suck in a gasp, feeling the way his tongue flicks over my clit before he sucks and teases, sending me into overdrive. Desperate to see him, I prop myself up on my elbows to watch the show, and it's the most erotic thing I've ever seen—the way his mouth works over my pussy, even more so when he adds his fingers to the mix and pushes them up into me, massaging my walls.

"Oh, God, Logan," I groan, my head tipping back with undeniable pleasure as my fingers grab hold of the sheets beneath me, barely holding on.

His tongue runs past my clit with just the right amount of pressure, and my world detonates. I come harder than I thought possible, my legs wrapping around his head and refusing to release him. I feel his grin against me, but he doesn't dare stop. He keeps working me until I ride out my high, and when I'm finally able to breathe, the world returns to me.

"Holy shit," I pant as Logan climbs back up my body, a proud grin lingering on his lips. He crowds me, taking his time before closing the gap and kissing me deeply, letting me taste myself on his warm lips.

"Are you sure you want to do this?" he asks as we come up for air. "I could take you somewhere, make it special."

"No," I whisper, running my hands up his back and into his hair, the idea of stopping destroying something deep within me. "This feels right. I don't want to wait a second longer."

Logan's lips come down on my neck and I let out a needy moan before sliding my hand between us and taking hold of his thick, veiny cock.

Logan lets out a deep groan, his eyes fluttering with pleasure as I pump my hand up and down before running my thumb over his tip. His hand comes down over mine, squeezing tighter and slowing my movements. "Are you ready?" he murmurs.

I nod as he meets my stare, making sure I truly want this. Finding whatever it is he's searching for, he reaches for his side drawer and pulls out a condom. He tears it open with his teeth and rolls the latex over his thick cock before finally guiding himself to my entrance, the anticipation building rapidly within me.

My fingers dig into the strong muscles of his back, and I take a shaky breath as he slowly begins to push inside of me, stretching me like never before. I close my eyes, getting used to the foreign feeling of having someone inside of me, but it doesn't hurt, not even a little. Though that could have a little something to do with the many toys in my bedside drawer.

"Are you okay?" he asks, his lips brushing across mine.

"Yeah," I whisper, a wide smile spreading over my face, never having felt quite so full. It's intoxicating. "I'm okay."

Logan smiles against my lips before dropping them to my neck, and I involuntarily tilt my head, giving him all the access in the world. "Fuck, Elle. You feel so good, but please, for the love of all that's holy, tell me I can move."

A grin takes over me, butterflies storming through my stomach. "God, yes."

With that, he gets started and, once again, I lose my fucking mind.

He draws back, still taking his time, and with every little movement he makes, my world is sent into an overwhelming bliss. In. Out. In. Out. It's more than I ever knew it could be.

Logan takes me right to the edge, and I dig my nails into his back. I never knew it could be like this. Having such a deep connection with someone while sharing such an erotic, sensual moment together is everything and more. It's the most intensely beautiful moment of my life and has me wondering why the hell I've waited so long.

Logan continues to move, and it doesn't take long before I get the hang of things and truly become an active participant in this addictive dance. My whole body comes alive, and I feel on fire—the best kind of fire—and it doesn't take long before I'm exploding around him.

My nails dig in as I cry his name, my pussy convulsing as I reach my climax. The high rocks right through my body, sailing through my veins. My head flies back and my toes curl just like I'd always imagined. Seeing me come undone has Logan coming right along with me with a deep groan, his head buried in the curve of my neck.

I'm panting, desperately holding onto him as he falls to the bed beside me, pulling me into his arms as he goes. "Fuck, babe," he says, catching his breath before pressing a kiss to my forehead. "Are you okay?"

My heart swells seeing how much he cares. I was right to have waited, and I'm so damn proud to have stood my ground. If I had thrown it away recklessly, this moment would never have been so special with him.

Propping myself up on his chest, I look down at the man who is changing my life for the better and making me feel things I never dreamed I was capable of. "I've never been more okay in my life," I tell him.

Logan reaches up and tucks a stray lock of hair behind my ear, his dark gaze so warm and full of life. "I'll never get enough of you."

"Really?" I grin as I lower myself to him and run my lips along his neck before coming up to lock his lips on mine. "Why don't we test that theory?"

Logan's lips pull into a wicked grin as he grabs me by the waist and lifts me onto him. I straddle him, his thick cock already in my hand. "I like the way you think," he tells me, then just like that, he lets me explore his body all over again, only this time, I'm in control.

Chapter Nineteen

LOGAN

I t's finally the day I've been waiting for—the first game of the
season.

There's something so thrilling about skating in front of
thousands of people, each one of them screaming your name and
cheering you on. Knowing I have the crowd's support always pushes
me to my best, and I'll never get enough of it. The fact that tonight is
a home game only makes it that much better.

This season is going to be different. I'll have Elle standing at the
sidelines, those big blue eyes watching my every move and spurring
me on. She's never been to a hockey game in her life, not even during

college or when her brother was younger and still playing. So, it's up to me to show her what it's all about. Though she's supposed to be on the sidelines watching and waiting to see if any of the players suffer any injuries that will require her immediate attention, but that's beside the point.

The past few weeks with her have been incredible. She's come out of her shell and has truly been living, no longer suffering under a cloud of debt and working herself to the point of exhaustion. She's living each and every day like it's her last, and it really fucking suits her.

I've been a mess of jittery nerves and excitement the entire day. I always get this way at the start of the season, and I have no idea why. The second I step onto the ice, it disappears, and I get in the zone. I must admit, having Elle around managed to calm my nerves. Maybe it's the prospect of not knowing how strong the other teams have become in the off-season, or maybe it's the weight of being the captain on my shoulders.

With only a few minutes to spare, I grab my things and head out to my truck, knowing Coach will bust my ass if I even think about arriving late to the arena. It would have been nice to spend the day with Elle, but she's been there for hours already, making sure she has everything prepped and ready for the off chance she'll be needed.

She's also a mess of nerves being her first game and all, but as promised by Tony, she has a temporary senior therapist working with her, so it should help ease her mind. Though she really doesn't need it. Elle's done an amazing job of mending me up. I only feel it every now and then when I push myself too hard. But that's not on Elle, that's on me not doing enough stretching before and after training, which Elle makes sure to remind me of each and every time I complain about it. On the plus side, now that I'm healed and not walking around with a limp, Jax and my brothers have quit making jokes about my "broken dick."

Making a quick detour before heading to the arena, I jump down from my truck and quickly hurry inside, all too aware of the time. "Yo," I say, knocking on the door and pushing my way into the room, not bothering to wait for an invitation.

Brendan looks up and groans the second he sees me. "What the fuck do you want?" he mutters with his usual attitude. Though by now I've come to realize this is just his way of being a protective brother toward the guy who's dating his sister. He's an angel to everyone else.

"I'm breaking you out of here," I tell him. "Grab your shit. Let's go."

"What?" he grunts, staring at me like I just flopped my dick out onto his leg and asked him to pet it. "Are you allowed to do that?"

"Fucked if I know," I shrug, resisting the urge to remind him that I'm Logan fucking Waters, meaning I can generally do whatever the fuck I wanna do. "But I'm not about to let you watch me dominate the ice from your shitty little phone."

"You're taking me to the game?" he questions, still staring, his brow arched in disbelief.

"Would you prefer I take you on a date instead?" I ask as I push his wheelchair across the room and right to his bedside. "I'm not into dudes, but I'm sure I can find it within myself to show you a good night. And if you're a good boy and use your manners, I might even make you scream at the end of the night."

Brendan lets out a heavy sigh. "You know I fucking hate you, right?"

"Ahh," I tease, indicating the chair again. "If only that were true."

I play with the idea of scooping his ass out of bed and plonking him in the wheelchair to hurry this shit up, but I know that wouldn't go down well. Brendan would rather face plant onto someone's dick and accidentally deep throat it before asking his sister's boyfriend to help him. So instead, I stay quiet and let him do his thing.

It takes way too long for him to get his ass into his chair, and every minute I'm not at the rink is another minute that I risk getting my ass handed to me by Coach. To speed things up, I grab a hoodie out of his closet before pushing him out the door. A nurse turns the corner and I quickly dart him back into the room, my heart racing. "Fuck," I curse, hoping she didn't see.

Brendan looks up at me with disapproval, his gaze narrowed. "You didn't get this little excursion cleared, did you?"

"Of course I didn't," I grunt. "I told you, I'm breaking you out of here. Nobody has time for that kind of paperwork. Besides, Elle said your doctor is all for you doing positive things."

"I don't quite think this is what he had in mind," Brendan mutters, his eyes sparkling with mirth, probably thinking he's caught me out on something. "I can guarantee you didn't talk to Elle about this either. Man, she's going to destroy you."

I shrug my shoulders. "I figured it was better to ask for forgiveness rather than permission."

"Dude, you're fucked," he laughs.

"Nah man," I say, peeking out the door to make sure the coast is clear. "She'll be thrilled we're spending time together. We're bonding."

"Righteo," he grunts as I determine the coast is clear and push him out the door again.

We make a break for it, and I bolt toward the exit, pushing him in front of me and bypassing the empty nurses' station. Once I get him out the door, we're home free, and I let out a breath of relief. The only question now is how the fuck am I going to sneak him back in tonight? Though I'm sure they will have noticed his absence by then and called Elle, who I'm sure will fill them in, but until then, it's all James Bond shit.

We get to my truck and he looks up at the beast with concern, and I can all but see the wheels in his mind turning, trying to figure out how the hell this is going to work. "Dude, how am I supposed to get in there?"

A wicked smirk stretches across my face as I meet his stare. "I guess we're about to find out if you find being in my arms as thrilling as your sister does."

"Get fucked."

I shrug my shoulders as if he actually has a choice. "It's either that or I can tie you to the tow-ball and roll your ass there."

"Fine," he grunts. "But make it quick. I don't want anyone to see."

I grin and take my sweet ass time hoisting him up into my truck, taking pleasure in the way he groans and grunts every step of the way.

Then the second it's done, I make my way around the back of the truck and haul the wheelchair into the bed before finally hauling ass to the arena.

We make small talk along the way, and before we know it, I'm parking in the athletes' parking lot and helping him down. I wheel him in through the players' entrance and introduce him to as many of the guys as possible, and the way this bitch starts fangirling has me wondering if I picked up the wrong asshole from the rehab facility.

Brendan and I make it to the main arena, and I can't help but look around, taking it all in. There's nothing quite like game night. The arena is completely decked out for the game. Music is playing as the fans pour in through the doors and climb the grandstand to find their seats. Fans point me out, and I sign a few autographs and shake hands before excusing myself and Brendan, certain Coach Robinson would be looking for me by now.

"Wow, aren't you Mr. Popular?" Brendan muses as I deposit him into the V.I.P. section.

"Comes with the territory," I tell him as I squat down to reach his height, getting to the real reason I brought him here, desperately needing him to find the motivation to keep going. "Look, I'll make you a deal. If you work your ass off to get back on your feet, I'll get you back on the ice with some of my guys."

"Really?" he questions with hope in his eyes.

"You've got my word."

"Even when you inevitably fuck up and Elle dumps your sorry ass?"

I roll my eyes at his enthusiasm. "Dude, that's not going to happen. You'll be walking her down the aisle before I let her get away."

"Pretty confident about that," he scoffs.

"Can't afford not to be."

He's quiet for a short while. "Fine," he says, holding his hand out, a new excitement brimming in his eyes. "You got yourself a deal."

I nod my head and shake on our deal. "Good. Text me if you get cold, and I'll get you a jersey with my name on it," I grin as I stand up. "I know how you like having me all over you."

"I swear, man. If I could beat your ass, I would," he murmurs as he averts his gaze to take in the magnitude of the arena, once again, turning into the tough love younger brother.

A booming laugh rumbles up my throat as I duck out of the seating area and back into the hole. I make my way into the locker room, bypassing Elle's office, and I make sure to stop and send her a wink before making my way into the locker room.

The second the boys catch sight of me, they start whooping and cheering, but they're only doing it to give me a hard time rather than actually cheering for their captain. "Knock it off," I grunt as I dump my shit in my bay and start getting ready.

The locker room soon turns into a mess of boys warming up and taking practice shots, and it's not long before Coach Robinson is coming in and giving us his first pre-game motivational pump-up speech of the season.

He gets that shit over with and discusses our plays before checking in with all the new kids on the block and making sure that they're good to go. After all, our games are highly televised so there's no room for mistakes.

Our team is finally called for the beginning of the game, and I lead my boys out of the hole with my head held high, those pre-game nerves finally beginning to settle. We walk past Elle's door and she grins as we pass her, though it's damn clear she's checking me out in my gear, and judging by the grin on her face, she hasn't worked out I busted her brother out of prison just yet. Though, I'm sure she will in the next few minutes.

We break out into the arena, and the sound within the building is deafening. I look up into the stands and find my family sitting exactly where they said they would be, decked out in the Thunder's colors, scarves, blankets, and foam fingers. The only difference is Cass is wearing a jersey with Jax's name on the back, but that's a loss I'll have to deal with. Even Jace and Lacey are sitting up beside Sean and Sara.

Brianna sits in the sea of Thunder colors—the odd one out— wearing the colors of our opponents. Her twin brother, Bobby, Jax's best friend, was drafted to the New York Titans, and just like Jax, tonight is his debut game in the NHL. He's going to bring everything he's got, but Brianna will soon see that she's chosen the wrong colors tonight.

We step onto the ice and the crowd goes wild, welcoming their favorite team back to center stage for what's bound to be one hell of a game.

Jax skates up beside me with a grin the size of Texas stretched across his face as he looks up at the massive crowd. "This ain't college hockey anymore," he says.

"No, it's not," I say to the kid who has been a little brother to me for longer than I care to remember. "Are you ready for this?"

"Fucking born ready," he confirms before taking off.

I watch after him, realizing he truly is ready. He skates past Bobby and they give each other a nod, whereas in any other situation, they would be fist-bumping and jumping around like a bunch of dickheads. But here, it's important for the fans that they put on a show.

I can't help but feel that this is exactly where Jax was meant to be, just like the rest of the team, only there's something special about being able to share the ice with the kid. I can't wait to do it for the rest of the season, and hopefully, many more seasons to come.

The start of the game is called and the players get into position. I stand front and center, right before the opposition, waiting for the ref to drop the puck. I look over to the team's box and find Elle watching with wide eyes, her excitement spurring me on.

The puck is dropped and it's on.

Chapter Twenty

ELLE

Holy shit. This game is fucking epic.

I've been here for hours already, checking over the players' files who have current injuries and familiarizing myself with any players who have ongoing issues just to be safe. Though I've been working for the Colorado Thunder for a few months now, so I know every detail of their files as though they were etched into the back of my eyelids.

Either way, I can't afford to screw up tonight. Come the end of each period, I need to be on the ball, ready for anything that could come my way. After all, ice hockey is well known to be a brutal sport.

Injuries could happen in the blink of an eye.

That alone has my nerves riding high. Logan is used to taking a beating on the ice. You can't be the captain of an NHL team without escaping a beating by the opposition every now and then. To be honest, judging by how good he is, he's probably the one who hands people their asses during these games, but it still has me scared he could get hurt.

His whole family sits above us in the grandstand and it's great to see them here, not that I'll have a chance to say hi tonight. Over the past few weeks, I've been able to get to know them better, and I feel as though I've slotted straight in.

My whole outlook on life has changed since getting to know Logan. There's no other way to explain it, but to say that he has freed me from myself. I told him that I was falling in love with him, but after the past few weeks together, there's no doubt in my mind that I'm already there. I'm one hundred percent madly and truly in love with the big boofhead, and I wouldn't have it any other way.

We're only a few minutes into the game and it has completely sucked me in. The guys are on fire. It's fast-paced and scary as hell, but it's the most intense thing I've ever seen. I've never liked sports, but tonight, I'm their biggest fan. Logan stole the show the second the puck was dropped to the ice, and in that same instant, he showed me exactly why he's been captain of this team for so long.

The rest of the team instantly fell in with him. Some of them moved around him and went on the defense, others skated up beside him, ready for if he needed to pass the puck, but that's not what really caught my eye.

What has the drool running down my chin is the way he moves across the slick ice. His eyes are sharp as if he knows where each and every player is on the ice at all times. He's fast, strong, and deadly. I've never been so turned on in my life. Don't get me wrong, I've watched him during training, and he's incredible, but this right here is a whole new level of impressive. Logan is dominating the ice and the game has barely begun.

I wasn't expecting it to be this loud either. I must be the only person on the planet who had no idea what to expect from an NHL game, but I'm so glad I'm here.

Pulling my shit together, I force myself to concentrate on the players rather than the sexy beast dominating the ice. I need to be on my game tonight, ready and prepared if there are any injuries or signs of fatigue. I won't miss a single thing.

I watch the guys moving up and down the ice like lightning. From what I can tell, the Colorado Thunder looks as though they're much stronger than the other team, but I can't pretend to know anything about hockey.

They're only ten minutes in and have had possession of the puck for the majority of that time. We already have a point on the scoreboard . . . or is it called a goal? I don't know, but we've got one, and that's all that counts.

My phone starts ringing in my pocket, and if it weren't for the vibration against my ass, I would never have heard it. I pull it out to send the call to voicemail when I recognize the number scrawled across the screen. Shit. It's the rehab facility. They only ever call in an emergency.

Crap. If that asshole has overdone it, or attempted to walk again, I'm gonna . . . I don't know, I'll probably freak out and cry, and then once I've checked on him, I'll have no choice but to beat his ass.

Scrambling out of the box, I hurry back down the hallway to where I am able to hear the person on the other end. It's still too freaking loud, but it will have to do. "Hello?" I yell into the phone while using my other hand to try and block out some of the noise.

"Elle, it's Dr. Ellis here," he says. "Look, I uhh . . . don't know where to start, but do you happen to be with your brother?"

"Um . . . What?" I ask, confusion thick in my tone.

There's an awkward silence before Dr. Ellis continues. "Brendan isn't in his room or anywhere else in our facility, so we were wondering if you took him out for the day or if you had heard from him."

"You've lost my brother?" I spit, my tone hitching up a few octaves.

I hear the cringe in his tone. "Well . . . yes, it appears that way," he tells me regretfully.

My anxiety spikes, and I promptly begin freaking out, fear pounding through my veins. "He isn't in the bathroom? He takes a while in there sometimes."

Shit. This is not a good time for that little dimwit to go missing. Why would he do this to me, tonight of all nights? He knew how important this was.

"No, we've checked the whole facility. We thought we'd check with you before we started looking into the surveillance and getting the authorities involved."

"Crap. Okay," I say, desperately trying to calm my nerves. I'm sure there's a logical explanation for his whereabouts and that he's not lying in a ditch somewhere. "Let me give him a call and see if I can find him."

"Sure, let us know how it goes," he says before hanging up.

Not sparing a single second, I bring up Brendan's number and impatiently wait as the phone rings out. "Answer your phone, you little turd," I spit into his voicemail before calling again, and again.

He picks up on the third call and a very small part of me relaxes. "Yo, Elle. What's going on?" he asks, way too fucking cheery not to be suspicious.

"Where the hell are you?" I demand, skipping the pleasantries.

There's an amused laugh, and I have to strain to hear him over the sound of the cheering crowd. "I'm closer than you think," he says, making me want to strangle him.

"Brendan. I'm not in the mood for your shit. Where the hell are you?" I demand. "Tonight is too fucking important. I'm working. I can't be running around after you, scared as shit that you're going to do something to hurt yourself."

"Jesus, woman. Calm down. I'm at the game," he laughs. "Your boyfriend is pretty good by the way. Don't tell him that, though. His ego could use a few kickbacks."

"What?" I yell before running out of the hallway and back into the stadium. My gaze lifts to the V.I.P. section to find my brother grinning down at me with a goofy as fuck grin across his stupid face. "You little turd. How the hell did you get here?"

"Logan broke me out. Take it up with him," he says, that wide grin turning wicked as he makes a show of ending the call.

God, that little prick. If he weren't already in a wheelchair, I'd put him in one myself. Needing to call the doctor back, I quickly glance back toward the ice before bailing back down the long hall and hitting redial on my screen. "Elle, tell me you've got some good news for me," Dr. Ellis says.

"Yes, I've found him," I say with a heavy sigh. "I'll have him back in a few hours."

"Good. We'll see you soon."

"Thanks," I say before hanging up the call.

After pocketing my phone, I walk back out to my position in the players' box with a scowl across my face. I want nothing more than to get on that ice and drag Logan off by his ear, but that probably isn't the best idea right now, so his scolding is going to have to wait.

Somehow managing to keep my eyes on the game, I watch as Logan darts up and down the ice, continuing to dominate. Watching him turns the flames within me into tiny little puddles of joy, which only irritates me more.

God, why does this man have to have such an effect on me? It's driving me insane.

I look up at Brendan and see nothing but excitement on his dorky little face as his eyes struggle to keep up with the fast-paced game, and I realize he's completely in his element. This is where he wants to be, and I know deep down it's killing him that he can't be on that ice right now. It probably doesn't help that I'm flaunting Logan around. It's probably a constant reminder of what he can't have.

One day he's going to be back up on his feet, and he'll want to get back on the ice, but it'll be over my dead body that he'll ever play a risky game like hockey ever again. But at least he'll be able to feel the ice under his blades.

"Fuck," Coach Robinson curses as the rest of the players get to their feet and start screaming out. The crowd burst into outrage, and I find my eyes flying back to the ice to see what I've missed.

Crap.

Fear rattles me, finding Logan pinned against the boards by a man who must be at least one hundred feet tall and weighs a ton.

"Come on, Logan," Tony curses from beside me as Logan pushes the asshole to get him off him. The guy stumbles back and drops Logan to his feet, but before Logan can flee, he grabs him again and slams Logan back to the boards, bringing his knee up in a devastating blow to his thigh, right where his torn muscle was nearly finished healing.

The Thunder players rush in and rip the asshole off him, which causes Logan to drop to the ice in pain. Jax swoops in and grabs Logan off the ice while the ref comes in and starts saying a whole lot of shit I don't understand. The big guy is sent off the ice, and I could be wrong, but I'm pretty sure they call it being in the sin bin.

Logan comes over to the side with Jax right by his side as the rest of the team crowds around. His eyes meet mine, and he gives me one of those panty-dropping winks, letting me know he's okay, but I can tell by the look on his face that he is in a world of pain.

"What the fuck was that?" Coach Robinson demands, stealing Logan's attention.

He shakes his head. "I don't know. The fucker's had it out for me since the start of the game," Logan says.

"I know," Coach scowls, clearly pissed. "Right, get off and let Elle check you out."

"I'm fine," Logan says. "I can keep going."

Bullshit.

"I don't give a shit," Coach says, flexing his authority and shutting Logan up. "You're out until Elle can assess the damage. I need to know if that bastard has just ruined the rest of your fucking season."

Logan reluctantly steps off the ice, and it's clear he's a million shades of pissed off right now. He rips off his gloves and helmet and dumps them on the bench before following me out of the box and down the hallway. I don't miss the limp in his step, but I keep my mouth shut until I can get a good look at it.

We step into my office and Logan keeps the door open, probably so he can keep listening to the game. He sits at my desk and doesn't waste a second unlacing his skates. He kicks them off and makes quick work of the rest of his gear before making his way to the massage table.

"You okay?" I ask as he leans against the table and turns to face me.

Logan reaches for me and pulls me into his arms. He rests his head on mine and lets out a breath, and I try not to be disgusted by the man-stench or sweat. "Yeah," he says with disappointment heavy in his tone.

I know he's not, but I let it go. He clearly isn't ready to talk about it yet. "Come on," I say as I push him back to the table. "Let's see if you can get back on the ice."

Logan does as he's told, and I get to work, quickly oiling up my hands before pressing them down into his muscle. He cringes, but that could either be bruising from getting hit or from his previous injury. "What's the pain like?" I question.

"It hurts, but not as bad as when I first did it," he explains.

I nod as I continue to work. "So, there's a very excited moron in a wheelchair sitting up in the stands," I mention as I rub deeper into his leg.

"Yeah, I saw that," he says, playing dumb.

"Logan," I groan. "You kidnapped my brother."

"Yeah," he laughs, that spark returning to his eyes.

"Thank you," I say. "I want to strangle you for it, but it means the world to him to be here."

Logan's arm snakes out, reaching up for me. He pulls me down until our lips meet in the briefest kiss. "Anytime, babe."

I kiss him again before pulling back and focusing on my work, all too aware that we're on a time crunch right now. As the seconds tick by, a big red mark begins appearing from the blow, and I'm relieved to find it an inch or two too low. The asshole missed his mark, but it's clear he was aiming for it, meaning word of his injury has started to spread.

I rub into the muscle a little more and deem Logan safe from harm, though his muscle is definitely tense after skating so hard during the game. I lightly press into the red mark on his thigh. "It's just deep bruising here. You'll be fine, but you should take it easy. You're putting too much strain on the muscle."

"I can skate?" he questions.

"Wait until the next period and spend the break stretching through it, but yes, if you do that and back off a tiny bit, you should be fine unless that dickwad decides to take another shot at you."

"He'd be a fool to try that shit again," Logan grunts as he gets up and starts pulling on all his gear again. The crowd roars and starts chanting the Thunder's war cry letting us know they've scored another goal and Logan grins at me with a boyish charm in his excited eyes. I can't help but grin back.

"You didn't hit him back?"

Logan takes my hand and leads me back down the hallway. "No. I play clean. I don't get off on beating the shit out of dickheads like that, despite how much I might want to."

"Why did he do it? Do you know him?"

"No, but there's always one in every team. I'm the biggest threat so they think if they can take me out, they'll have a better chance at taking the win. It never works because the team is only as good as their weakest player. My boys know how to pick up the slack when I'm out. That's why we're the current defending champions," he explains.

I roll my eyes as we step back into the arena. "Proud much?" I tease.

"Damn straight, babe," he laughs as he steps back into the box and gives Coach Robinson the verdict. Though I notice he skips the part about backing off, and I realize I'll be spending my night at Logan's place trying to loosen his muscle, but I really don't mind. I would have ended up there tonight anyway.

The game goes on, and true to his word, Logan stays off the ice until the next period.

The game comes to an end with the Thunder remaining the defending champions, and the noise in the arena is incredible. I've never heard anything like it, but I know for a fact this is where I want to be, and I have absolutely no plans to change that. The atmosphere in here is something I'll never grow tired of, and the fact that I also have Logan to share it with only makes it that much better.

The boys disappear into the locker room, and I head into my office to get started on tonight's paperwork, making sure to document everything. I find myself lost in my work when Logan knocks at the door and I realize I've been at it for over an hour. "Come on," he says, those dark eyes so damn soft. "I'm taking you home."

"I don't think so," I laugh as I turn to face him. "You need to take my brother home and explain to them where the hell he's been."

Logan walks straight into my office and scoops me up out of my chair. "He's already in the hallway, ready to go. But there's no denying where he's been. The foam finger and Thunder jersey are dead giveaways."

I look up at Logan and fall in love with him all over again. "Kiss me," I tell him.

"My pleasure," he murmurs before pressing his lips to mine.

"What's taking so lo . . . ugh," Brendan whines from the door of my office. "Dude, get off my sister."

I grin against Logan's lips, and just to make a point, he kisses me deeper before reluctantly pulling back. I grab my bag and soon find myself curled up in the warmth of Logan's truck, driving Brendan back to the rehab facility.

Logan helps break him back into his room while I apologize to as many nurses and staff as possible, explaining what my moronic boyfriend had done. In the end, Brendan had a great time, and I couldn't have asked for anything more.

Half an hour later, Logan and I are wrapped in his sheets, and just as I thought, I'm busy trying to relax his muscle while fighting off hands that keep grabbing my ass. "Wait," I laugh.

"Nope," he demands as he grabs me and throws me down to the mattress. His hand slides down my body and into my panties, and my body instantly comes alive with his touch. I've become such a whore for my man. I simply can't get enough.

My panties somehow find themselves kicked off at the end of the bed before my legs are wrapped around Logan's waist. And without even a moment of hesitation, Logan pushes inside of me, filling me to the brim before giving me everything he's got.

Chapter Twenty-One

LOGAN

What a beautiful fucking day for a wedding.

Just like Sean and Sara, Cass and Jax have hijacked my parents' estate to hold their wedding, and once again, I wouldn't have it any other way. Though I suppose it's not exactly hijacking when they've been living here while they build their own home. This place is perfect, and it's where we all feel closest to my parents, so it makes sense. I wouldn't be surprised if Carter and I also held our weddings here one day. Not that I can ever see Carter actually tying the knot.

The whole process of decoration and table settings started two days ago, and it's pretty damn clear this is going to be one hell of a grand wedding. The place is decked out, even more so than when Sara got her hands on it.

I do my best to keep out of the way of the hundreds of people coming and going as they put it all together. It's a fucking madhouse. It's ridiculous. I just want to fast-forward to the actual wedding rather than suffer through all the other bullshit that comes along with it.

I stand with Jax, Bobby, and my brothers on the second level of the estate. Music blares from the speakers, and we're already a few drinks in as we get dressed in our matching suits, looking like a bunch of sophisticated dickheads. I take a look at us all and can't help but think Mom would be loving this if she were here right now. She'd be running around with her camera, straightening our ties, and pinching our damn cheeks.

Fuck, I miss her.

I can't believe she isn't here to see her little girl get married.

The thought has me drifting out the door and up the stairs to the massive top floor. I knock on the door and hear my sister calling out from within. "If that's you, Jax, you can take your bitch ass right back downstairs."

"It's me, dork. Open up."

The door flies open, and I find myself looking down at the most beautiful woman in the world. I wrap my arms around Elle and pull her into me, not giving a shit if she gets makeup across my suit. "That's not a nice way to talk to your sister," Elle scolds as she tips her head up to kiss me.

I run my hands down the champagne-colored silk gown that wraps around her breathtaking body. I'm so proud of my sister for asking Elle to be one of her bridesmaids. I think she, just like the rest of us, has realized that Elle is going to be a part of our lives until the end of time and wanted her to be a part of her special day. And for me, that only makes today that much better. Not to mention, I'll get to dance with her rather than some other bridesmaid.

I push her back gently so I can fully take her in, my gaze dropping over her gorgeous curves, following the silk gown right down to her toes before trailing right back up again. I run my finger along the tiny spaghetti strap that holds up her dress as I take in the sexy as fuck plunge that shows off her cleavage.

Unable to help myself, I push the strap off her shoulder, and she quickly rushes to pull it back in place. "Stop that," she scolds, smacking my hand away.

"I can't wait to get this off you," I murmur as I press my lips to her neck, wondering just how quickly I could get her up against a wall.

"Get a room," Brianna calls.

Elle pushes me back with a smile before taking my hand and dragging me into the room. I take a look around at the rest of the bridesmaids and they look absolutely stunning, especially Sara with her little baby bump protruding from her golden dress. Sean is going to die when he sees her, either that or come in his pants.

I walk further into the room and turn the corner to find none other than my baby sister standing in the mirror, looking radiant in her wedding dress, decked out with the makeup, hair, and veil. My eyes are glued to her as she goes about putting her earrings in while the photographer goes nuts with the camera.

"Woah," I breathe, taking it all in.

Cassie looks up at me through the mirror with the brightest smile on her face. "Hi," she whispers, her eyes filling with unshed tears of happiness.

I walk toward her and watch as she slowly turns around to give me the full effect, and I can't resist pulling her into my arms. "You look beautiful," I tell her.

"Are you sure? It's not too much?" she questions, looking up at me through those eyes that are so much like our mom's.

"No. It's perfect," I tell her, pride swelling in my chest. "I was just checking if you're doing okay."

"I am."

"Okay, well if you get cold feet and want to bolt, my truck's parked by the door with the keys in the ignition."

Cassie rolls her eyes and swats at my arm. "Shut up," she laughs. "I'm not going anywhere."

"Alright," I say as I grab someone's champagne glass and knock it back before filling my pockets with all the little treats they have on the coffee table. "I should head back downstairs. I didn't tell the boys I was leaving."

"Oh, sure," Cass says. I turn and head back for the door, but Cassie's soft little voice stops me in my tracks. "Logan?" she asks with the smallest hint of nerves creeping into her tone.

"Yeah?" I ask as I head back toward her. She reaches out and takes both my hands in hers and looks up at me with watery eyes. "What's wrong?" I question.

"No, no. Nothing's wrong," she says, fighting back the tears so she doesn't ruin her makeup. "It's just . . . call me cliché, but I had always hoped Daddy would be here to walk me down the aisle." She pauses for a moment before looking up at me. "Since you're my favorite brother and all, I was hoping it might be okay if you were to do it?"

Emotion swells in my chest, and I have a hard time containing it, feeling as though I could drop to my knees and weep for everything she's had to go without. I couldn't imagine how she must be feeling not having Mom and Dad here with her today. As I meet her teary stare, I know there would be no greater honor. "I wouldn't have it any other way," I tell her.

Cassie pulls me in and gives me the tightest hug. "Don't tell the boys I said you were my favorite," she smiles.

"They already know," I inform her. "We had bets on who you'd ask."

"Did you win?"

"Yep," I say before scoffing. "Sean was adamant it was him."

She rolls her eyes as she lets me go and practically pushes me back out the door. I send Elle a flirty wink as I pass, making sure to get an eyeful of that sweet ass as I go. "I can't wait to see that dress on my bedroom floor," I inform her.

Elle's eyes are filled with hunger as she stares back at me, dragging that bottom lip between her teeth. "You and me both," she murmurs just as Cass closes the door between us.

I grin to myself as I make my way back down to the guys only to push through the door and find all eyes on me. "Where did you go?" Carter grunts, refilling his drink.

"I was checking on the girls," I tell them.

"And?" Sean questions.

"And they look fucking beautiful. You should see her," I say, referring to Cassie.

Jax discreetly slips his hands into his pockets, trying to cover the fact that he's nervous as fuck. "Is she all good?" he questions, pacing by the window.

"Yeah," I grin. "But I let her know my truck's out front with the keys in it if she needs to make a quick escape."

His face drops and loses all its color. "Fuck," he grunts. "Be right back. I need to unplug your battery."

"Relax, dude. She isn't running," I laugh. "She looked more than ready."

An hour later, the wedding planner knocks at the door and tells us it's time to go, and the boys start walking out, but I hang back, ready to head back up to Cass. "I'll see you down there," I tell them. They each turn to look at me with confused, questioning expressions, and I let them in on the secret. "I'm walking Cass down the aisle."

"Fuck," Carter grunts as he reaches into his pocket and hands me a twenty while Sean just nods, and averts his stare, not wanting to let on how fucking jealous he is. But Jax just smiles, accepting I won't be there for a while, and with that, heads out the door with the boys on his six.

Making my way back upstairs, I wait with the girls, somehow turning into their little bitch boy while they finish their final touches, and before we know it, we're standing in the grass, the girls' heels sinking in as the sun shines on our faces.

The music starts, and I feel the nerves begin to radiate off Cassie. I step in close, looping my arm through hers and letting her know I'm right here if she needs me.

The wedding planner sends Elle on her way, and I can't help but watch her walk, her hips gently swaying and gaining the attention of every man in the crowd. "Look at that ass," I murmur to Cass way too loudly, making Elle turn around and shush me.

"Yeah, it's a nice ass," Cass agrees with a nervous laugh.

Sara and Bri are sent down the aisle next, and then finally, it's our turn.

The nerves continue to plague her, but the second we turn the corner and she lays eyes on Jax, she calms, and I know without a doubt, she will never need another person in her life, not as long as he stands at her side.

I'm absolutely blown away by how many people have shown up to celebrate their wedding. The whole Colorado Thunder team is here, including management, marketing, and the personal trainers. Even all of Jax's friends from his college team—Miller, Tank, Xander, and their girls.

A very uncomfortable Brendan sits in the back row, looking out of place in his suit, but at least he was able to break out of his rehab prison for the day, so that's gotta be a bonus. I was worried they'd never let him leave after the last time, but the added motivation of possibly getting back on the ice has done a world of wonders for him.

We get to the bottom of the aisle, and I hand Cassie over to Jax before taking my place next to my brothers and watching as our little sister vows to commit herself to Jaxon for the rest of her life, in sickness, in health, for richer or poorer.

The ceremony is short and sweet, just as I knew it would be, and before I know it, Jax is storming into her, gripping Cassie's waist, and slamming his lips against hers in the most inappropriate kiss I've ever seen at a wedding.

The eager onlookers cheer for the newlyweds, and just like that, it's time for the fucking photos.

Kill me now.

By the time the photos are done, Carter and I are positively drunk and have Sean running around after us, desperately trying to keep us under control. The girls are well on their way to Tipsyville and have had an absolute blast coming up with new and improved poses for the photographer, whom they have all deemed the sexiest man alive.

And all I can think about is that today has been nothing short of magical.

The photographer takes Jax and Cass away, leaving the rest of us free to enjoy ourselves for the next half an hour. Then with a stupid grin, I turn toward the rest of the bridal party, but before I can make any suggestions, Elle bolts toward me, grabs my hand, and pulls me away.

She drags me down to the back of the property and into the trees, and I hardly have a second to think before she crushes her lips to mine and starts pulling my shirt out from my pants.

My, oh, my. If this is the game my girl wants to play, then by all means, I'm going to rise to the fucking challenge.

Elle makes quick work of my pants, and I'm hard within seconds. Then just when I think I'm about to rock her world, the little she-devil drops to her knees and takes my cock right in the back of her throat. "Fuck," I grunt, having to brace against a tree as she peers up at me through a thick row of false eyelashes.

She works me up and down with her skilled mouth, her hand moving right along with her, and I feel like I could die in this ecstasy. She pushes me right to breaking point, her tongue roaming over my tip as I do everything I can not to knot my fingers into her hair, knowing I'll more than fuck it up.

Elle takes me deeper, and a loud groan tears from the back of my throat until I simply can't take it anymore. I need to be inside her.

Gripping her arms, I pull her to her feet and whip her around, her back flat against my chest. My hands bunch in the fabric of her silk gown, and I pull it up her body until the soft skin of her sweet ass rests against my straining cock. Then bracing herself against the tree, I bend her over and slip my hand between her legs, feeling just how fucking ready she is.

Elle pushes her ass back against me, and I push my fingers deep inside her sweet cunt, giving her just a taste before dragging them down to her clit and rolling tight circles, watching the way she squirms and jolts under my touch. "Tell me, baby. What do you want?"

"Fuck me, Logan. Make me scream."

I groan low in my chest, unable to wait another second, and after lining my cock up with her slick entrance, I slam deep inside. Elle cries out my name, pushing back harder against me to take me deeper. Holding her hips to control her wild need, I go to town, my fingers digging into her skin.

I slam into her over and over, taking her just how I know she likes, and I watch with a desperate hunger as she slips her hand between her legs and rubs tight circles over her clit. The Elle I first met would never have done this. She was shy, and her cheeks would flush at just the thought, but tonight, she's not holding back. Over the past few months, she's let her true self shine through, and I fucking love it. My girl is a fucking vixen, and it's the sexiest thing I've ever seen.

Her pussy clenches around me, and as I push deeper into her again, she comes hard, reaching her climax, and it drives me fucking wild. As she convulses around me and rides out her high, I thrust into her one more time, and it's exactly what I need to come right along with her.

As we both come down, Elle straightens, and I reluctantly pull myself free from her sweet cunt. "Holy shit," Elle pants, turning to fall into my arms.

"What was that for?" I question, pressing a kiss to her forehead and giving us just a moment to catch our breath before we start fixing ourselves and attempting to look presentable for the rest of the night.

"Why do you think?" she grins as she looks me up and down, that hunger returning in her eyes. "Have you got any idea how good you look in that suit? Goddamn." Elle steps right up to me and runs her finger across my chest. "It's irresistible. I couldn't wait any longer."

Dipping my head, I catch her lips in mine and kiss her deeply before pulling back to meet those breathtaking blue eyes. "I love you," I tell her, meaning every fucking word.

Elle throws her arms around my neck and holds my stare, everything she's feeling conveyed in her eyes. "I love you, too," she whispers, her body pressed up against mine.

I go to kiss her again when Brianna's voice tears through the trees, calling out for us, and I realize we've been gone for longer than we should have been. We start making our way back up to the house, hand in hand, and feeling as though nothing could possibly get better than this.

"This home is amazing," Elle murmurs as she looks up at the gorgeous estate my parents had built from the ground up.

"It really is," I agree, taking it all in.

We catch up to the rest of the bridal party and hurry to join the others. It's just about time for the reception, and all the guests have already gathered inside and found their seats. Music plays from within the room, but I don't have time to dwell on it as Cass catches my eyes with a ferocious glare of her own, telling me she knows exactly where I've been and what I've been doing.

All I can do is laugh as I shrug my shoulders and grin back at her. What can I say? I don't regret it one bit.

The emcee starts talking over the music and welcomes everyone to the wedding of the year before he introduces the bridal party. Bobby heads in first with some chick Cass met when she was living in New

York. Next up is Sean and Sara, followed closely by Carter and Brianna.

I hear our names next, and I lead my woman inside the decked-out grand hall, holding onto her so fucking proudly. The room blows me away, but I'm quickly distracted by my teammates sitting in the back, being rowdy as fuck as they cheer for Elle and me.

Leading her past the guests and across the room to the bridal table, I help her into her seat and lean over her shoulder before pressing a kiss to her cheek. "We're next," I murmur before leaving her with her jaw hanging open in shock.

I grin as I take my seat, loving the look that remains on Elle's face. Yeah, she wasn't expecting that shit, but I don't care. I have every intention of marrying this girl, and I can't fucking wait.

Chapter Twenty-Two

ELLE

What an amazing night.

I'm having the best night of my life, and I have Logan to thank for that. Without him, I never would have been here and been able to be a part of Cassie's bridal party. I've never been a bridesmaid before. In fact, I've never actually been to a wedding before . . . Well, I'd gone to a small handful as a kid, but it's a whole new experience as an adult. Not to mention, being in love myself, I have a whole new perspective on it.

The ceremony was breathtaking, and it was incredible to have Logan across from me, staring at me like I was the only woman in the world.

But fuck, this dress. It must be the second most amazing thing about this day. Not to inflate my own ego, but I look fucking amazing. I've never worn silk before, and I swear, it just floats across my skin and makes me feel like a goddess.

Then Logan had to go and touch me, and I was a goner.

One thing I know for sure, I'm going to be buying a shitload of silk from now on.

I sit at the bridal table, waiting for Cassie and Jax to enter, but I can hardly concentrate after the bomb Logan just dropped on me. We're next? As in, he wants to marry me? What the fuck is wrong with this guy? Who would want to marry me? I'm next-level fucked up with more baggage than anyone has the right to have, but if he is willing to take me, flaws and all, then I'm all in.

Nothing would make me happier than marrying Logan Waters, which is ridiculous, right? I've only known him a few months, but it was more than enough time to know he's the only man I will ever love until the end of time.

I just hope that feeling doesn't change for him, otherwise, I'm screwed.

The bride and groom walk in and the guests go insane, cheering for the happy couple. It's absolutely ridiculous the amount of noise coming from this room. But I guess that's what happens when neither the bride or groom have any parents or extended family to invite. I swear, the whole room is packed with friends only, apart from the triplets, but they hardly count.

The reception gets underway and once again, I find myself blown away by the event. Drinks are flowing, music is playing, and what's better, we all get fed for free.

Once all the formalities are over, the real party gets started, and as soon as he can, Logan swoops me out onto the dance floor. The guys on the team let their hair down and dance until their little hearts can't take it anymore, and considering their fitness levels, it's a lot.

Cassie introduces me to a few of her girlfriends, Dani and Sophie, and I find myself laughing in stitches from how ridiculously hilarious they are, and might I add, very bad influences, but who gives a shit? I'm having the time of my life.

The only frustrating part is the way Max keeps trying to undress me with his eyes, trying to catch my stare as if he has any kind of chance with me.

I understand why Jax invited him, but for my sake, it would have been nice if his invite got lost in the mail. I've had to dodge his advances countless times over the past few weeks, and he doesn't seem to be getting the hint.

He's faked injuries just to come into my office and ask ridiculous questions that any professional athlete would more than know the answers to. Not to mention, he blatantly asked me out last week, and even after reminding him I was with Logan, he continues to try his luck. The asshole makes my skin crawl, but for the benefit of the team and the camaraderie they share, I haven't told Logan about it. I don't know how he would react, but I'm positive it wouldn't be good, plus I don't want to think about how a rift between players would affect their game.

Spotting a waitress from across the room with a tray of champagne glasses, I go about my business, stalking her until I have one of those pretty glasses firmly in my grasp. I lift the glass to my lips, but my body is yanked to the side and dragged into a coat closet before I can even get a taste of the sweet champagne.

I let out a gasp but swallow it as a pair of warm lips press down on mine. By the taste and feel of the man currently pinning himself against my body, it's pretty damn clear it's Logan, but it's that familiar scent that gives him away. I fucking love how he smells. It's so addictive and has my knees threatening to give out beneath me. It's also clear by the feel of his straining cock in his pants that he intends to repay the favor from earlier, and I fully intend to let him.

Logan makes quick work of screwing me into oblivion before I find myself collapsing against him, trying to find my breath. "That gets better every time," I tell him with a satisfied grin, needing to hold onto him just to stay on my feet.

"I know," he smirks, his eyes sparkling with a wicked satisfaction. "It's because I'm a stud."

"You're an idiot," I laugh as we get dressed and slip out of the closet. We head back to the party, and I'm pleasantly surprised to see the same waitress walking by once again since I have absolutely no idea what happened to my last glass.

"Where the hell have you been?" I hear a familiar voice scolding from behind me.

I whip around to find Brendan impatiently waiting for my answer, only Logan goes and makes things worse. "I was showing your sister appreciation for how fucking good she looks in that dress," he says.

Well . . . That's not going to go down well.

"What did you say?" Brendan demands, his eyes widening in disgust.

I jab my elbow into Logan's side and grin at the whoosh of air that escapes his lips. "What do you need, Bren?" I question as I push Logan away toward the crowd of hockey players that have taken possession of the open bar.

"Were you seriously just fucking your boyfriend during a wedding?" he asks.

I shrug my shoulders. "What are weddings for?"

"Ugh," he groans, thoroughly repulsed, which only makes this better. "I thought you'd at least keep it classy."

"Nope," I grin. "You should have seen what he did to me out in the bushes earlier. Now that was definitely not classy."

A laugh bubbles up my throat just as someone bumps into me, and my glass of champagne goes flying right out of my hands and spills right across Brendan's lap. "Crap," I gasp as Bren hastily starts cleaning himself up.

The person who bumped me turns around, and I nearly hiss at the moron, not surprised in the least to find he's a sloppy drunk. Max cringes before looking down at my brother. "Oh, shit. Sorry dude," he says as he calls for a waitress to help us out.

"Don't worry about it," Brendan spits, more than annoyed. "I'll sort it out myself."

At that, Max holds up his hands with a silent apology before slowly backing away from my very pissed-off brother, and the second he's gone, I wheel Brendan out of the room and into the oversized bathroom. I help him get cleaned up, and it's not long before he's ordering an Uber, more than ready to call it quits for the night.

"Did you want to stay the night?" I ask him, hating the thought of him leaving on such a bad note. "There are heaps of rooms upstairs. I'm sure Logan wouldn't mind."

"Nah, it's okay. I'd rather go back," he tells me, dumping the champagne-filled towels into the sink and rolling his wheelchair back out of the bathroom. "I have a therapy session early in the morning."

"Okay," I sigh, hating that he's not having the best time. "Let me take you outside. I'll wait for the Uber with you."

He nods and waits patiently as I duck back inside the massive room and quickly find Logan. He pulls me into his arms, more than ready to drag me back to the dance floor, but I push him off before he can get ahead of himself. "Brendan needs to get out of here, so I'm gonna sit with him outside while we wait for his Uber."

"Okay, do you want me to come?"

"I can handle myself," I smile.

"Don't I know it," he says before giving me a quick kiss and sending me on my way with a delicious spank to my ass. I rush back toward the foyer, only to have Max blocking my way. He holds a new champagne glass out to me and cringes again. "Hey, I'm really sorry about spilling your drink all over your brother," he says, offering me this new glass. "Consider it a peace offering."

Needing to get around him, I hastily take the glass from him and offer an awkward smile. "It's really okay. You didn't need to get me a new drink, but thanks," I say politely. "I appreciate it."

"Is your brother alright?" he asks. "I feel like shit."

"He'll be fine. He's made of tough stuff," I say fondly as I try to walk around him.

Max steps in front of me, looking down at me in concern. "Are you leaving so soon?"

"No," I say, trying to peer around him to see where Brendan had gone. "Just waiting with Brendan for his Uber. He's taking off now."

"Oh, okay. Well, tell him I'm sorry," he says before finally moving out of my way, and I don't spare him another glance before rushing past him and out into the night.

"Took long enough," Brendan grumbles as I find him waiting by the grand entrance.

"Shut up, turd," I grin before spinning his chair and giving him a push while trying to hold onto the champagne flute between my fingers. We make it out the door, and I'm instantly hit with the chilly Denver air. "Shit, dude," I curse as I stop pushing and cross my arms over my chest, trying to keep them warm. "You're going to have to wheel yourself."

"I'd offer you my jacket, but you spilled champagne all over it."

"That wasn't my fault," I object.

"Righteo," he grunts.

We shiver as we wait for the Uber to show, keeping ourselves entertained with ridiculous conversation while I sip on my champagne and find a bench to sit on. My head starts to spin, and I realize I've probably had one too many drinks, but that was bound to happen sooner or later.

"Are you okay?" Brendan asks.

"Yeah, just a little shit-faced," I laugh. "It might be time to cool it on the champagne."

He rolls his eyes. "Maybe you should head back inside. I'll be okay out here."

"No, no. Your Uber will be here any minute," I say. "Besides, I'm not about to leave my baby brother waiting out in the cold by himself. If you're gonna shiver to death, then we'll shiver to death together."

"Fine," he says with a heavy sigh, knowing a lost cause when he sees it.

We wait a few more minutes, and my head grows worse, but I keep a smile plastered on my face so he doesn't worry. The Uber's headlights finally appear at the bottom of the longest driveway on earth, and I get up and push Brendan to the curb before helping him into the Uber, and by helping, I mean, I don't do shit.

The Uber drives off after I promise to call Brendan in the morning, and the second he's gone; I can finally give in to my spinning head. I walk back toward the seat I'd just vacated and find myself a stumbling mess.

Shit. This isn't right. I've been wasted more times than I care to admit, and this has never happened.

My vision begins to blur, and I fall back into the seat before dropping my head in my hands and closing my eyes for a moment. I need to lay down, but the second I do that, the night is over, and I'm not ready to call it quits. I just need to sober up a little.

Maybe a good power spew would help.

I try to get to my feet but trip over my heels just as an arm shoots out and saves me from eating dirt. "Hey, are you okay?" a voice asks through the night. "You don't look so good."

I turn to see Max by my side, and I blink a few times as his face grows blurrier by the minute. "I umm, I don't . . . Logan," I tell him, the words struggling to come out. "I need Logan."

"Sure thing," he says as he starts leading us away.

With each passing second, it gets worse, and I collapse my whole weight onto Max, struggling to keep my feet under me. "I don't feel . . . well."

Max doesn't respond, just keeps leading me away, and something doesn't feel right, but I can't work it out. Where's Logan? Why isn't he taking me to Logan? All the questions hurt my head, and my eyelids grow heavy, but I force them to stay open as my head really starts throbbing. "Where are you taking me?" I slur.

"It's okay," Max finally says, leading me into the shadows of the thick trees. "I'll have you back to your boyfriend in no time."

What? What does he mean by that?

This isn't right. I need to find Logan, and if Max isn't going to help me, then I'll have to find him myself. Determination pounds through my veins, and I try to push Max off, but he holds onto me tighter. "Let me go," I slur, wobbling on my feet.

"You ain't going anywhere until I'm finished with you, baby girl,"

Max says, finally coming to a stop in the thick bushes.

"I need Logan," I tell him again. Why doesn't he understand?

Max lets go of me, and my legs instantly give out, and I fall to the ground, scratching up my knees and palms. Everything hurts, and I'm pretty sure my dress is torn to shreds, but at least from down here, the world seems to have stopped spinning, at least a little.

Max kneels before me, and I find my eyes growing heavy again. Sleep. I just want to sleep. Max? What's Max doing here?

"Max," I murmur.

"That's right, baby," he says as he reaches toward me.

I hold my hand out so he can help me up, only he doesn't reach for my hand, he reaches for the strap that holds up my dress. He pushes it down my arms and I try to pull away. "Stop it," I rumble, my words straining to come out.

His hand comes out and slaps me hard across the face, and I fall back to the ground, scratching up my arms and chest. I try to hold my hand against my face to stop the pain, but I can't control it. I can't control anything.

"Shut up," Max demands.

Why is he hurting me like this? He said he'd find Logan. I need to find Logan.

Max grabs my dress again and with one simple twist of his wrist, tears the fabric away from my body. "No," I cry as my eyes grow heavier and my ability to fight back dwindles to nothing. "Stop. Please stop."

Then as Max reaches for my underwear, tearing it right off my body, I succumb to the darkness, leaving myself in Max's vile hands.

Chapter Twenty-Three

LOGAN

"Have any of you fine ladies seen my woman anywhere?" I ask Sara and Bri as I throw my arms over both their shoulders.

"Nope," Brianna says as she throws back the rest of her drink. "But when you find that little hussy, tell her to get her ass on the dance floor. Sara is slowing me down."

"Shut up," Sara laughs. "If I wasn't pregnant, I would have drunk you under the table by now."

I ignore their banter and move to the next crowd. Where the hell could she be? She took Brendan out half an hour ago, and there is no way an Uber would have taken that long to arrive. I pull out my phone and dial her number, but it rings out, though I'm not surprised. There would be no reason for her to have taken her phone with her, it's probably still in her purse under the table.

"Yo, Tony," I ask as I pass him. "Have you seen Elle?"

"Yeah," he laughs. "She told me she was going to find a real man."

"That explains why she walked right past you," I throw over my shoulder as I continue my search, more than proud of my quick wit, though I'm sure Tony will make sure I pay for it later.

I head out front and walk all the way down to the driveway, but as expected, she isn't here. Dashing back up the stairs, I check my old bedroom, making sure she didn't decide to take herself to bed, but there's no sign of her here either. Besides, if she was tired, she would have come and told me so she could drag me along with her. She hates sleeping alone now, and damn it, I'm right there with her. A night without her in my arms is a night I never want to see.

Just to be sure I didn't miss them, I pull my phone out of my suit pocket and bring up Brendan's number, quickly giving him a call. "What's up?" Brendan answers almost immediately as if he'd been busy playing on it, probably asking random chicks for nudes.

"Hey, are you still with Elle?" I ask.

"Nah, Uber came ten minutes ago. She didn't look so great. She's probably gone somewhere to lay down."

"Alright, thanks, man," I say, ending the call.

I head back downstairs and find Carter and Sean at the bridal table, each sitting back with a drink in hand, watching their girls on the dance floor, except there's a strange, depressed look in Carter's eyes. "Have you guys seen Elle?" I question as a hint of worry seeps into my tone, certain I should have found her by now.

"Nah, have you checked upstairs?" Carter asks, turning his eyes on me.

"Yeah, she's not up there."

"Out front?"

"Nope."

With that, both their eyes begin scanning the room until those concerned creases appear between their brows. "She wouldn't have gone out back?" Sean questions, knowing just how daunting the backyard can be at night, especially to someone who doesn't know the area. Don't get me wrong, it's beautiful out there by the lake and the bushes, but there's not much lighting, and anyone could easily get lost.

"I don't know, man. I don't see why she would."

"It can't hurt to look," Sean says, getting to his feet. "Come on, I'll help."

"Yeah, I'm up for a stroll," Carter says, getting to his feet after downing the rest of his drink.

"What's up with you?" I question as we head for the back door.

He looks back over his shoulder and waits until we've cleared the door to answer. "It's Bri," he says with a sigh. "I think the wedding's getting to her. She keeps hinting that this is what's next for us."

Sean scoffs at that. "Let me guess," he starts. "That's freaking you the fuck out."

"Hell, yeah," he says as he brings up his hand to rub the back of his neck. "What's wrong with what we've got now?"

"Nothing," I say, "but a woman like Bri isn't going to be satisfied with just that. She's the commitment type. For some godforsaken reason, she loves you, and staying with her is going to require a big fucking wedding and a shitload of kids running around."

"Don't say that," he groans, never having been one to see a future like that for himself. Carter would be content if it were just him and Bri for the rest of their lives, though he might relent and get her a puppy, but that's it.

"What's the problem with marriage and kids?" Sean asks as we start looking around the yard.

"Nothing," Carter says. "It's just not what I've ever pictured for myself."

"Well, you need to figure that shit out," I tell him as my eyes continue scanning the yard. "Bri's not going to wait forever, and you don't want to push her away in the meantime."

Carter lets out a frustrated sigh as he pulls his phone out of his pocket and turns on his flashlight app. We all follow suit as we get deeper into the yard.

"Elle?" I call out.

"It's fucking simple," Sean says continuing the conversation. "Do you love her?"

"Yeah," he says as if it truly is the simplest thing.

"Then I don't see your problem."

Carter sighs again, and this time I understand where he's coming from. Carter and I have never been the commitment type, but that's changed for me. Sean is different. He wanted to marry Sara the second he met her all the way back in high school. He practically proposed the second their ages deemed it acceptable.

"Yo, what's that?" Carter says as he points his phone flashlight in the direction of something near the tree line.

We all head over to the shiny object that seems to reflect against the light.

The closer we get, the worse my stomach drops. I'd recognize that shiny little object anywhere. After all, I was only staring at my woman in it all night. I dash over and confirm my thoughts. I pick up the champagne-colored high heel and turn to show my brothers.

"Are you sure that's hers?" Carter asks, knowing damn well it is. "All the girls are wearing the same shit. It could be any of theirs. There's no reason to panic yet. Besides, they all had their shoes off. There's a pile of them under the table so they could keep dancing without their feet getting sore."

"Dude, you were just watching the girls on the dance floor. They were all there except for Elle."

"She wouldn't have wandered into the trees, would she?" Sean asks with concern, peering out into the dark bushes.

"I fucking hope not," I grunt. These bushes are huge, and it's dark as fuck out here. If she has wandered in here, without her phone, and after drinking all day, she could be in trouble.

I do what any concerned boyfriend would do and dive straight into the trees. "Elle?" I call as the boys do the same thing.

I walk deeper and deeper, searching everywhere.

Come on, Elle, where the fuck are you? I hope she isn't hurt or passed out. "Elle," I call louder, only to get no response.

Babe, tell me where you are.

Panic tears at my chest the more I hear the boys calling out for her and getting nothing in return. Each passing second makes me want to crumble to my knees. I spend another few minutes searching when I find a piece of torn silk amongst the sticks and fallen leaves, and I pick it up, scanning over it as my stomach sinks. There is no mistaking it, the material is from Elle's dress.

"Carter. Sean," I call out.

They start making their way over, but I keep searching deeper into the trees. I hear a rustling from my left, and I head that way, stepping around a bush and coming face to face with my worst nightmare.

My heart sinks.

Elle lays motionless on the dirty ground, her skin covered in grazes and bruises as Max hovers above her. Elle's torn panties are discarded in the leaves, her legs spread apart, as Max holds his dick in his hand, two fucking seconds away from pushing inside of her.

I see red.

"Get the fuck off her," I roar, flying toward the fucker and gripping him by the back of his suit. I throw him off my woman, his back slamming against the trunk of a thick tree. He grunts in surprise but doesn't have a chance to react before I come down over him, nailing him again and again with as many blows as it will take for my rage to subside.

My knuckles split, and his face looks like a fucking blood bath, but

I've barely even started. "Fuck," Sean grunts behind me. He races in, desperately trying to break me away from Max, but I overpower him with ease. "Stop it," Sean booms. "You're going to fucking kill him."

"Good," I grunt before I suddenly find both my brothers at my arms dragging me backward. I fight against their hold, trying to break free, but against the two of them, it's impossible. "Let me go," I demand.

"No," Carter says, maneuvering me around so he can get in my face. "Go check on Elle. We'll deal with him."

Hearing her name is like a bucket of iced water over my head and has my gaze snapping in her direction. The fight leaves me, and the boys drop my arms as Max disappears from my thoughts. Fuck, I hope she's okay. I scramble through the bushes, rushing toward her before dropping to my knees and pulling her into my arms. "Babe," I say, giving her a slight shake, the panic tearing at my chest, hoping like fuck she's going to be alright. "Can you hear me?"

Elle doesn't respond, but at least she's breathing. She's clearly unconscious, and I realize this is much more than just drinking too much. Did he give her something or did he knock her out?

I gently scoop her up into my arms, making sure to protect her precious head, and I make my way out of the trees, knowing the boys will do whatever it is they need to do to deal with Max.

Making my way up to the house, I go in through the back entrance, so I don't disturb the wedding, and take her straight up to my old bedroom. I lay her on my bed and find some clothes before hastily pulling them on, trying my hardest to offer her all the privacy in the world. After heading into the bathroom, I come out with a wet washcloth before sitting down on the edge of the bed and cleaning her up the best I can. Preferably, I'd like to get her in a shower, but that's going to have to wait.

The more scratches and grazes I clean over, the more that rage starts to return, but knowing Elle needs me right now is the only thing keeping me from going back out to the bushes and annihilating the fucker.

I sit beside her in the bed watching her sleep, getting some relief knowing she's safe. A knock sounds at my door, and I find Carter and Sean, each with bloodied knuckles.

"Is she okay?" Sean asks, concerned.

"I think so," I tell them. "Is he dealt with?"

"Yeah. We took him up to the front gates and called the police. He's gone," Carter says before cringing.

"What is it?" I demand.

"We found pills in his pocket," he says.

"Shit," I curse. "Do you know what they are?"

"No," Sean says. "You should get her down to the hospital. They can run her blood and check her over."

"No," I tell them, shaking my head, knowing she'll prefer to stay right here. "Let her rest. Can we get a doctor out here instead? Or a nurse? I think she should do a rape kit, just in case we hadn't made it there in time, but nobody is touching her until she can consent to that. Got it?"

"Yeah, of course," he says as he looks past me into the room, sadness in his eyes. "The police asked if she'd be comfortable giving a statement, and I said yeah, but obviously that's up to her how she wants to handle this."

"She would want to," I tell him, glancing back at her. "I'll take her down in the morning."

The boys nod and go to leave, but Carter looks back. "I'll call the home doctor and let you know when they're here."

"Thanks," I say, and with that, they head back toward the stairs. "Hey," I call out and wait as they turn back. "Don't tell Cass about this. I don't want her worrying on her wedding day. She should be enjoying her night."

"You got it," Carter agrees before they disappear.

I close the door and climb back into bed with Elle, pulling her unconscious body into my arms and holding her tight. I will her to wake up but, seeing as though it's the middle of the night and she's been drugged and drinking, it probably won't happen for a while.

Lying awake, I listen to the music from downstairs seeping up through the massive house, unable to find enough peace to close my eyes. The more I think about what happened, the more I need to do something to somehow make this right.

Despite my need to stay right here next to her, I tuck the blanket over Elle and slide out of the bed. I grab my suit jacket and pull it on before I dash downstairs and head back into the party and look for the one man who'll be able to give me the peace I'm searching for.

I find him among the other guys from my team and head over, dread filling every inch of my body.

"What's up with you?" Tony asks as I step into his side. "You look like shit."

"Don't I know it," I grunt. "Listen, can we talk for a moment?"

His brows furrow, watching me. I've never approached him like this. He's a smart man, so he knows something is up. "Sure," he says.

I nod and lead him through the estate and into a private room, where we can have a proper conversation without one of my teammates coming and slurring about how fucking wasted they are.

"What's up?" he asks as I close the door behind me.

"It's Max," I say before explaining everything that has gone down tonight while doing my best to mask just how fucked up my knuckles are from the beating I gave him. The more I talk, the more horrified Tony's expression becomes.

"Fuck," he finally grunts as he slams his drink down on the table, his whole body shaking with rage. "How's Elle?"

"Sleeping. We have a doctor coming to check her out and see what's in her system."

"Good," he says. "If it's okay with her, could you let me know those results?"

"Of course," I say with a grim nod.

"You spoke with the cops?" he asks.

"Not personally, but my brothers dealt with them."

"Okay," he says, slipping into manager mode. "We'll deal with it in the morning, but rest assured, effective immediately, he's on suspension pending an internal investigation."

"Good," I say, knowing exactly what's going to come out of that investigation. The Colorado Thunder has always been known for its excellent reputation. We don't put up with bullshit and never have. At the moment, it's my word against his, but as soon as Elle can give a statement and they find out what's in her system, his ass will be out of here and locked up for attempted rape.

How dare that fucker pull that shit on my woman?

"The press is going to have a fucking field day," Tony grunts as he picks up his drink and throws it back. "Tell Jax thanks for the invite. I'm going to head off. I need to get ahead of this before it blows up in the media."

"Sure thing," I say.

"Thanks for bringing it to my attention. Had you waited until morning, it would have been all over the news and too late to do damage control."

I nod and watch as he leaves the room, too fucking grim to even respond.

I throw on a smile and ditch my suit jacket, all too aware of Max's blood splatters staining the material, then certain I'm ready, I head back into the party. As much as I want to be upstairs with Elle, I know she's safe and sleeping. Right now, Cass needs me to be present for the best day of her life. I'll stay for another half hour, give her a few more dances before quietly slipping out again. By then, the doctor should be here.

Just as expected. I stay at the party for half an hour, pretending that my mind is solely on enjoying Cassie's day before heading upstairs with the doctor. She goes about her business and requests that we have her checked over once she regains consciousness.

The doctor heads out, and after scouring through the estate's security footage and finding what I need, I climb in beside Elle once again. I pull her into me and find relief in having her safe in my arms, but the gnawing guilt eats me alive.

I can't believe I let this happen. I knew Max was into her, and I knew he was a fucking weirdo. I should have looked out for her. Gone with her to send off Brendan. Where the fuck was I when she needed me the most? Fucking around getting drunk with my friends.

This, I will never forgive myself for.

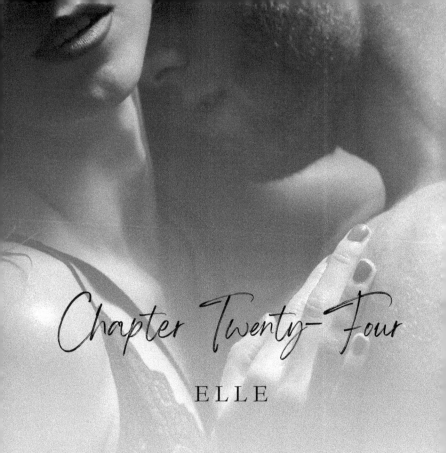

Chapter Twenty-Four

ELLE

My head hurts.

Why the hell does it hurt so bad? I roll over and inhale, and a warm smile spreads over my face. There's no place else I'd rather be.

Logan's arms pull me in tighter, but for once, I wish he would loosen up a bit. My body aches, and the need to fall back asleep crashes through me. I try to open my eyes, but that only makes everything worse. So instead, I snuggle in under the blankets and groan.

What the hell is going on? Did I really drink that much?

"How are you feeling?" Logan murmurs in that sexy just-woke-up voice as he moves around the bed to get a good look at me.

"I feel like I've been run over by a truck," I tell him.

"That's expected," he says before leaning in and pressing a kiss to my head. "I'm so fucking happy you're alright."

"Huh?" I grunt as I slowly try to open my eyes again. The pain hits, but with Logan so close, he blocks out the majority of the light. "What do you mean *alright?*"

His face sobers, his eyes widening with horror and guilt. "You don't remember?" Logan questions.

"Remember what?" I question, unease beginning to rush through my veins, not liking his tone one bit. "I remember drinking . . . a lot, partying, being screwed within an inch of my life, and putting Brendan in an Uber. Then . . . not much. Did I pass out?" I groan in embarrassment, remembering how my head was starting to spin after saying goodbye to Bren.

"Not quite," Logan says with a cringe as he runs his hand down my side. I hiss out in pain. What the fuck was that? "Shit, sorry, babe."

"What happened to me?" I question as I try to sit up.

Logan helps me and immediately hands me a glass of water and some painkillers. "Here, take this," he says. "It should help."

I do as I'm told like a good little girl before looking at Logan in concern, not liking his expression at all. "Spill it. Did I make an ass of myself?" I ask as I look down and find myself covered in grazes. I try to cross my legs under the blankets, but my knees protest in pain. Great, they're probably scratched up too.

"Babe," he says in a soothing tone as he reaches out and takes my hand, but not in his usual claiming way. This feels more like he's trying to comfort me. "You know that part of your night you can't remember?"

"Yeah?" I prompt.

Logan cringes, clearly not wanting to tell me whatever it is that I did, but he's not about to leave me out in the dark. He lets out a breath and regret shines brightly in his dark eyes. "Max slipped you some pills," he says.

"What?" I grunt in shock. "No, that's not possible," I say, shaking my head.

"Yeah, babe. It is," he says as panic crashes through me and overwhelms my system. "Security footage shows him putting pills into a champagne flute then handing it to you."

I think back to last night and remember the exact moment. "He spilled my drink and got me a new one to apologize," I say in confusion. "Why would he do that?" I ask, looking to Logan for answers as horror and dread have tears already filling my eyes. "What did he do?"

"It was very dark last night, so the footage was hard to see, but from what we can tell, after Brendan left, you sat on a bench. When you got up, you tripped and Max caught you. There was a conversation and then he led you away."

As he talks, bits and pieces start coming back to me. "I wasn't feeling well. My head was spinning, and I asked him to take me to you. I kept telling him that I needed you, but he was going the wrong way. I couldn't . . ." Logan closes his eyes, clearly battling with some sort of inner conflict, but I don't question it as more memories start to come back to haunt me.

I gasp as I recall hands tearing my dress and hitting me. My hand flies to cover my mouth, but Logan reaches out and pulls me to him. "It's okay," he soothes as he holds me.

My tears quickly stain his shirt, but he doesn't dare pull away. "Shit," I cry. "Did . . . did he?"

"No," Logan says. "At least, I don't believe so. We got there in time."

Relief comes over me, but it isn't enough to take away the panic that still surges through me. "How could I be so stupid? That's the first rule of drinking. Never accept a drink from anyone. Always get your own and make sure you see it being opened. Never let it out of your sight."

I fell for the oldest fucking trick in the book.

"I hope it's okay, but I allowed a doctor to take a sample of your blood so we can work out what he gave you," Logan explains. "I also think it's in your best interest to get a rape kit done, you know, in the off chance we weren't there in time."

I nod my head, really not giving two shits that Logan had my blood tested. It was the responsible thing to do, and I would have done the same if the situation were reversed. But the idea of having to go into a hospital and requesting a rape kit makes this too fucking real.

"The police would like a statement, but if you're not up to it, that's fine. We have the security footage to back it up, so you don't need to do anything you don't want to do."

"It's okay, I'll give a statement," I mumble as I look up at Logan, my eyes sore from crying. "Did I ruin the wedding?"

"No," he says. "Cass and Jax don't know a thing about it, but I'm sure they will soon. Max is off the team pending investigation, so it won't be long before they find out."

"Them and the rest of the world," I grunt, realizing a scandal like this is going to end up on international news. Brendan is going to hear about it, and the guilt he'll feel about leaving me there . . . shit.

"Are you okay?" Logan asks.

I think it over for a moment, and to tell the truth, I have absolutely no idea. What nearly happened would have been awful and devastating in every way, but it didn't. I'm physically fine—apart from a raging headache, cuts, and bruises—but mentally, that's a different story, one I haven't figured out yet.

My breath comes harder, and I try my best to push the terrifying thoughts away. It was a close call, that's all. Logan got there in time. Max has been dealt with, and there's more than enough evidence to make an open and closed case, so I have no reason to panic, right? It's time to move on.

"Can I let you know?" I whisper into the too-quiet room.

"Of course," he murmurs as he shuffles us around and pulls me onto his lap. He drops his head to my shoulder as he gently strokes my back.

A soft sigh escapes his lips, and I realize for the world's chattiest man, he's being way too quiet. "What's wrong?" I ask as I raise his head to meet his eyes.

Logan presses his lips together before letting it out. "I feel like I failed you. It's my job to keep you safe, and I wasn't looking out for you last night. I should have gone with you, not let you out of my sight for one fucking second."

"Don't do that to yourself," I tell him, cupping his face in the palm of my hand. "This is not your fault. If anything, it's mine. Max has been nonstop hitting on me since I started working for the Thunder. I turned him down each and every time. I was the one who didn't tell you. I didn't report him to management, and I was the one who accepted a drink from someone I shouldn't have. None of this is on you."

Logan looks at me with those eyes that I love so much, and I can tell he isn't buying what I'm saying. If anything, I'm probably making it worse, but he needs to hear it. "Hey, how would anyone have known that he's that fucked up?" I question, trying to lighten the mood.

He leans back against the headboard, and I climb right up into his lap, straddling him and ignoring the pain. "You know I love you, right?" I ask as I rest my forehead against his.

"I know, babe," he smiles before catching my lips in his.

"Despite the ending of the night, I still had a really great time," I tell him.

"I know," he replies as he wraps a hand around my neck, holding me to him. "You looked fucking radiant."

I bring my hand up and run it down the side of his face, which is when I notice the dirt under my nails. "Ugh," I groan. "I don't look radiant anymore."

"What are you talking about?" he questions.

I turn my hand around so he can see the state my nails are in. "Did I not shower last night?" I ask in disgust.

"No," he scoffs. "You were sort of passed out."

"Logan," I groan.

"What were you expecting me to do? Throw you in a bath with a floaty and hope you didn't drown?"

I roll my eyes as I push myself up off him and scoot to the edge of the bed.

"What are you doing?" he questions.

"Showering," I reply as I try to stand. "I feel like I still have the taint of him on my skin."

"I did give you a sponge bath," he informs me with a grin that makes him look like the worst kind of pervert. "But, if you want to do the rape kit, it's best not to shower. At least, that's what the doctor told me last night. You'll be washing away the evidence."

I bite the inside of my cheek as I turn to face him, not quite sure what I want to do. "You said you had enough information to convict him, right? The footage, plus my statement, and I'm assuming yours as well."

Logan nods. "My brothers were with me when I found you, so they'll be giving statements too."

"Do you think that's really enough?" I ask, fidgeting with my hands and averting my gaze. "I just . . . the thought of a rape kit seems so . . . I don't know. Violating. And I just, I'm content believing that you made it in time. If I were to do it and find out that something more did actually happen . . . I just . . . I think it would destroy me."

"It's okay," he tells me, standing in front of me and dropping his hands to my arms and slowly rubbing up and down. "I don't want you to do anything you don't want to do. If you feel it's too much and you just want to shower, that's fine. We'll get him with everything else."

"Are you sure? I can shower?" I ask. "I just . . . I need to wash him off me. I feel so dirty knowing he touched me."

"Yeah, babe. I'm sure."

I swallow hard and step into him, wrapping my arms tightly around him and resting my head against his chest for just a moment. "Did you want me to come with you to shower, or would you prefer to be alone?"

I shake my head and meet his haunted stare. "I don't want to be alone right now."

Logan holds me tighter and presses a kiss to my forehead, the emotion thick in his tone. "You'll never be alone, Elle. Not with me."

A few moments later, I find myself basking in the warmth of the shower and watching as the soapy bubbles slide down my skin, taking the memory of Max with them. They disappear down the drain, and I hope to God they'll never be seen again. "I know you probably don't want to think about it anymore, but I just have one question."

"What's that?" Logan asks, holding me under the warm spray of water.

Taking his hand, I gently brush my thumb across his split knuckles, before looking up and meeting his stare. "I thought you were a lover, not a fighter?"

"I am," he scoffs, a sad, forced smile spreading across his face, trying to lighten the mood for me. "But when it comes to someone I love, I'd do just about anything. In fact, I think I fucked him up pretty bad."

"Shit, Logan," I curse, my eyes wide as I struggle between the need to get revenge and what's right. "What about your contract?"

Fuck. I couldn't live with myself if he lost his contract because he was defending me.

"Don't worry about me," he says, running his hands down my wet hair and pressing a kiss to my forehead. "Tony has it covered."

Thank God.

"Logan," I whisper, looking up at him. "Before you, I was a shell. It was just me and Brendan, and we lived in our own version of a nightmare that we couldn't wake up from. Then you came along and woke me up. You breathed new air into me, and I feel like I'm finally alive. The last eight years have been so damn hard, but for the first time I feel like I have something to look forward to, and it's all thanks to you."

His arms wind around me and pull me in close, his lips pressing against my temple. "You have no idea how fucking good that feels."

"I think I have a pretty good idea," I tell him.

"You're my whole fucking world, Elle."

"Right back at ya, Captain."

Chapter Twenty-Five

LOGAN

I walk into the arena for the final game of the season, more than ready to stand with my boys as we defend our fucking championship title. Having the championship game held in our home arena is just the cherry on top of the best fucking cake in the world.

As expected, we've had to go through all the bullshit that comes with being at the top of the leaderboard. The media at the games has been insane, plus the paparazzi have been on point. Not to mention the intense press conferences. Being the captain, guess who gets thrown right in the limelight the most? Yeah, me.

There's nothing I hate more than sitting down and giving a press conference, talking to the media, and posing for all their damn photos. The only thing keeping me from losing my shit this year is Elle. She's my rock, my world, and I can't wait to marry her.

I just have to get through this last game and end the season the way it's supposed to be finished. Being the championship game means it's going to be the hardest game of the year. We're up against the best.

The LA Storm. Fucking Miller Cain and Tank. *The dream team.* They're friends of Jax's, but tonight, they're our rivals.

It's still hours before the big game, but there's a lot of shit to get through, such as this full team meeting. We only have these when something serious has gone down or to give management a chance to talk themselves up, which I assume is what's happening today.

At least they have lunch on offer.

As usual, I beeline for the lunch buffet and make myself a nice full plate that anyone would be proud of. The only downfall is sticking to my strict diet, but come tomorrow morning, I'm binging on whatever the fuck I want. I might even help myself to a nice juicy hamburger with loaded fries and chili.

I can't fucking wait.

I get comfortable in my seat and down my lunch, being careful not to spill anything on my team suit while I wait for the rest of the team to arrive. The remainder of the day is going to be insane. Championship game days always are.

Following this meeting, we have media interviews where they'll be questioning any scandals the team has endured this year. Then as usual, they'll go right ahead and ask each of us about our personal lives to see if there are any uncovered stories they can splash all over the news.

Luckily for me, I'm squeaky fucking clean.

Following the meeting and interviews, we'll get together to discuss game tactics while Elle and the senior therapist check over all the players to make sure they're all good for tonight's game. Then it's warm-up time for the guys to go over their practice shots and try not to freak out, and that's where I come in. None of the guys will be freaking out on my watch.

One by one, the guys make their way into the massive conference room, all heading straight for the food before settling into their seats. A few minutes later, Elle makes her presence known at the door, looking sexy as fuck in her team suit that management demands she wears.

The boys get a good look and drown her in wolf whistles, letting her know just how appreciated she is. She struts across the room, putting on a show in her fitted suit and heels, all while trying not to burst into laughter.

Elle struts past me, but she won't be going anywhere soon. My arm snaps out and grabs her around her waist before hauling her back to my lap. She lets out a girly squeal which is quickly swallowed by her laughter as her arms fall around my neck.

"You look amazing," I tell her.

"You don't look too bad yourself, Captain," she responds before giving me a kiss that only serves to make the boys rowdier.

"Get a room," Jax calls out as the rest of the boys voice their own opinions.

"With pleasure," I say, standing with her securely in my arms before heading for the door.

"Logan," Tony demands as he enters the room. "Put the girl down. Until the end of the night, Elle is still ours. We need her focused today, not swooning over her boyfriend."

She looks up at me, and I see true disappointment flashing in her eyes, and I lean down to give her a kiss. "Don't worry, babe. As soon as this game is over, I'll make it up to you."

"Is that a promise?" she questions.

"You bet your fucking ass it is," I tell her as I take her back to my seat and get comfortable.

"And you'll do that thing I like?" she murmurs as she hops off my lap to take the seat beside me so we can at least appear to be professional.

"I'll do all the things you like," I promise, taking her hand in mine.

Elle's face flames, and she has to look away to stop her grin from breaking her face in two.

"Alright," Tony says to the room. "Settle down. We have a big day today, so I want to get this part over with." He waits patiently as the boys settle down into their seats and provide him with their undivided attention.

"Okay," he starts. "I want to open this meeting by saying what a great job you've done so far this season. You've all shown great commitment to the team, and that commitment comes through loud and clear in our results. Not one of you has lacked in your training, on ice or off, so please give yourself and your teammates a round of applause."

At that, the room bursts into applause with the boys and management all nodding in agreement, and I have to say, I'm right there with them. The boys have shown amazing commitment this season, and that shows on the leaderboard. They have all worked their asses off and deserve nothing less than the win tonight, but it's not going to be handed to us, we'll have to put up one last fight.

"Other acknowledgments this year. I'd like you all to thank team management for all the work they've put in this season, our lovely physiotherapists, our trainers, and our PR team. We would not be where we are today without your dedication and hard work. It certainly does not go unnoticed."

Again, the team breaks into applause, voicing their approval.

"Next up, our trusted captain, Logan Waters. Another successful year where you have proven that you were the right choice for captain. Again, you have managed to keep these boys inspired, motivated, and most importantly, in line. Good job, Logan."

I nod my head, accepting his thanks, and wait for him to move right along. Elle squeezes my hand, and I look at her to see a brilliant smile staring back at me. "I love you," she mouths.

"Right back at ya, babe," I murmur.

"Last but not least," Tony continues, finally moving the attention off me. "Coach Robinson and the coaching staff. What a fantastic job you've done this season."

As expected, the room bursts into absolute chaos for our beloved Coach Robinson. The boys get up out of their chairs and crowd him, and he's suddenly thrown upon shoulders and demanding to be put down, but that shit isn't about to happen any time soon.

The boys eventually calm down, allowing Tony to get onto the more serious topics.

"Get your asses back in your seats," he demands. "We've got a lot to cover." They do as they're told with a few stragglers detouring back past the food buffet on the way.

"Alright. Down to business. We've had some disappointments this year with both Dave and Max. Both rocked the team's name in the press. However, we have come through the other end much stronger. I'm sorry to play this card on you all, but keep in mind that you are all replaceable. As you move on, another player will come, so as you saw with Max, one strike and you're out. Please remember this during your off-season. What you do reflects on us as a team, so keep it classy, boys."

Tony then goes on to remind us about our media interviews and after-game press conference. He then goes over all the ways to avoid certain questions and how to word certain things to make you look like a glowing star with the brightest future in the league.

On and on he goes with all the shit that we don't want to be here to listen to, but as a good bunch of guys, we sit patiently and wait until he's ticked off all the items on his list to discuss.

"Hang in there, guys. We're nearly done," he encourages but what does he expect out of a bunch of guys?

"So, as you all recall," he says, pointedly looking at my woman. "At the beginning of the season, I made a deal with Elle." That perks us all up. I watch in amusement as the guys sit a little taller and throw one hundred percent of their attention toward both Tony and Elle, curious as to how this is going to play out.

"For those who don't remember, Elle was promised that if she put in the work and showed that she was capable of handling the responsibilities of being our senior therapist, that the job would be hers. And I have to admit guys, Elle is a fucking star. She has shown incredible dedication to our team and put up with all of your bullshit while simultaneously doing a great job. So, Elle, if you are still interested, I'd like to formally offer you the position of Senior Physiotherapist for the Colorado Thunder."

Elle gapes at Tony, and it's a few seconds before she finally recovers. "Are you serious?" she squeals as her hand squeezes in mine, though I'm not entirely sure she realizes she's doing it. "What about Kate?" she asks, looking at the other senior therapist who has since become a good friend.

"As serious as a heart attack. I have spoken to Kate, who has agreed that you deserve this position. She will also be staying on for the foreseeable future. So, what do you say?" he says with an excited grin.

"Hell freaking yes," she says with big eyes and a smile that threatens to tear her face apart. "Thank you so much. I won't let you down."

"I know you won't," he says before dramatically making a point of sitting down and relaxing so he can give the boys a chance to go ape-shit crazy, which of course, they do. Only this time, I don't let them beat me to her.

I pull Elle into my lap while circling my arms around her and pressing my lips to hers. "Congratulations," I tell her.

She smiles back at me with love in her eyes. "Thank you," she says.

"You deserve it," I tell her before she's pulled away from me and thrown into the air by the guys chanting her name. I'm so fucking proud and happy for her, but right now, with the guys throwing her around like a fucking ragdoll, I want nothing more than to bust their balls.

If they hurt her in any way, shape, or form, I'll be tearing them up into little pieces and feeding them to Louie, which would only be a waste, as I'm sure he really isn't into eating humans for dinner.

Elle lets out a squeal as the boys get a little too rowdy, and I swoop in to save my woman.

"Alright, alright. Settle down," Tony says. "We still have a little time before the pre-game press starts, so I'll give Coach Robinson the floor to discuss game tactics for tonight."

With that, Coach gets up and makes his way to the front of the room.

"Please remember, no matter what happens tonight, there will be post-game celebrations at the Hilton Hotel, and you should all be there," Tony says as he signs off for the time being.

Coach steps up, front and center, getting right down to the reason we're here. We go over everything, and I make sure to memorize each and every word spoken by the coaching staff. After all, once we're on the ice, it's up to me to lead these boys to victory.

Once the meeting is done, shit goes crazy. Some of the guys are sent for interviews while Elle and Kate steal the small handful of guys who have injuries or issues that need to be looked at before the game. Management opens the ice for any last-minute training, and pucks fly across the ice while players check over their skates, blades, sticks, and gear.

The afternoon flies by, and I soon find myself dressed and ready to get on the ice for the final showdown of the season. The arena is packed to absolute capacity, while the press is everywhere with their expensive cameras and crew. The lights flash and music blasts throughout the whole building as fans of both Denver and LA pile into the grandstands for what is bound to be the show of the decade.

Fuck. I'm a strange mix of excitement and nervousness, and I'm busting to get out there and get the game started, but apparently, I have to stick to a fucking time schedule. I hate feeling like this, but the second I get on the ice and in the zone, it will all fade away.

I know we can beat this team. We've worked our asses off for this moment, but they aren't going to make it easy, and they sure as fuck aren't just going to hand us the championship. If we make even one mistake, we could give it all away. Not to mention, the LA team now has their new shining stars, Miller Cain and Tank Meyers. But to me, they're still kids and just a couple of friends of Jax's. These two on a team haven't lost a single game for the past two seasons, but this is the big leagues, and they're in my house now.

Some official-looking woman comes in and tells us it's time to start heading out of the hole. We line up by the door, with me in the lead and my boys falling in behind. Coach brings up the rear along with the rest of management, trainers, and of course, Elle and Kate.

When the door opens, the sound flowing in is incredible. We head up the hallway and come out of the hole into the arena. The grandstands are a sea of Thunder and Storm colors, swamped with foam fingers, lights, and jerseys.

We're announced to the arena and shit goes crazy, and I find it impossible to wipe the grin off my face. I look up into the family and friends' section our team has reserved and see my whole family sitting with Jaz and Brendan.

We step onto our ice, and I feel it in my bones. This is our night. We will take that big-ass trophy straight back to its home in our foyer, declaring us, once again, the National Champions.

I come to the center of the ice, ready to get this shit started, and find myself facing none other than Tank Meyers. "Sup, kid? Are you ready to see how the big boys play?" I grin.

He shakes his head and grins right back. "Bring it on, fucker," he says. "You haven't got anything I ain't seen before."

"We'll see about that," I tell him as the ref drops the puck.

I swoop in and own that puck, but it was fucking close. I take off with the big bastard right on my heels. Shit, he's fast, but not fast enough. Just as I knew he would, Jax comes right up beside me and saves me from the hell that Tank is about to rain down over me.

Jax collects the puck with ease, managing to dodge Miller in the process and slide it straight across the ice as the Storm's defense really kicks in. I make myself open and scoop it straight up as I dart toward the goal with the rest of my boys on my six.

I can't shake Tank, but I didn't expect to. At least I know he skates clean, and I don't need to worry about him slamming me into the boards anytime soon, but he'll try all that fancy footwork shit on me, just as Jax does. But I'm ready for it. The only thing I worry about is his speed. There's only a small handful of players on this ice who can keep up with me, and Tank is one of them. This is exactly where all the tactics we talked about in our meeting come into play. We need to play it smart tonight.

I shoot the puck back to Jax and instantly pull back, letting Tank and the rest of his team fly straight past me. Jax immediately shoots the puck back, and I take my shot at the goal, letting the puck fly free.

The goalie hardly sees it coming. The puck flies straight past him, and I watch in amusement as the goalie throws himself across the ice, trying to block the puck, but it's too fast and comes to a stop in the back of the net.

The buzzer sounds and the music blares through the arena as the crowd roars their approval. Jax flies around the back of the net and finds me on the other side, and we slam into each other, which has him losing his footing and falling to his ass.

Jax scrambles to get up, but with all the gear it takes a little longer, giving me plenty of time to give him shit for it. I hold a hand out and help him up while I try to control my laughter. "Everyone saw that, didn't they?"

"Sure fucking did, kid," I laugh. "That one will be played on the ESPN blooper reel until the end of time."

"Ahhh, fuck," he grins as he pushes me away.

Tank and Miller skate past, and Jax just can't help himself. "Who's the fucking dream team now, bitches?" he laughs.

"Games still young, Jax," Miller says in amusement as Tank just shakes his head.

This game is going to be hard, but so fucking worth it. I can't wait to play out every damn second of it.

Chapter Twenty-Six

ELLE

This game is so freaking good. I sit on the very edge of my seat, not wanting to miss a second. The boys are up against the LA Storm, which is the team Miller and Tank are on, so that probably means their girlfriends are in the grandstands. There's no doubt about it, no matter who wins tonight, it's going to be one hell of a good after-game celebration.

I've never been so busy. This team is fucking good, and they're keeping my boys on their toes, which means, they're keeping me on mine, too. Honestly, it kind of sucks because I want nothing more than to sit here and watch the game. But I'm working, so I've spent half the game in my office with player after player on my table. It's good that I have Kate with me to pick up some of the slack.

So far, there have been a few big incidents with guys being tripped or slammed into the boards, but nothing the boys can't handle. No fists have flown yet, but I'm waiting for it. It's the championship game, and with a bunch of dudes wanting nothing more than to win, it's bound to get ugly at some point.

I'm just glad I don't have to worry about Logan. He plays clean, and I'm happier because of it. I don't know how I'd feel if he was the kind of guy starting fights on the ice and constantly being thrown in the sin bin. Though, if that were the case, he wouldn't be captain.

Logan has been on fire tonight, but from how good Tank is, he has to be, which makes it damn clear why Logan is the captain. He's good, and it turns me the fuck on. I can't wait to get him home tonight. Maybe I'll have to bombard him in the locker room after the game. I'm not sure I can wait until we get home.

The game is so close. The teams have been scoring goal for goal, we're just lucky that the Thunder is one up. Poor Tony looks as though he's about to have a heart attack. He's been on edge since the puck dropped and it's the funniest thing I've ever seen.

The crowd roars, and I join in as Logan makes his third goal for the night, making me want to scream at the top of my lungs that he's my man and that none of these thirsty bitches constantly throwing themselves at him can have him. That's right, whores, he's sleeping in my bed tonight and every other night.

There are five minutes left on the clock, and I have two guys on the bench who need attention, but Coach has demanded they wait in the box. Honestly, I don't think I could get them in my office even if I tried. It's crunch time. The boys are up by two now, and they are exhausted. I know they still have plenty of fuel left in their tanks, and even if they don't, I know they'll find it somewhere.

They zoom up and down the ice at a pace I still can't comprehend, like seriously, they're doing this shit on tiny fucking blades. It's ridiculous. The arena is in chaos with everyone already on their feet. The game is too close for my liking. Anything could happen.

I watch with wide eyes as Jax steals the puck, only to have it taken straight off him by Miller. He flies down to our goal, but Logan swoops in like the hero he is and intercepts his shot only to have it taken straight off him by Tank, who shoots right for the goal.

The puck sails past our goalie and the crowd goes wild.

Oh shit.

This game is getting closer by the second, it's too fucking intense. I can't handle it. We're still one up but with only four minutes left on the clock. This is still anyone's game.

The clock continues its countdown. With Jax, Logan, Tank, and Miller stealing the show. I swear, there are hardly any other players in the game, well none that anyone notices today anyway.

The boys are continuously up and down the ice, blocking each other's advances and attempts at the goal. I still hardly understand what's going on, but I know it's damn good. This is the type of game that will be remembered for years to come.

Two minutes to go. The crowd is going nuts, and my eyes are

constantly flicking back and forth between the clock and the ice.

A minute left.

Forty-five seconds.

Thirty seconds.

Shit. If I was a nail biter, I'd have none left.

Twenty seconds to go, and Logan shoots back up the ice with fierce determination in his eyes. The boys back him up while the opposition races to catch him, but he's too far ahead.

The whole stadium holds their breath as they watch my man. He brings his arm back, preparing to shoot, and the goalie tenses, ready to fly in whichever direction is needed.

Logan strikes and the breath catches in my throat. The stick connects with the puck and it shoots forward, hurtling through the air toward the goal with a speed I can't physically follow. The goalie dives for the puck, and I throw myself to the boards to get a better look.

The puck comes through on the other side, slamming into the back of the nets before falling to the ice. The buzzer sounds and the Thunder fans go insane.

There are still six seconds left in the game, but we all know it's over.

Jax barrels into Logan, and they slam their chests together before giving each other a tight hug. The whole team tears their gloves off, throwing them across the ice before yanking their helmet off.

With six seconds to go, the boys are forced to pick up their shit off the ice and complete the final few seconds. But they're just going with the motions now, the other team not even trying as the eager crowd begins their countdown.

The final buzzer sounds, and my boys reclaim their title as National Champions.

Confetti cannons shoot up into the grandstands, while the rest of the team jumps the boards to celebrate with the players who just brought the game home.

I find myself standing on my chair, jumping up and down, cheering for my boys. Fuck. I'm so happy right now, I can hardly contain myself. I'm so fucking proud of them, but mainly Logan. I'm so happy for him. This is what he has worked for all season, and it's paid off in the biggest way.

I'm jumping and cheering so much that I don't notice my man approaching and find myself being hauled off the chair and thrown over his shoulder with his hand firmly on my ass. He takes off into the middle of the ice and shuffles me around so I can see the view he's been looking at all night.

I look up in the stands and am awed. This is more than incredible. Confetti falls from the sky as a sea of Thunder jerseys applaud for my boys, the sound booming through the arena. "You did it," I tell him as he whips me back around to face him.

"That was the hardest game I've ever played," he admits.

"And you killed it."

He grins wide, and unfortunately, he has to take me back to my seat so they can accept their trophy and talk with the press. I head into my office to grab my bag. I can get through all the paperwork tomorrow. Tonight's for celebrating.

I head up into the grandstand and wait with Logan's family while he finishes all his interviews.

Logan finally comes out and instantly draws me into his arms before telling everyone where to meet for the after-game party, which I'm assuming is going to be massive. I just hope I don't get drugged at this one.

Logan and I jump into the car and he heads toward the Hilton Hotel with a constant string of comments about the game and how freaking great it was. Then he turns to me with horror written all over his face. "What's wrong?" I ask, searching his eyes for any hint of what's on his mind.

"Louie," he says. "I forgot to put him back in his cage."

"What?" I screech as he pulls a U-turn to head back toward his place.

Panic surges through me knowing Logan tends to forget to close the windows from time to time. Shit. My baby. I hope he's okay.

Logan and I have been living together for the last few weeks, and it's been amazing, the only thing Logan struggles with is having a pet to be responsible for. It's been a challenge for him, which I thought he was getting used to, but apparently not. Though he had the biggest game of his career to date, so I guess I can let him off the hook, as soon as I know Louie is safe.

Hell, Louie is probably flying around the house having the time of his life, swearing at all the birds outside.

We turn down his long-ass driveway, and I have to hold in my curses as he drives way too slow for my liking. "You better come in too.

It's a big house, he could be anywhere."

"You think I had any intention of actually staying in your truck?" I scoff.

Logan tries to hold back a grin as he parks, and the second I can, I bail out of the truck and race up the stairs. I wait impatiently as he searches for the right key on his massive keychain, and I'm just about ready to yank them out of his hand when he finally gets it open.

The door swings wide open, and I push past Logan. "Louie?" I call. "Where are you, you little bastard?"

I get no response, but that's typical when he's not in his cage. Logan comes in behind me and walks in the opposite direction, and I head upstairs while he stays down. "Louie," I continue calling.

"Babe," I hear Logan calling from downstairs.

"What?" I call back.

"I found him, but the fucker's not coming down," he tells me.

God, do I have to do everything around here? "Just grab him," I tell him.

"He keeps flying away and calling me a bastard," he says.

"Fine. I'm coming," I say as I dash down the stairs. "Where the hell are you?"

"Living room."

I head that way and groan to myself. Freaking Louie, he's such a naughty boy. I step into the dark living room. Why the hell hasn't Logan got the lights on if he's looking for the stupid bird? Am I the only one with brains around here?

I flip the switch and instantly get a chorus of SURPRISE booming through the living room.

What in the ever-loving fuck?

I gasp in shock as I stand motionless on the spot. The room is crowded with my friends, the whole team, and of course, Brendan too. But Logan, fucking Logan is dead center in the middle of the room, down on one knee.

"What the fuck are you doing?" I ask as he grins up at me from the ground.

"Shut up and listen," he demands as chuckles come from all around the room.

I ignore his demands as I take it all in. My eyes quickly swivel around and find Jaz, who gives me a beaming smile.

"Hey," Logan says. "Eyes down here, babe."

I do as I'm told and focus on my man, who actually does have Louie, safe and sound, perched on his shoulder. "I love you," he starts before pulling a little velvet box out of his pocket. "I've told you a million times that you're my world, but I want so much more than that. I want to come home every day knowing that you'll be there, not as my girlfriend, but as my wife. You, me, and Louie. A family," he says as he opens the box to show off a beautiful engagement ring. "Elle, will you do me the greatest pleasure of becoming my wife?"

Tears of joy spring to my eyes as I look down at this amazing man, but just as I go to respond, Louie's little birdy voice comes breaking through the silence "Ahhh, fuck no. Bastard. Ya big bastard."

Laughs break out across the room and I roll my eyes at my silly bird, unable to help the grin that settles across my face. "Are you sure?"

I ask Logan.

He laughs as he looks at me. "I've never been so sure in my life."

I nod my head as the tears start to fall, and I can't help but crash right into him, my lips fusing to his. "Yes," I murmur against his lips. "Yes, I'll marry you."

"Thank God," he breathes, his arms locking around me as the room erupts into chaos. Logan manhandles me to get me off him so he can fix the shiny white gold diamond ring on my finger.

"Holy shit," I laugh, meeting his admiring stare. "I love you so much."

"I love you too, babe," he tells me as all of our family and friends begin crowding around and offering their congratulations.

We get to our feet, and suddenly it's the biggest party I've seen. "Wait, don't we have to get to the Hilton?" I ask.

"No, babe," he laughs. "There was no party at the Hilton."

"What?" I demand. "It was all a lie?"

"Damn straight."

Wow, my future husband is a liar in the best way and got everyone I know to go along with it. I can't believe this is happening. My whole world was turned upside down when I accepted this job, and I'll never go back. I can't wait to live my life with him and see what the future holds for us.

Shit, I can only imagine what fresh hell little Logans would be like to raise.

Looking around me, I take in all my friends and soon-to-be family. I know my parents and sister aren't here anymore, but I finally feel like

I have it all, and it has everything to do with Logan.

He's it for me. I hold his heart and he holds mine.

He's my life.

My love.

Until the end of time.

Epilogue

ELLE

2 YEARS LATER

"How's married life treating you?" Jaz asks as I meet up with her at our favorite café.

"So far, so good," I smile. "He hasn't managed to kill Louie yet, so I guess that's a good sign."

"He better not kill Louie," she laughs as she goes about pouring water into each of our glasses. "I miss hearing his squawking through the walls every day."

"I know, but now you have Brendan to listen to."

"Ugh, don't remind me," she groans. "He's had a different girl over there every night for the past few days."

"Yuck," I mutter, my lips twisting in disgust. "I didn't want to hear that." After I fully moved out of my apartment, I decided I really didn't want Brendan moving with me. I mean, I love the little turd, but it didn't feel right bringing him with me to Logan's place, even though he insisted Brendan could come. It was about time Brendan had his own space anyway. He's not a kid anymore, and he needed to learn to do things for himself.

"I think you did," she demands. "Maybe you can talk some sense into him or at least get him to pick just one of the girls and stick with her. Preferably the blonde. She's not as . . . loud."

"Jaz," I groan. "Stop, you're going to make my ears bleed."

We give our orders and I sit back in my chair, the movement making the sweet little baby girl inside my stomach kick me in the ribs. "Ow," I groan, rubbing my ribs. "That's not nice, my sweet baby."

"She kicking again?" Jaz asks as she flies across the table and places her hand on my protruding stomach.

"Yeah," I laugh, moving her hand to the right spot. We both sit silently waiting to see if this baby will kick again, but as usual, whenever Jaz touches my stomach, all movement ceases.

"Sorry," I cringe. "I don't think it's going to happen." I'm 38 weeks pregnant, and to say it's getting a little squishy in there is an understatement. I'm just happy it's almost over. This pregnancy is killing me. Women all over the world are always saying how beautiful pregnancy is, but I'm hating it. I can't wait to get this watermelon out of me.

"Damn it," Jaz grunts. "I swear, your baby hates me."

"Yeah, probably," I laugh.

"That'll change when she's sixteen and her overprotective mother refuses to let her out of her sight."

"You stay away from my daughter," I tell her. "No corruption is going to be happening in this baby's future."

"We'll see," she smiles.

Our lunch comes out, and we make quick work of annihilating it. Well, kind of. I have to eat in small bites and wait before taking another, otherwise, my stomach gets squished and if the baby moves, I end up throwing it all up. It's just great. It's like a little party trick that Logan usually gets the brunt of.

I'm paying the bill when my phone starts ringing in my pocket, and I pull it out to see Logan's name across my screen. "Hey, what's up?" I say as I try to juggle putting my change back in my wallet while using the other hand for the phone.

"What are you doing?" he questions.

"I'm with Jaz. We just finished lunch."

"Cool, can you come down to the arena? I have a surprise for you."

"Okay," I say slowly, not trusting his version of a surprise in the least. "I'll be there in ten minutes."

I hang up and pocket my phone before finding Jaz. "You want to come to the arena with me? Apparently, Logan has a surprise."

"Sure," she says as she collects her things off the table. We walk out to my car and jump in. "What kind of surprise?"

"No idea," I say as I start up my car. We drive to the arena and soon find ourselves standing by the ice, looking at Logan in confusion. "What's going on?" I ask.

"I told you, I have a surprise," he says.

"What kind of surprise?" I ask, repeating Jaz's question from earlier.

Logan grins back at me, refusing to say a word as he nods to the entrance. I turn around and see my brother walking through the door with a pair of skates hung over his shoulder.

A massive smile takes over my face as understanding dawns on me. He's been walking for the past year now, but it started really slowly. He could only take a step or two at a time, and it was shaky to say the least. He then progressed to a few steps at a time with assistance.

It was my wedding day where he surprised the hell out of me and got out of his wheelchair, threw the walker away, and walked me down the aisle. Logan had to catch him at the other end, but it meant the absolute world to me.

He has come further and further ever since. Though he started to notice the way I would casually loop my arm through his when he was walking. It didn't take him long to realize I was only doing it just in case he fell. He shut that shit down real fast, but seriously, one fall could ruin it all, and I'm not about to take that risk.

"You're going to skate?" I ask him as he gets closer.

"Yep," he says in excitement.

My hands begin getting all fidgety as the nerves seep in. "You'll stay to the side, right? And hold the boards?" I ask.

Logan slips his hand into mine, easily taking away some of my nerves. "Relax," he tells me. "He'll be fine. I'll be with him the whole time. Besides, I made a deal with him, and I intend to keep it."

"What are you talking about?" I ask.

"Remember the night I abducted Brendan from the rehab facility?"

"Yeah?" I prompt, still pissy about that.

"I told him if he got back on his feet, I'd have him up on the ice with all the boys."

"Shit," I groan. "All the boys are here. You know he'll get too excited and take on more than he can handle."

"Um . . . You know I can hear you, right?" Brendan says.

I ignore him as I face my husband. "He'll be fine, I promise. It might kill me, but I won't leave his side."

"Fine," I grunt. "But if he falls, it's on you."

"Will you punish me?" he grins.

I roll my eyes and give in. There's not a lot I can do about it. He's been walking on his own for over a year, so I should be thankful he's managed to wait this long before getting back on the ice.

I take a seat and watch as they lace up their skates and get on. "I can't watch," I say to Jaz who's looking on in awe.

"You should," she tells me. "He looks like a kid in a candy store."

I look up, and just as Jaz said, he looks absolutely ecstatic. Once again, I have another reason to love my husband just that much more.

They get Brendan comfortable on the ice before the rest of the team gets on, and I pull the plug when someone suggests getting him a stick and throwing a few pucks on the ice.

They hop off, and I wait for Logan to put his skates away before rushing up to him and throwing my arms around his neck. "Thank you, so much," I say, squishing my stomach into him to get as close as possible.

"Anything for you, babe," he says.

I reach up onto my tippy toes and give him a kiss when I feel something wet on my legs. I step back from Logan and look down as my heart begins to race.

A gasp comes flying out of my mouth before I look up at my husband with wide eyes. "Logan?"

"Yeah, babe?"

"I'm really sorry," I tell him. "But my water just broke all over your shoes."

"What?" he grunts, his eyes bulging out of his head. He looks down and notices the wet patch on the ground, running down my legs and covering both our shoes. "It's time?"

"Yeah," I smile up at him as we get that much closer to meeting our baby girl. "It's time."

Never Gonna Happen

Thanks for reading

If you enjoyed reading this book as much as I enjoyed writing it, please consider leaving an Amazon review to let me know.

For more information on the Denver Royalty series, find me on Facebook –

www.facebook.com/sheridansbookishbabes

Stalk me

Join me online with the rest of the stalkers!!
I swear, I don't bite. Not unless you say please!

Facebook Reader Group

www.facebook.com/SheridansBookishBabes

Facebook Page

www.facebook.com/sheridan.anne.author1

Instagram

www.instagram.com/Sheridan.Anne.Author

TikTok

www.tiktok.com/@Sheridan.Anne.Author

Subscribe to my Newsletter

https://landing.mailerlite.com/webforms/landing/a8q0y0

More by Sheridan Anne

www.amazon.com/Sheridan-Anne/e/B079TLXN6K

DARK CONTEMPORARY ROMANCE - M/F

Broken Hill High | Haven Falls | Broken Hill Boys | Aston Creek High | Rejects Paradise | Bradford Bastard

DARK CONTEMPORARY ROMANCE - REVERSE HAREM

Boys of Winter | Depraved Sinners | Empire

NEW ADULT SPORTS ROMANCE

Kings of Denver | Denver Royalty | Rebels Advocate

CONTEMPORARY ROMANCE (standalones)

Play With Fire | Until Autumn (Happily Eva Alpha World)

PARANORMAL ROMANCE

Slayer Academy [Pen name - Cassidy Summers]

Ingram Content Group UK Ltd.
Milton Keynes UK
UKHW011615210623
423807UK00004B/162